DUAL DECEPTION

DUAL DECEPTION

A PROJECT MOLKA NOVEL
FREDRICK L. STAFFORD

This is a work of fiction. Names, characters, businesses, places, events, and incidents are either the products of the author's imagination or used in a fictitious manner. Any resemblance to actual persons, living or dead, or to actual events is purely coincidental.

Copyright © 2020 Fredrick L. Stafford
All rights reserved.

No part of this publication may be reproduced, stored in a retrieval system, copied in any form or by any means, electronic, mechanical, photocopying, recording, or otherwise transmitted without written permission from the publisher.

My Thanks

To all the PROJECT MOLKA readers and supporters. The journey is still just getting started.

PROJECT MOLKA

At the peak of her warrior skills, Molka resigned from an elite special forces unit and chose veterinary medicine as her post-military career. She opened a small clinic, built a small practice, and sought to live her life in humble obscurity.

And she did—until the Traitors Scandal intervened.

Her country's foreign intelligence service—known as the Counsel—suffered an unprecedented disaster when moles burrowed in deep for 10 years popped up and exposed the identity of almost every covert operative.

In a small state with many enemies sworn to annihilate it, the safeguarding role of covert operations is indispensable. The Counsel, gutted and demoralized, fell into panic mode.

In the short term, they used a few uncompromised retired operatives—along with some career bureaucrats who never qualified for field work—to fill the gaping void. The results disappointed, to put it mildly.

In the long term, new operatives would be recruited and formally trained, but the process would take several years.

It was the time in between when the country faced the most danger.

The Counsel's solution was Operation Civic Duty—more often called the Projects Program. They recruited ordinary citizens who held what they deemed a useful skill or skills. Each citizen recruit—or project, as they were dubbed—received some quick, very basic operative training before being sent straight out to complete what the Counsel called a task.

It sounded desperate and borderline suicidal, and it was. Even so, they found willing projects everywhere: university students, factory workers, athletes, scientists, housewives.

But the Counsel's prize recruit was Molka.

Their best recruiter, Azzur, told her as much when he came to her office. He said she was the preferred age range—not yet 30—maintained superb physical condition, retained a useful skill set from her military service, and could claim an excellent cover. Who could be suspicious of a person who lives to help animals?

He told her that the Counsel required her help. She told him she was a patriot, but she had already done her duty. She wasn't interested. Please leave her alone.

He smiled and left.

He came back a week later with more information for her. Azzur can always find more information. He told her all about her worst special forces mission, how that mission led to the unavenged murder of her little sister, Janetta. He said the Counsel knew the identity of the one responsible and where this one hid. And if Molka completed 10 tasks for them, her 11th task could be personal. They would give her the identity and location of the one she would die to kill.

She agreed to the Counsel's offer.

She agreed to serve under Azzur.

She agreed to become his project.

Project Molka.

PROJECT LAILI

Born to a drug addict mother and a father killed in a gang fight before she was born, Laili's life started rough.

And it went downhill from there.

But young Laili determined that it would not be her fate to live in a filthy, foodless, one-room ghetto apartment being abused by the various men her mother brought home.

So, at age 13, she ran away to Europe with a man. The authorities returned her. At age 15, she ran away with another man to the United States. The authorities returned her. At age 17, she ran away with yet another man to New Zealand. The authorities returned her.

By age 18, Laili had grown into an exceptional beauty, with a virulent disrespect for authority. And when it was time for her compulsory military service, she decided to use extreme disobedience to get herself dismissed. All she wanted to do was get away from her home country and forget she had ever lived there.

As usual, she pushed things way too far. She was not given a discharge; she was given two years in a military prison.

While Laili waited to start her sentence, an army psychiatrist, who examined her before her court martial, wrote a report based on his findings and interviews he conducted with her training sergeants and commanding officer. The report stated Laili showed genius level intelligence, and when interested, she responded remarkably well to training. Also, from her runaway travels, she spoke very good English, excellent French and Spanish, decent German, and passable Russian. Her anti-authority behavior was likely a, "trust no one but yourself," defense mechanism developed from her horrendous childhood.

The psychiatrist passed his report along to an old army friend who served as the Counsel's top recruiter for their controversial Projects Program. If anyone could harness and exploit Laili's raw abilities and useful skills, it would be Azzur.

Minutes into their first meeting, Laili physically attacked Azzur. Azzur quickly and violently subdued her and then offered her a cigarette and a chance to avoid serving in prison by serving him.

She agreed.

Azzur put Laili through accelerated training in weapons, martial arts, helicopter piloting, and veterinary technician procedures. Her results in each were beyond off the charts.

In Laili, Azzur knew he possessed the most gifted operative recruit he had seen in his 20-year career. However, he also knew her extreme volatility was a prohibitive handicap to her vast talent reserves.

In normal times, Laili would be rejected for covert duty as too high risk. But thanks to the Traitors, the times were not normal.

Perhaps if he paired Laili on her first task with his star project—Project Molka—she would learn to temper her inner demons and maximize her potential.

Azzur stamped Laili's file: approved.

She became Project Laili.

CHAPTER ONE

***O**UCH!*

The hard puncher floored Molka with a surprise straight right to the chin when she walked in the door. And if she had ever been hit harder by another woman, she couldn't remember when. But she would always remember that an oil worker's bar in Pasadena, Texas on a Friday night was no place to start a fight.

Actually, Molka didn't start the fight.

The brat did!

The brat being: her new partner, Laili.

Molka sprung back to her feet, landed a front kick on the puncher's chin—returning the flooring favor—and kept advancing toward Laili's Alamo-type position.

The lean, long-legged, long blond-haired, green-eyed, 19-year-old beauty—hypersexualized in a tiny black crop top, tight jean short-shorts, and platform sandals—stood trapped behind a corner table by eight other irate women.

Laili fired alternating kicks to fend off their double flank slap and punch attacks.

Twenty plus oil worker men watched and laughed and cheered and jeered the unfair "catfight" and the jukebox blared out moment appropriate Outlaw Country.

DUAL DECEPTION

Molka hadn't come dressed for combat either. She arrived straight from her acting class at the community center attired comfortable-cute in a white sundress and new bright-white-canvas sneakers. She had taken care all evening not to get either dirty, but Laili's distress call made her caution moot.

Laili's eyes locked on Molka. "It's about time! And they just called the cops on me too!"

Molka grabbed a cue from atop a pool table and tossed it to Laili. "Rolling extraction! Can you make it?"

Laili nodded. "Yes! Hurry!"

Molka turned to leave and get the truck.

Another brawler babe pointed at Molka and yelled: "That's her partner! Don't let that bitch leave either!"

Clad in western shirts, Wrangler jeans, and cowboy boots, four hardworking, hard-drinking, hard-fighting, daughters of the Lone Star State formed a skirmish line across Molka's exit path to do just that.

Molka admired such women.

She would have liked to be friends with them.

They did not feel the same, and they expressed their sentiments with cussing, spitting, and wild swings targeting Molka's head.

Even so, Molka didn't want to hurt them too badly. It was their bar and their town and their republic. And they hadn't invited Laili to bring her nonsense into any of them.

Molka used moderate front and side kicks to push them back and kept moving toward the door.

Behind her, the pool cue helped Laili hold her own and prepare to make an escape hole for an exit run. Using her freakish-fast reflexes and incomparable dexterity, she forced the women surrounding her to give ground to keep teeth.

Molka's forward push toward the door continued. In her peripheral vision, she caught a skinny girl behind the bar cocking her arm to throw something. Molka glanced over her shoulder and tracked a brown flying blur heading toward Laili.

CRASHHHHHH!

If the bar girl had to heave a full bottle at Laili's head, why did it have to be Crown Royal? Why not opt for a cheaper brand that would have done the same damage? Shame to waste the good stuff.

Either way, it missed Laili, and everyone else, and shattered on the bar's prized relic: an autographed, authentic Houston Texans jersey mounted in a glass case on the wall.

The tragedy didn't go over well with the oil worker men, and they started to yell for everyone to "whoa up," and that, "the law would be there directly; let them handle it."

The Texas ladies blocking Molka heeded their calls.

Her route to the door cleared.

Exploit it.

She fast-twitched into a run.

Two strides in, a non-conformist cowgirl grabbed Molka's ponytail from behind and yanked. Hard.

Molka's mother had used to do the same thing to her when she was being bad, to get her attention.

She had hated it as a little girl.

She wouldn't tolerate it as a grown woman.

Playtime's over.

Molka spun around and fired an elbow strike into the hair puller's nose.

Cartilage crunched; blood ran.

Molka spun back and advanced again.

A woman swung a punch at her face.

Molka ducked it and fractured her ribs with a side kick.

Another woman swung a face-aimed punch.

Molka slipped it and gashed her head with a front kick.

Another woman tried to kick Molka.

Molka eluded it and rocked her world with a hammer fist.

Laili yelled approval: "Yeah! Fuck them up!"

Another woman attempted to tackle Molka.

Molka broke it and round house kicked her unconscious.

They wanted no more from Molka.

But she wanted more from them.

But the police were on the way, and Azzur would not abide her and Laili getting arrested.

Molka made it to the door and yelled to Laili, "Thirty seconds!"

Laili yelled back: "I'll be there!"

Molka ran in the humid, night air to a gigantic, dual rear-wheeled, diesel-powered Ford pickup truck parked three rows back. She fired it up and cooked rubber pulling out and aligning the truck for a pass by the bar's front door.

DUAL DECEPTION

Laili burst from the bar and swung the cue at her pursuers.

Molka approached Laili from behind at about jogging speed.

Laili flung the cue to back off the attackers, faced her body in the same direction the truck traveled, and looked over her shoulder.

As Molka passed by her, Laili grabbed the truck bed's side and vaulted herself up into the bed deft as a gymnast.

Rolling extraction executed.

The entire lady mob surged from the bar and launched a longneck beer bottle bombardment. Two exploded against the truck's side.

Laili poked her face through the open rear window slider. "Go fast! Go hard!"

Her command wasn't necessary. Molka fried more rubber leaving.

When they cleared the parking lot and pulled onto the main road, Molka asked, "Anyone following us?"

Laili checked their rear and then poked her face back in the window. "One white pickup. Two bitches inside. Can't believe they want some more."

"They're probably trying to get our plate number for the police. We need to lose them. But we're about to get slowed down in traffic ahead."

"Turn there!" Laili pointed through the window to a dark, narrow side street ahead on the left.

Molka cut across oncoming, honking traffic, made the turn, and found the street to be a narrow dirt access road. Impenetrable woods ran along the right side, and a fence fronting a deep ravine ran along the left side.

After about 100 yards, Molka stopped, cut the lights, and checked the rearview mirror.

Laili crawled to the truck bed's rear and squinted into the darkness. "I think we lost them." The white truck made a high-speed sliding turn onto the road and raced toward them. "No, we didn't!"

Molka stamped the gas.

But the smaller white truck moved faster. The gap closed quickly, a double barrel emerged from the passenger window, and took a low forward aim.

"Oh shit!" Laili ducked.

BOOOOM!

Shotgun pellets pinged the rear bumper.

Laili yelled up toward the rear window. "Double barrel 12-gauge! They're trying to shoot a tire out!"

Molka zigged hard right.

Laili slid and slammed into the truck bed's left side.

Molka zagged hard left.

Laili slid and slammed into the truck bed's right side.

BOOOOM!

More pellets hit the tailgate.

With both barrels fired, Laili peeked back. The white truck had stopped. "What are they doing, reloading?"

Molka stopped too.

"And what are you doing?" Laili said.

"Dead end coming," Molka said.

Laili spun to look. Three hundred yards ahead, the road ended at more impenetrable woods.

"They're going to keep us boxed in," Molka said. "Until the police get here."

"No, they're not," Laili said. "Here they come again."

The white truck started moving toward them at low speed.

Molka put the truck in reverse, sped backwards, jerked the wheel hard right, and spun the massive vehicle 180 degrees to face the white truck.

"Cool!" Laili said. "Where did you learn to do a J-turn?"

Molka grimaced at the approaching headlights. "I can't believe I'm going to do this again." She turned her headlights back on.

"Do what again?" Laili said.

"Play chicken. Hold on."

"Oh shit!"

Laili dropped and hugged the wheel well.

Molka punched it.

The white truck kept coming.

Collision in 100 yards.

Molka kept coming.

The white truck kept coming.

Collision in 60 yards.

Molka kept coming.

The white truck kept coming.

Collision in 40 yards.

Molka kept coming.

The white truck kept coming.

DUAL DECEPTION

Collision in 20 yards.
Molka Kept Coming.
The White Truck Kept Coming.
Collision In 10 Yards.
MOLKA KEPT COMING.
THE WHITE TRUCK KEPT COMING.
COLLISION IN FIVE YARDS.

The white truck panicked, veered to its left, crashed through the fence, and disappeared into the deep ravine.

Molka buried the brakes and stopped where the white truck had gone through.

Laili raised her head, surveyed the results, and smiled, excited. "That was badass!"

Molka exhaled adrenaline. "One of these times, I'm going to be wrong about the other chicken."

They both jumped from the truck and peered over the ravine's edge. The white truck rested at the bottom, wedged nose-first into the opposite bank. The driver and passenger—shaken but showing no injuries—exited their wounded vehicle.

Laili laughed. "You two again?"

Molka also recognized them as two of the women who had Laili trapped behind the table when she had first arrived at the brawl. She called down to them: "Leave your weapon in the truck. We're armed too." She lied.

"It's empty," Woman One said.

"You guys ok?" Molka said.

Woman Two said, "Hell with both y'all!"

"Do you need an ambulance?" Molka said.

Woman Two repeated, "I said, hell with both y'all!"

"We're ok," Woman One said. "We don't need an ambulance."

"Are you sure?" Molka said.

"Yes."

"Alright. We're leaving then."

Woman Two said, "Y'all come back to the bar and see us real soon. Especially you, blondie."

"Maybe I will," Laili said. "Just make sure you bring your sexy husbands again."

Woman Two said, "Hell with both y'all!"

Woman One said, "Who are you two, anyway?"

Laili sprang back into the truck bed, glared down on them, and raised two middle fingers high. "This is who we are, bitches! And don't ever forget us!"

"Um…she speaks for herself," Molka said. "I would appreciate it if you forgot me immediately. Have a good night."

CHAPTER TWO

With Laili moved into the passenger seat, Molka left the access road, got back onto the main road, drove to an I-45 South onramp, and headed toward their temporary accommodations. Forty miles away on Galveston Island, a Counsel associate on an extended vacation had allowed them use of his spacious home, along with the pickup truck they rode in.

Laili viewed her face in the sideview mirror, finger tapped a split on her lower lip from the fight, and spit blood out the window. "Those Texas bitches are tough and relentless. You have to give them their props."

"How did you get from the community center to that bar?" Molka said.

"I asked some guy hanging around outside to give me a ride."

"Ok. Very foolish. Then how did you get in a fight with every woman there? And by the way, the drinking age here isn't 19 like back home. It's 21."

"That's why they asked me to leave."

"You started a fight over that?"

"No," Laili said. "The fight started when I gave this hot guy a little booty-shaking dance." She grinned. "He loved it. Every other guy there was loving it too."

"I'm sure they were."

"Then that fat bitch who was driving the white truck walks up and tells me to get away from her husband. So I said, 'ok, fuck you very much for telling me that, bitch,' and started dancing for another guy. And the other bitch in the white truck comes up and says to get away from her husband. I slapped the shit out of her and went back and slapped the shit out of the first bitch too. That's when all the bitches jumped in on me."

"And that's when you called me to come help," Molka said.

"Took you long enough."

Molka laughed. "Well, you—"

"I know what you're going to say. That I have a big loud smart mouth. Yes. I admit that. So what? I can back it up."

Molka laughed again. "No. I was going to say you found out that you don't mess with another woman's man in Texas. You don't mess with Texas period, I've heard."

Laili spit out the window again. "Shut up, bitch. I was bored. I wanted some action. We've been stuck here over a month, and I'm tired of hanging out with you every night at all your tediously dull self-improvement classes. I mean, the only one that was somewhat cool was when you learned to drive that big boat. Even though it took you three sessions to get what I figured out in one hour. What's up with that, anyway?"

"I'm not a girl genius like you who can read the manual before she goes to bed and wake the next morning an expert. I have to apply myself and study hard."

"That's your problem," Laili said.

"I know that, but—"

A sheriff's vehicle flew past them. Molka watched it speed on ahead after someone else. She continued. "But if you wanted to fight tonight, you could have just waited until we got home and fought me. I would still love to finish the one you started in Vancouver."

Laili smirked. "Stop talking trash. You don't want Azzur to kick you out of the program any more than I want him to kick me out. You're just lucky the fighting ban he put on us is saving your ass."

"You mean yours."

"Whatever, bitch." Laili turned on the radio, scanned through several stations—all commercials—and turned it back off. "I suppose you're going to snitch on me to your precious Azzur about tonight?"

Molka raised annoyed eyebrows at Laili. "What do you mean, my precious Azzur?"

"He's always like, Molka can do this, and Molka can do that, and Molka has done this, and Molka has done that, blah, blah, blah, who gives a fuck."

Molka accelerated and passed around a semi-truck. "Azzur's never said anything like that to me."

"Are you going to snitch on me or not?"

"No," Molka said. "You can snitch on yourself to him. I got a message during my class. He'll be here tomorrow to brief us on our task. We're about to find out if you can really back up your big loud smart mouth."

CHAPTER THREE

Molka and Laili waited on opposite ends of the brown leather family room couch for Azzur to return.

Their project manager was fit for his early 50s, dark complexioned, with neat, gray-specked black hair. He stepped out minutes after he arrived to retrieve something from his rental car. But before leaving, he placed his usual brown leather satchel on a coffee table in front of the couch, removed a standard briefing tablet, and synched it to the room's 60-inch flat screen.

Laili lounged with a canned energy drink, wearing black sleeping boxers and a gold t-shirt featuring a lioness, which somewhat matched the small tattoo on the right side of her neck.

Molka wore a blue tank top and blue running shorts. Like her long, dark, ponytailed hair, they remained sweat soaked from a run in steamy hot, early October, East Texas. When she brushed some loose bang strands from her large oval blue eyes, her glistening bicep flexed nicely. A month of regular gym sessions had definitely toned her already athletic body back up.

Laili pinched her nose at Molka. "Uuk. You stink so bad."

"So do you," Molka said. "But at least my stink is a clean stink from my run. Your hair still reeks of stale cigarette smoke and beer from the bar last night."

DUAL DECEPTION

Laili burped energy drink. "I just woke up. I haven't gotten around to my morning shower yet."

"Too late now. It's almost 2PM."

Azzur re-entered wearing a fluorescent yellow hazmat suit. He carried a bright yellow metal case displaying *"Hazardous Material"* decals.

He placed the yellow case on the fireplace hearth, removed the suit's protective mask, and addressed the women.

"Pharmaceutical fentanyl is a synthetic opioid pain reliever. Approved for treating severe pain—typically that experienced with advanced cancer—it is 50 to 100 times more potent than morphine. Illegally made fentanyl is sold for its heroin-like effects. It is often mixed with heroin and/or cocaine as a combination product—with or without the user's knowledge—to increase its euphoric effects. In the US, illegal fentanyl is now the most commonly used drug involved in fatal overdoses with over 25,000 deaths per year by some estimates and rapidly growing."

Azzur placed his mask on again, walked back to the case, released the latches, and opened the lid. He removed metal tongs, used them to grasp and remove a tiny empty glass vial from the case, and carried it toward Molka and Laili.

He held the vial two feet from their faces. The closer view revealed it contained a minuscule quantity of white powder.

Azzur's voice was muted through his face protection. "That tiny amount of fentanyl is enough to kill a fully-grown adult male." He returned to the yellow case, replaced the vial and the tongs, re-secured the latches, and moved back toward Molka and Laili. "Within two weeks, 1,000 pounds of illegal fentanyl—enough for hundreds of millions of lethal doses—will be smuggled by an individual into our country. The ramifications of introducing such a large quantity of a super-killer substance into our population of only nine million could be unimaginably catastrophic."

"Who's the smuggler?" Molka said.

Azzur removed his mask and gloves, picked up the briefing tablet from the coffee table, and swiped. On the big TV screen across from them, a bald-shaven, trim bearded, handsome young man's headshot appeared.

Laili sat up and pointed. "I know who he is! That's Paz! He's a championship gamer. Well, he used to be." She smiled. "I had a little thing for him, way back when I was a gamer myself. When I was just a kid."

Molka rolled her eyes. "Said the 19-year-old kid."

Laili smirked. "Shut up, bitch."

Azzur lit a cigarette from a pack beside the tablet. "Laili is correct. He is Mr. Paz Davidov, age 22 and former noted professional video game player. He is also our prime minister's nephew."

"I remember this guy too," Molka said. "Didn't his grandfather leave him billions and then he did something ridiculous with it? Like he bought a big yacht so he and his rich loser party-boy friends could cruise around the world getting trashed?"

Azzur blew smoke. "His late billionaire grandfather established an exceedingly generous trust fund for Mr. Davidov, his sole grandchild. With his new wealth, Mr. Davidov—already considered the family's black sheep—purchased an opulent mansion in Haifa and this custom-fitted, 200-foot mega yacht." He swiped to a wide shot of a massive, stunning, sleek, modern white vessel.

Laili whistled. "Sweet."

Molka pointed at the yacht's image. "What's that green flag flying from the back with the initials TP on it?"

"Duh," Laili said. "Team Paz. That's the name of his gamer crew."

"Mr. Davidov named her *Outcast*," Azzur said. "Then he hired a captain to pilot her, and with his young friends, sought to drink his way from port-to-port until he circumnavigated the globe."

Laili smiled. "How fucking cool is that?"

Molka rolled her eyes again.

"However," Azzur said, "their tour of debauchery has ended on Saint Thomas in the US Virgin Islands, where Mr. Davidov has become engaged to this woman." He swiped to a model-stunning young woman smiling in a red bikini on a white sand beach. Her ash hair flowed with confidence, her lips curled mischievously, and her steel-blue eyes were penetrating. "Miss Caryn Thorsen, age 20."

"She's beautifully gorgeous," Laili said.

Molka agreed. "That's one way of filling out a bikini."

Azzur continued. "The manager of Mr. Davidov's trust fund has required Mr. Davidov to return home before the 30th of this month to sign notarized documents under penalty of forfeiture of his trust fund. Therefore, he must leave Saint Thomas within 12 days. He and Miss Thorsen are to be wed on the last possible day."

"I have a comment," Molka said. "I know Paz is not one of our best and brightest, but even he can't be stupid enough to try and bring that much dope into the country."

"He has no idea he is about to smuggle it, thanks to Miss Thorsen's father, Mr. Donar Thorsen." Azzur brought up a professionally taken photo of a thin middle-aged man in an expensive silver slim-fit suit standing on a marina dock filled with huge luxury yachts. His gray hair was slicked back with conceit, his lips pursed seriously, and his steel-blue eyes were penetrating.

Laili nodded. "I can see where his hot daughter gets her hot looks from."

Azzur scanned for a place to flick ash. Laili popped off the couch and handed him her energy drink can.

He used it for an ash tray and continued. "Mr. Thorsen, age 51, has Danish roots that go back to the colonial days of the US Virgin Islands, and he has long been considered a respected businessman. Drug trafficking is a relatively new endeavor for him, started when he accrued some large debts. He has partnered with a Belize-based cartel to bring marijuana destined for the US into Puerto Rico using a boat charter service he operates. But now, with fentanyl production currently exceeding US demand, and at the suggestion of his cartel partners, Mr. Thorsen sees his daughter's marriage to Mr. Davidov as a great opportunity to open a pipeline of the highly addictive—and much more profitable—fentanyl into new and underdeveloped Middle East markets through our country."

"What a sick fuck," Laili said. "I hate drugs and I hate drug dealers."

"I cannot blame you," Azzur said. "Considering the ravages both have wrought upon your family."

Laili gazed past Azzur out the sliding glass door. "Thanks for reminding me."

He went on. "Mr. Thorsen's main legitimate business is ownership of the largest marina destination in the islands: Yacht Marina Grande." He swiped to a website photo of a mall-like complex fronting a large marina. "The property features upscale shopping, fine dining, a day spa, and the aforementioned boat charter service, but its main function is the berthing and care of mega yachts such as Mr. Davidoff's. This is how cartel members were able to gain access to the *Outcast,* install a hidden smuggling compartment deep within her, and load the fentanyl without Mr. Davidov's knowledge."

"Sneaky," Molka said.

"Also shipping with the fentanyl are 100, 400-ounce gold bars as a courtesy fee the cartel will pay their new partners in our country."

"How much are 100, 400-ounce gold bars worth, daddy?" Laili said.

"If current market trends continue, approximately 100 million US dollars."

"They consider a 100 million-dollars a courtesy fee?" Molka said. "Ha. I'm working for the wrong people."

"Immediately after the wedding," Azzur said, "the newlyweds are to honeymoon cruise back to our country on *Outcast,* where Mr. Davidov is to introduce his new bride to his family and to her new home in Haifa, and then openly campaign against the prime minister's party in the upcoming election."

Molka chuckled. "Ooops."

"Meanwhile, cartel associates waiting in our country will clandestinely board *Outcast* and remove the hidden fentanyl and gold for their new partners. And they do not fear discovery because the cartel believes—with good reason—our security and customs people will not seriously search the prime minister's nephew's vessel."

"It's a clever scheme," Molka said.

"It gets even more so." Azzur blew smoke. "Almost immediately, Miss Thorsen will insist upon frequent yacht visitation cruises between Haifa and her beloved old Virgin Island's home. On each of these trips, the *Outcast* will carry back another massive fentanyl load. It is believed Miss Thorsen is fully aware of the scheme and is, in fact, coordinating it."

"That dirty little whore," Laili said. "Poor Paz."

Molka raised a hand. "Ok. I know this an irrelevant question because you wouldn't be here. But isn't the simple solution to just give our drug enforcement people this information? They can save the country from this fentanyl disaster, Paz from himself, and take credit for the biggest drug bust in our history. Maybe anyone's history."

Azzur stubbed out and lit a new cigarette. "The prime minister feels once it is exposed to the public that their nephew married a drug lord's daughter—let alone also being duped into a major drug trafficking plot—it would be a devastating national embarrassment. Not to mention detrimental to the prime minister's party in the upcoming election."

Molka smirked. "But this won't be a devastating national embarrassment or hurt the prime minister's party in the upcoming election. Because unlike all our law enforcement agencies, we—I mean the Counsel—don't answer to the government or have any government oversight. The Counsel answers directly to the prime minister. Which means this potential disaster will never be exposed to the public."

"That is correct," Azzur said.

Alright," Molka said. "How are we going to stop what will never officially have almost occurred?"

Azzur swiped the tablet and started a slide show presentation featuring spectacular island paradise-like scenes. "The US Virgin Islands are an unincorporated and organized territory of the United States located in the Caribbean east of Puerto Rico. It consists of the main islands of Saint Croix, Saint John, and Saint Thomas, and many other surrounding minor islands, few of which are inhabited. The total land area of the territory is 133.73 square miles. The population is approximately 110,000 with an Afro-Caribbean descent majority. Official language: English. Primary economic activity: tourism. The territory's capital is Charlotte Amalie on the island of Saint Thomas, which has a deep-water harbor that was once a haven for pirates and is now one of the busiest ports of call for cruise ships in the Caribbean, with about 1.5 million cruise ship passengers landing there annually."

Laili beamed. "It all looks so amazing, daddy."

Azzur continued. "A wealthy associate of ours, Mr. Benjamin Levy, enjoys a quiet retirement there with his wife on Saint Croix island. And although not a pet owner himself, he believes the US Virgin Islands are underserved in veterinary care. Therefore, he has decided to open an animal hospital in Charlotte Amalie. You two are his first employees, hired to assist in setting up the hospital for opening. Of course, there is nothing to set up, and the hospital will never open. It only functions as a cover for your legends: veterinarian and vet tech."

"Wait," Laili said. "You made me rush through that vet tech training course, and I'm not even going to get the chance to use those skills? What a waste."

"Nothing I ask you to do is wasteful," Azzur said. "To maintain a legend, you must be able to speak on it competently should anyone ask. Hence your training."

"Well, try not to speak on it too much," Molka said. "It takes at least two years to become a truly competent vet tech."

Laili sneered. "Whatever, bitch."

Molka shifted around on the couch and cast a scowl on Laili. "I've asked you, and I've told you, to stop calling me that, brat. Now I'm insisting."

Laili shifted around on the couch and viewed Molka without fear. "Whatever...bitch."

Azzur hit Laili with a formidable gaze. "Laili."

Laili smiled. "Yes, daddy?" She hopped up again and helped herself to one of Azzur's cigarettes.

"Do not forget this is your first task," Azzur said. "Molka has been given credit for completing three, and before that, she served our country with honor. She has earned her right for basic respect."

Laili mocked shame. "Yes, daddy." She looked back to Molka. "Sorry I called you a bitch...ugly."

Azzur let her sarcasm slide. "Oh, I almost forgot to mention, at the prime minister's recommendation, the Counsel has approved each of you—upon completion of this task—for eight vacation days in the US Virgin Islands and a bonus of 15,000 US dollars."

Laili rocked back and kicked feet at the air. "Yeh!"

"Ok." Molka smiled. "That makes up for all the range ammo they never reimbursed me for. But dangling that type of incentive reward shows how huge this is for the prime minister."

"That is correct." Azzur carried the tablet to a leather recliner across the room and sat. "In a moment, I will brief each of you separately, but the overall objective of your joint task is twofold and is as follows: After Mr. Davidov leaves the island for home, one of you will secure the *Outcast* so the fentanyl and gold can be offloaded by us and do so in such a manner as to be without his knowledge. An asset will assist in this operation."

"Who is the asset?" Molka said.

"The asset was recommended by our American Corporation friends."

Molka addressed Laili. "The Corporation is the nickname for the American's main foreign intelligence service."

Laili scoffed. "I know that."

Azzur continued. "But before Mr. Davidov even leaves for home, and prior to their wedding, the other one of you will break up Mr. Davidov and Miss Thorsen's nationally embarrassing relationship. And do so in such a manner as to make Mr. Davidov believe it was his idea. You will have exactly 10 days to accomplish this task."

Molka sighed. "Another honeypot operation. Alright. I suppose I can enchant Paz, make him fall in love with me, and get him to dump Caryn Thorsen. But I'm not going to bed with him. That's not negotiable."

"You will not be the one enchanting Mr. Davidov," Azzur said. "Laili will."

Molka's face recoiled. "What? No. Her? That's a job for a grown woman. Don't you think she's too young?"

"It is not that she is too young." Azzur blew smoke. "It is that you are too old."

# CHAPTER FOUR

Azzur sent Laili—who was doubled over in loud uncontrolled laughter—out of the room.

Molka waited until the laughter cut behind Laili's bedroom door closing and addressed Azzur. "Just how old do you think I am?"

"Mr. Davidov prefers his women to be more girl than woman," Azzur said. "In any case, securing the fentanyl and the gold bullion from the *Outcast* is the more crucial element of the task and should go to the senior project."

Molka sat back and folded her arms. "I'm not yet 30. I'm not too old."

"How did your yacht pilot training progress?"

"I can get one underway and on course, no problem. But docking is…very tough. They use thrusters and…well…it takes a lot more practice than I've had."

"Docking won't be an issue for you. The key to your phase of the task is working with the asset, this man." Azzur swiped the tablet. "Captain LJ Savanna." On the big screen, a white man—dressed in all black—leaned on the railing of a black boat. His wavy, shoulder-length dark-brown hair was parted on the side and featured a perfect bang flip. Hazel eyes twinkled at the camera, and beard stubble covered his angular face, which was split by a large, gleaming, slightly crooked, grin. A gold hoop earring shined from his left ear.

"Is it just me," she said, "or is he trying a bit too hard to look like a charming rogue?"

"Captain Savanna's name is likely an alias and little is known about his background. He is believed to be in his early 40s and purportedly a retired naval officer from an undisclosed country. He lives on a small private island he owns, and named Katelyn Island, located in the waters between the US and British Virgin Islands."

"What's his profession?"

"Several things: entrepreneur, raconteur, and pirate."

Molka's eyebrows rose. "Pirate? Really?"

"For the past seven years, Captain Savanna has operated a very lucrative extortion racket. He pays informers to provide him with the travel schedules, navigational routes, and destinations of privately owned luxury mega yachts cruising the Caribbean. Using these logistical tips, he and his crew of well-trained specialists intercept and seize these vessels while at sea—in a spot of his choosing—along with their exceptionally wealthy owners and passengers, who are then brought to Captain Savanna's island and ransomed."

"However, they are not held as terrified hostages, rather as honored guests. Captain Savanna entertains them for several days while the guests' family members or representatives arrange payment of a negotiated *tribute* to Captain Savanna for their loved one's or employer's safe release. The payments are made through varied and changing untraceable accounts in various countries and appear to be completely legal."

"Why haven't I heard about this?" Molka said. "He's like a…modern-day pirate of the Caribbean."

"The story has not been widely told because none of his victims have filed a criminal report. To the contrary, they have all expressed how much they enjoyed the experience. And among the elite yachting set, it is now considered a badge of honor to be chosen for ransoming by the captain. It is even said in their circles that you have not really arrived until you have been a guest of Captain Savanna, the 'Gentleman Pirate.'"

Molka shook her head. "Rich people are crazy. So how is this 'gentleman pirate' going to help me secure and offload the *Outcast* without Paz's knowledge?"

"Captain Savanna has not been informed about the *Outcast*'s secreted cargo, nor the plot which put it there. And he is never to learn of it. He only knows he is being offered an irresistible tip, that being a flash drive containing the complete planned route and navigational coordinates for the *Outcast*'s return voyage home, obtained by us from her captain's personal computer. You will give this flash drive to Captain Savanna at the appropriate time, and he will use this tip to seize and ransom his biggest prize to date: the billionaire playboy Mr. Davidov, who also carries the added prestige of being the nephew of a sovereign state's prime minister."

"And why would we offer him such a prestigious opportunity?"

"Captain Savanna has been told that the prime minister wishes to bring their wayward nephew under control by putting him at the mercy of a pirate. However, for legal reasons, Mr. Davidov cannot ask the manager of his trust fund to make the very large tribute payment that will be demanded by Captain Savanna to secure his release. Therefore, Mr. Davidov will be forced to appeal to—if not beg—the prime minister for assistance."

Molka smirked. "And the prime minster will use that cry for help as leverage to muzzle Paz before the election."

"That is the plan as far as Captain Savanna will know. However, before any ransom is paid, a hostage rescue team from our navy's special operations unit, Flotilla 15, will conduct a rescue operation on Captain Savanna's island and free Mr. Davidov."

Molka nodded impressed. "Flotilla 15. They're really really good. So the prime minister is hedging their bet. If Paz isn't persuaded to stop openly campaigning against the prime minister's party by having his ransom paid, he will be persuaded when he finds himself worthy of the prime minister sending one of our best special ops units to free him. Which, I have to say, is quite sleazy politics."

"Mr. Davidov's rescue by Flotilla 15 also serves another purpose," Azzur said.

"I hope so."

"Flotilla 15's neutralizing of Captain Savanna and his crew during Mr. Davidov's rescue will give you the opportunity to take control of the *Outcast*. You will pre-position yourself nearby Katelyn Island in a small boat, observe the operation's start, move in, seize *Outcast*, and bring her to a nearby assigned coordinate, where a contractor team will offload the fentanyl and gold for us onto another vessel. The *Outcast* will then be set adrift as if to seem she broke lose during the chaos of the operation. Mr. Davidov will later be returned his vessel none the wiser."

Molka raised her hand. "I have a few tough questions."

Azzur lit another cigarette. "As I expected."

"You said Laili's going to break up Paz and Caryn Thorsen's engagement. After that, are her and her father still going to let Paz leave with the drugs and gold?"

"Yes. That deal has already been finalized. They will just come to the realization it is to be a one-time endeavor."

"Ok. And Flotilla 15's neutralization of the captain and his crew during a hostage rescue op could mean permanent neutralization. Is that really necessary?"

"Captain Savanna is too valuable an asset to be permanently neutralized at this time. Flotilla 15 will be ordered only to detain Captain Savanna and his crew while Paz is freed."

"Unless they try to resist, of course."

"Next question," he said.

"What's the Counsel going to do with all that fentanyl and gold?"

"The fentanyl can perhaps be weaponized for use against our enemies."

Molka frowned. "Weaponized narcotics. Bullets and bombs are never enough. They always want something else. Why not just destroy that horrible stuff and feel good about it?"

Azzur blew smoke. "I suppose I must come to accept your moral protestations before every task."

"And the gold?"

"While 100 million is a pittance to the big illegal drug consortiums, it is an easily convertible commodity and a boon to our small cash-strapped organization." Azzur's eyes moved from Molka to an imaginary point in the distance beyond her. "Many planned operations I long thought infeasible can now be reconsidered. The possibilities are exciting. Very exciting."

"I'll have to take your word on that," she said. "How will I connect with Captain Savanna?"

Azzur refocused on Molka. "Our associate in the US Virgin Islands, Mr. Levy, is acquainted with Captain Savanna. They play chess together. He will make the introduction. Mr. Levy will also pick you up at the Saint Thomas airport and take you to your apartment located above the new animal hospital."

"Our equipment?"

"Give me a list," he said. "Mr. Levy will have it waiting in the apartment."

"Alright. I'll do my best. When do we meet for debriefing?"

"I will be with the contractor team when you bring *Outcast* to the rendezvous point. Until then, I will monitor your task from San Juan, Puerto Rico aboard our navy's newest warship, the INS *Geula*, which is arriving there on a goodwill tour."

"And is also conveniently carrying, I assume, Flotilla 15."

"That is correct. Which will put them, and me, less than one hour's flying time away from both Saint Thomas and Katelyn Island." Azzur rose, moved across the room to his brown leather satchel, removed another briefing tablet, and handed it to Molka. "In addition to your own, that also includes Laili's detailed instructions. Commit them to memory as well."

"Double the pre-work." Molka clutched the tablet to her chest. "Oooo...lucky me."

"I know Laili is immature and disrespectful. She is also very naturally talented with scary ability."

"I don't disagree with either of those statements."

"And I appreciate the patience and restraint you have shown in regard to her." Azzur flicked ash. "For the most part."

"And my 'for the most part' is wearing thin."

"Laili's behavior is the result of an abusive childhood, and so far, a very abusive life."

"Well, she's not the only one in the world who can claim that. So it doesn't give her a free pass to be insufferable."

"Agreed," Azzur said. "However, she is the best I have at the moment to help complete this task."

"But aren't you concerned that since she had a thing for Paz in the past it might complicate her judgment?"

"I believe your concerns might stem from what occurred with you on your previous task."

"No." Molka tugged on the base of her ponytail. "I've forgotten all about that."

"As you have said." He blew smoke. "However, I am not concerned. Laili is drawn to more mature, authoritative types, into which category Mr. Davidov does not fall."

Molka grinned. "So she calls you daddy because she really has daddy issues and not just because she's kissing up?"

DUAL DECEPTION

"Give Laili any guidance you can. And keep in mind—as an added incentive perhaps—that at the conclusion of this task there is a great chance you will never see her again."

CHAPTER FIVE

"**H**ey ugly?" Laili said. "You know what's worse than being ugly?"

Molka, leaving the family room, faced Laili re-entering.

Laili grinned. "Being ugly AND old!"

Molka answered the barb with a stone stare and departed.

Laili spread her arms and watched Molka walk away. "What, you want to do something?"

"Laili," Azzur said. "Come in here for your briefing."

Laili skipped in and plopped back on the couch across from Azzur, who smoked in the recliner again.

"How is your French these days?" he said.

"Pas trop mal, papa."

"Good. You will be traveling to the US Virgin Islands via Paris with a French passport." He removed a passport from his satchel and passed it to Laili. "You will be known as Giselle Binoche."

"Ok, daddy."

"Your legend's backstory is you are a native French girl who took the vet tech job in the far-away Caribbean to escape an abusive relationship. Therefore, you will affect a French accent on this task to conceal your Israeli identity. Mr. Davidov has never traveled to France and will not detect any irregularities."

Laili nodded. *"Pas de problème, papa."*

Azzur went back to his briefing tablet and swiped through several more Caryn photos displayed on the big screen; each one more striking than the next. "To get to your target, you will have to get past his fiancée, Miss Caryn Thorsen. And although she just turned 20 years old, do not let her youth mislead you. Her father has groomed her since she was a girl to take over the family business. And she does supervise much of the day-to-day operations at the Yacht Marina Grande complex. Like you, she can be very formidable in her own ways."

"Don't worry," she said. "That dirty little whore won't be a problem."

"One other thing I want you to be aware of." Azzur swiped to a photo of a Hispanic man in his late 20s and dressed for clubbing.

"Dude has a lot of gang tats," Laili said.

"This is Gustavo Ramos. He answers to Gus. The Thorsens hired him several months ago to act as a consultant for their boat charter service."

"Which means he's actually running their weed smuggling operation."

"Precisely," he said. "We do not have much on his background. We do know he is Cuban born and possibly served as a *sicario*—a cartel hitman—in the past. Try to recruit him as an asset, if possible, to get informational updates on the cartel-Thorsen fentanyl trafficking scheme, of which he may or may not have knowledge. I am confident you can handle Mr. Ramos should the need arise, but do not underestimate him either. Use caution."

"Ok, daddy."

Azzur set the tablet aside. "Before we proceed with your briefing, I want to give you something else to think about. You and Molka will have separate instructions and will largely work independently of one another, but you would be well advised to listen to any guidance she offers. Do you understand?"

"Yes, daddy."

"Good. Mr. Davidov is highly susceptible to suggestions made by beautiful young women. He can, and has been, manipulated by them. As a teen, he fell victim to several catfishing scams. And this past year, he was nearly duped by a Greek beauty into investing a vast sum into her father's failing newspaper."

Laili nodded. "Being rich doesn't always mean being smart."

"Precisely. Now I will explain to you exactly how to break Mr. Davidov to your will, and how to break him away from Miss Thorsen."

CHAPTER SIX

A big white banner with black letters stated:

**Gary's Shooting World
Fall Classic Practical Shooting Match
All Shooters Welcome**

A large outdoor shooting range lay beyond the banner and laid out on the range were several practical shooting courses.

Each course was constructed using a unique combination of plywood walls, large plastic barrels, and old tire stacks. Fixed metal and paper shooting targets, of various sizes had been placed among the obstacles.

The Practical Shooting Match involved handgun armed competitors—wearing ear and eye protection—moving as fast as they could through the course on a designated path and firing on the targets. At least one reload would be required to complete the course, and a range officer—holding an electronic shot timer device—followed behind them. The shooters were scored on a combination of speed and accuracy for each course—officially called a stage—and the overall best combined score from all the stages would win the match.

Molka and Laili observed the match from behind a sandbagged barrier with other shooters. Both wore a ponytail, a polo shirt, jeans, tactical boots, and holstered sidearms with a spare magazine pouch on tactical belts. Molka also wore her old pilot's watch on her left wrist.

Behind them, an aluminum grandstand held about 150 enthusiastic spectators. The gunpowder odor from hundreds of fired rounds mixed with the potent aroma from the surrounding sage bushes put a sting in the nostrils. And although the morning clouds and rain had cooled the day, the clear sky, afternoon sun reheated it fast.

A hefty man wearing a red shooting shirt—with *Gary* scripted on the front—a black cowboy hat, and a walrus-like moustache addressed the crowd with a wireless microphone. "Before we end this party, I wanted to thank y'all again for coming out and remind you of our big sale this weekend at Gary's Shooting World. Buy one bucket of bullets, get a second bucket at half price. That's Gary's Shooting World, off old Farm Road 517 in La Flore, where we say, 'If you don't like guns, we don't give a shoot!'"

Gary waited for his laugh-line to land and continued. "All right, we're about ready for the final stage with our top two shooters to decide it. So, let's meet 'em. Miss Molka, Miss Laili, step on over please." Molka and Laili complied. "Tell us a little about you, girls. Based on your crazy-good skills, I reckon you must serve in the military or law enforcement?"

Molka spoke into the mic. "I'm a veterinarian."

Laili spoke into the mic. "I'm supposed to be a vet tech."

Molka smirked at Laili. "We work together."

"Then where did y'all learn to shoot and move like that?"

Laili smiled at Molka. "Daddy took me to the range every day this summer."

Molka frowned at Laili. "I learned for self-defense reasons."

"Ok...sounds good, girls. Go load up at the Gary's Shooting World-sponsored, complimentary shooter's ammo table and get ready."

Molka and Laili moved to a table stacked with boxes of target ammo in various calibers.

Molka unholstered a Beretta 96A1, removed the magazine and her spare magazine and loaded.

Laili unholstered a Sig P320, removed the magazine and her spare magazine and loaded.

"You might as well not even shoot again," Laili said. "That cheap-ass little first-place trophy is already mine."

"We didn't come here to win a cheap little trophy," Molka said. "Azzur only suggested this because he wanted us to shake the rust off our shooting skills before we leave tomorrow."

Laili shook her head. "You've known him a lot longer than me, but you still don't get how his mind works, do you?"

"What do you mean?"

"Nothing. No, I mean how about a side bet between us?"

"Bet what?" Molka said. "Our debit cards draw from the same little account."

Laili pointed at Molka's left wrist. "How about your ugly pilot's watch?"

"You keep telling me how ugly it is. Why would you want it?"

Laili finished loading and holstered up. "Azzur told me your uncle was wearing it during the war when his helicopter crashed and he survived, and you were wearing it when you crashed your helicopter on a mission and walked away. You think it brings good luck. And that it's also the last thing you have connected to your family."

Molka finished loading and holstered up. "Azzur tells too much."

"That's why I know it's worth more to you than money. That's why I want it. Are you down?"

"I've already outscored you in every stage."

"Then you have nothing to worry about." Laili put out her fist for bumping. "Either you're down or admit you're defeated."

Molka bumped her fist. "I'm down."

Molka shot first. She moved through the course with power and precision, without a single wasted move. Her reload could have been used as an instructional video.

When she had finished, Gary consulted with the scoring official, uncorked a big smile, and clicked on his mic. "Ladies and gentlemen, we have a new match record!"

Impressed applause!

Laili's turn. She moved through the course with such ridiculous quickness that she seemed on the edge of losing body control and stumbling. Her reload was somewhat sloppy, but her cat-like recovery reflexes made up for the excess movements.

When she had finished, Gary consulted with the scoring official again, and he again uncorked a Texas-worthy smile and clicked on his mic. "Ladies and gentlemen, by a record narrowest of margins, we have YET another new match record! Congrats to our champion, Miss Laili!"

Enthralled applause!

In the pickup truck, getting ready to leave the match, Molka removed her loyal, lucky old pilot's watch and handed it over to Laili. "Shut your big loud smart mouth before you open it for a second and listen to me. Two things. One, don't ever wear it around me. Because if you do, I'll do something about it you won't like. And two, don't ever lose it. Because if I find out you did, I'll find you and do something about it you really won't like. And those aren't false promises. Those are honest threats."

Laili smirked but kept her big loud smart mouth shut.

PROJECT MOLKA: TASK 4

PROJECT LAILI: TASK 1

DAY 1 OF 10

CHAPTER SEVEN

"This is not what I expected," Molka said. "When I imagined a tropical island, I thought flat and mostly beach. But this one is made up of steep hills covered in lots of vegetation that overlook strips of beach and natural harbors."

"Yes," Mr. Levy said. "I've been told these islands are all peaks of ancient, submerged mountains and perhaps even extinct volcanoes."

"Interesting. All this beauty sitting atop something so volatile."

Molka was dressed flight-comfortable in a sleeveless pale-yellow dress, yellow canvas sneakers, a braided ponytail, and black-framed glasses. She rode passenger in the compact white Toyota that Counsel associate Mr. Levy had rented for her.

Mr. Levy had met her at Cyril E. King Airport on Saint Thomas Island and headed toward the downtown of the island's capital city, Charlotte Amalie. The wealthy retiree came corpulent and casual in sandals, shorts, t-shirt, and straw hat. His New York City accent hit the ear edgy after a month of smooth Texas twangs.

Molka noted the oncoming cars passing by on the right. "I'm going to have to get used to driving on the left side of the road."

"This is the only US territory that does that," Mr. Levy said. "It's a little awkward at first. The roads outside the city are also very narrow and steep, with a lot of blind curves. You might want to mention that to your partner too. Her rental car is parked at your apartment, by the way."

"Another thing I noticed flying in," Molka said. "Many other—maybe dozens—of hilly little islands with little or no sign of inhabitants. Are those part of the Virgin Islands as well?"

"Some. Some are wildlife refuges, some are privately owned, and some are just plain mysterious, and people don't discuss them."

In surprising early afternoon traffic, they cruised east on a main road named Veterans Drive, which ran beside a large, blue-green harbor on the right. On the left, gift shops, fast food restaurants, and strip malls mimicked the smaller touristy beach towns in South Florida that Molka had lived near in the spring.

The weather carried South Florida's heat and humidity too.

"You live over on Saint Croix Island," she said. "How far is that from this island?"

"Forty-two miles to my house."

"How did you get here from there?"

"I chartered a private boat," he said.

"I'm going to need to rent a boat while I'm here. Can you give me a recommendation?"

"What type of boat?"

"Something like a 28-foot bay with good power and a simple GPS Chartplotter."

"Do you need a captain too?"

"No," Molka said. "I can handle that myself."

"I'll make some calls for you."

They approached a group of larger buildings, starting with an imposing, old-looking red fortress.

"That's Fort Christian," Mr. Levy said. "Built by the Danes in 1672. It's a museum now. Across from it is the Coast Guard Station, and that's the police station over there."

They exited and drove up a curving road which climbed a steep hill. A resort hotel occupied the top. Mr. Levy pulled over outside the gated entrance, parked, removed binoculars from a case in the backseat, and passed them to Molka. "Azzur said you would be interested in this view."

Molka binocular scanned the big harbor below. In the background, three massive colorful cruise ships were anchored bow to stern alongside a large pier teeming with tourists. In the foreground, an upscale shopping and restaurant complex fronted an expansive, boat-filled marina: Donar Thorsen's Yacht Marina Grande.

The marina moored about 25 huge, magnificent yachts.

"Mega yachts, mega money." He laughed. "See one you like?"

She did. Moored at the marina's far end, the most mega yacht among the mega yachts: Paz Davidoff's *Outcast*.

Molka lowered the binoculars. "I'm ready to see your new animal hospital now."

Mr. Levy parked curbside on a narrow street a block off Veterans Drive. Small busy eateries and food stores dominated the area. He and Molka exited and faced a two-story, stucco building painted a gaudy orange. A wood-railed balcony ran the second floor's length and a sign in the middle of three big first-floor, display windows read:

**Future Home of St. Thomas Animal Hospital.
Not Hiring.**

"It was a mom-and-pop-type bakery as recently as a month ago," Mr. Levy said. "They lived in the apartment upstairs: two bedrooms, one bath, nice-sized living room, and a small kitchen. Good AC. It has an entrance from inside the bakery and an external one on the side. I had it furnished for you."

"Sounds good," Molka said.

He swept his arm at the pedestrian-heavy sidewalks. "As you can see, there's a lot of foot traffic around here during the day. But I picked this location because it's not near any of the bars, so it won't be noisy at night."

"I appreciate that."

Mr. Levy pointed to a gold Toyota parked on the curb ahead of their car. "That's your partner's. Shall we get your luggage and head inside?"

He removed a red travel bag and a black tactical gear bag from the trunk. He offered to carry them, but Molka politely declined and followed him inside the former bakery's front door.

DUAL DECEPTION

Except for an old glass display counter and a wonderful, faint baked goods scent, the space sat empty.

Molka pointed to the front windows. "I'll need to cover those so people walking by won't see what's not happening in here."

Mr. Levy grimaced. "Of course. I should have thought of that. Sorry. I'll take care of it before I leave today."

He led Molka through a backroom and upstairs to the apartment. The white-walled, brown-carpeted living space featured a green upholstered couch and matching chair, a two-seat kitchen table, and a little desk with a wi-fi router. Each small bedroom contained a twin bed, a nightstand, and a dresser. The bathroom was shower only.

"No TV?" Molka said.

"Azzur said you two wouldn't have time. The other things he asked me to obtain are in here."

She followed him into the kitchen. He bent and removed two large, sealed storage tubs from the cabinet under the sink and placed them on the counter.

Molka popped the lids. The first contained her preferred Beretta 96A1 and Laili's preferred Sig P320. Both weapons came in behind-the-back holsters and included custom-made suppressors and five boxes of ammo.

The second container held two sets of tactical binoculars, two sets of night vision goggles with headgear, a large envelope Molka knew from her briefing held 20,000 US dollars in task expense cash, and a shoebox-sized sealed package which she removed.

"That box was delivered to my home two days ago," Mr. Levy said.

Molka read the package's sender address: ICM Electronics. Lowell, Massachusetts.

He flashed a nervous smile. "My wife was afraid it might be explosives or something dangerous. She insisted I bring it over here immediately."

"No worries," Molka said. "Just phones."

Mr. Levy handed her the rental car keys, removed another set from his pocket, and passed her those as well. "For your partner's car. When does she get in?"

"In a couple of hours."

"Would you like me to pick her up too?"

"No, thank you," Molka said. "I'll take care of it."

"I hope everything is satisfactory?"

"Very satisfactory."

"Happy to do my part. I'm so honored I was asked to help."

"Mr. Levy, without help from friends like you, we couldn't operate."

His eyes glistened. "Thank you."

Molka opened the refrigerator—empty. "How will you handle my introduction to Captain Savanna?"

"The captain prefers a public meeting," Mr. Levy said. "He has very particular ideas about security. So, he asked me to host a cocktail party at my home tomorrow evening and invite all the elitist snobs in the US and British Virgin Islands. The captain loves to schmooze with the elitist snobs and is an absolute maestro in the art of it. I'll introduce you to him then."

"I've never been to an elitist snob cocktail party. What should I wear?"

"Informal is fine. We're even more laid back on Saint Croix. My wife and I chose it over this island because its less crowded. You know, with all the cruisers constantly overrunning it."

Molka opened the used microwave—clean. "I understand you play chess with Captain Savanna. How's his game?"

Mr. Levy smiled. "What a great probing question. He's an accomplished player. Master of the decoy."

"I don't play. What's the decoy?"

"The decoy is luring your opponent to move a piece to a square they don't want to be on. Most of his checkmates against me have come from using this tactic. Does that tell you anything?"

"Yes," Molka said. "But I'm not sure what it is yet."

CHAPTER EIGHT

"All the fucking way from Paris to Miami, this fucking kid would NOT stop screaming. And the fucking mom didn't even care. She just fucking sat there ignoring it. I wanted to strangle them both. I'm never fucking having kids."

Molka, driving her rental car, tolerated Laili's passenger seat rant as they exited the airport and headed toward downtown Charlotte Amalie, retracing the route Mr. Levy had used earlier.

Laili took Molka aback a bit by not arriving in her usual crop top and tight jean short-shorts ensemble. Instead, she sported an adorable red floral, V-neck dress and cute white sandals.

"What the hell?" Laili said. "Why is everyone driving on the wrong side of the road?" She pointed. "Wait! Stop there! I want to get a drink. And no lectures." She smiled at Molka. "The drinking age here is 18."

In the spirit of project cooperation, Molka stopped at the little open-air café-style bar Laili had pointed to. An outdoor market across from it bustled with dark skinned locals selling junk to white and burnt red-skinned tourists.

The bar's interior décor featured flags and old license plates from around the world—many signed by the donors—and ample cigarette smoke. Large ceiling fans somewhat mitigated the late afternoon heat for the 10 or so imbibing customers.

A shaggy, college-aged male pair hunching on the bar—one white, one black, both in t-shirts, swim shorts, and flip flops—checked Molka and Laili out all the way to a table next to the street side-railing.

Laili took the server girl's drink recommendation of a Painkiller: locally produced Cruzan Rum mixed with pineapple juice, orange juice, and cream of coconut.

Molka ordered a bottled water.

The drinks arrived, and Laili took a healthy pull from an oversized straw. "Damn, that's good! I need a cigarette now."

She surveyed the surroundings and smiled. "I love a good dive bar. They always make the strongest drinks. And this island is stunningly pretty. Did you see from your plane how clear the water is? What am I driving?"

"Same thing as me, in gold," Molka said.

"How far is our place from here?"

"Few blocks."

"That associate guy get all our gear?"

"Mr. Levy. Yes."

"Do you have my phone?" Laili said. "I'm supposed to text Azzur and let him know I made it."

Molka removed Laili's encrypted phone from her purse and passed it to her. Laili tapped out a quick text, read a reply, and went back to her straw.

"What did he say?" Molka said.

"Don't text him again."

"Same thing he told me. He also told me you and I should not text each other anything task related."

"Same," Laili said.

"So let's plan to meet at least every other day to liaison."

"What's a liaison?"

"It means we'll update each other and coordinate on our task. We'll do that at our apartment, but we'll consider this our first liaison meeting. Let's start with stating the individual goals of our task. Can you do that?"

Laili open-mouth sneered. "Of course. I get Paz to break up with that dirty little whore Caryn Thorsen before their wedding in 10 days. Then when Paz leaves for home, you get that pirate guy to kidnap him and his boat with the drugs and gold. While the navy special ops team rescues Paz, you steal his boat and bring it to contractors to offload. Then we get our bonuses and eight days of vacation in this paradise."

Molka nodded. "Good."

Laili smirked sarcastic. "Thanks, ugly.

"You're welcome, brat."

By Azzur's orders, Molka had memorized Laili's individual task instructions. She wanted to confirm that Laili had memorized them too. "What's your plan for Paz?"

"He spends every night with Caryn," Laili said. "Mostly on the *Outcast*, but sometimes at her dad's house where she lives. The only time they're not together is during the day when she runs her dad's marina. While she's doing that, Paz has been taking windsurfing lessons at a place called Sapphire Beach. I already signed up online for lessons there. That's where I'm going to start taking him away from her. What's your plan with the pirate guy?"

"Mr. Levy is going to introduce me to Captain Savanna tomorrow evening at a cocktail party he's hosting. I'll discuss a plan with him then."

"Well, just don't fuck your part up," Laili said. "Because I got mine handled."

"Nothing is decided until it's decided."

The shaggy pair of college guys at the bar unstuck themselves from their stools and approached Molka and Laili's table.

The white guy spoke first. "Afternoon. I'm Kyle; he's Sean."

"Sup," Sean said. "You ladies just get in?"

"Yeah," Laili said.

"Welcome to Saint Thomas," Kyle said.

"Thanks," Molka said. "Have a good day."

"Hey, don't be like that," Sean said. "We're just nice local guys, not creepers."

Kyle laughed. "Yeah, and don't worry, we promise we have nothing to do with the 'zombie girls.'"

"What's the 'zombie girls?'" Laili said.

Sean punched his arm. "Shut up, stupid. Don't even joke about that with the ladies."

Molka picked up her phone and searched.

Laili repeated. "What's the 'zombie girls?'"

Sean smiled. "Can we buy you ladies a drink?"

Molka read from her phone. "The 'zombie girls' are a mystery around here this summer and fall. They're tourist girls who go missing for a few days and then show back up in a zombie-like state and can't remember where they were or what happened."

"That's messed up," Laili said.

"Yeah it is," Sean said. "Very messed up. My boy shouldn't have said anything. We don't want to freak you out, especially since you just got here. Like I said, we're nice guys." He smiled again. "How about those drinks?"

"No, thank you," Molka said.

"A Painkiller," Laili said. "And a double shot of Cuervo. And a pack of menthols."

"You got it," Sean said.

"Be right back," Kyle said.

They went to fetch.

Laili laughed. "Guys are such idiots. They'll do anything a hot girl tells them."

"Well, tell them thanks and we're leaving," Molka said. "Because we are."

"Let's see what else we can get out of them first."

Their server waved at Molka and Laili from the bar and pointed at the drink, shots, and cigarettes the guys ordered. "Is this for you?"

"Yes," Laili said.

Kyle and Sean returned with Laili's requests.

"We got shots for us too," Kyle said.

Laili raised one. "Slam time."

The three kids powered down their shots, and Laili took a disposable lighter from her purse and lit a cigarette.

"What are you ladies doing tonight?" Sean said. "We know some great bars besides this one."

"We're heading home for the evening," Molka said.

"Why so early? The partying doesn't even get started here until after 10."

Molka forced a yawn. "It's been a long day and a long flight, and I'm tired."

Kyle looked at Laili. "Is she your mom?"

Laili exploded into laughter and fell from her chair for effect. "Yes! That old lady is my tired old mom!"

"I'm not her mom," Molka said. "And I'm not old and you little boys need to leave, or I'm going to get mad."

The boys took Molka's serious face, seriously.

"All right, baby," Sean said. "We give up. You're too tough for us." They laughed again, stood, and left the bar.

Laili sat back and sighed at Molka. "You're no fun."

Molka waved at their server. "Our bill please."

The server brought Molka the bill. Molka reviewed it and smirked. "The little punks put the drinks and cigarettes they bought you on our tab."

"Sorry," the server said. "They told me to do that. I thought when I asked if it was hers, she was ok-ing it for your bill. I'm so sorry."

"It's fine." Molka paid the bill and stood. "Coming?"

Laili stood, scanned the table, pawed through her purse, and scanned the table again. "Where's my phone? It was laying right here." She pounded the table. "Shit! They took it!"

"Great," Molka said. "She's been on the island less than an hour and she's already lost one of Azzur's expensive encrypted phones."

"Shut up, ugly. Let's go after them!"

Laili ran out and Molka followed her to the car. They mounted up and pulled out into the one-way street leaving the bar. They arrived at the corner cross street and searched both ways.

"There they are!" Laili pointed to the right. Half a block away, the pair walked in tandem on the sidewalk and vanished around the corner of a building.

Molka punched it and reached the point where they had disappeared. They walked a long, narrow alley unaware.

"Perfect," Laili said. "Drop me here and go around the block and cut them off." She jumped out.

Molka screamed the tires, turned hard at the corner, flew to the end of the street, turned hard at the opposite corner, and screech-stopped into an alley-blocking position. The pair—30 feet away—hadn't noticed Laili's stealth approach coming from behind them.

They identified Molka, startle-stopped, and spun to run.

Laili, on scene, dropped Kyle with a front kick to the chin and jumped on him.

Sean jumped on Laili.

Molka jumped from the car.

While Laili continued to wail punches on Kyle, Molka peeled Sean off her back with a side kick to his head.

Sean moaned and crawled to his feet.

Molka held out her hand. "Who has our phone?"

Sean pulled the stolen phone from his shorts, tossed it to Molka, and fled.

"I got it," Molka said and scanned for witnesses. "We need to leave."

Laili landed one more punch on Kyle's head and stood.

Kyle staggered to his feet. "You hit like a girl. Now I want to hear you scream like one." He pulled and deployed a butterfly knife.

Big mistake.

Laili spun a blur-fast roundhouse into his temple.

He went down and out.

Laili went to work on him again, dropping vicious body stomps with her thick-soled sandals.

Molka moved to stop her, but Laili stomped him one last time, ran back to the car, and got in. "Come on. Let's go after that other fucker and fuck him up too."

Molka got back in the car and sat unmoving.

Laili's fist slammed the dash. "Come on!"

"No," Molka said. "We're not here to fight with the local petty thieves. And we're not here to drink. And we're not here to party. We're here to work. And from this second on, that's all we should be doing until the task is completed. Understand?"

"You're not my fucking project manager. You can't tell me what to do."

Molka flipped Laili's phone back to her. "I'm not trying to tell you what to do. I'm trying to help you. Azzur gave you your instructions, but I am the senior project on this task, and I've had more covert operative experience than you, which isn't that much. So we need to put aside our little competitiveness and personality clashes and super-focus and work closely together if we're going to pull this off."

Laili laughed. "What, you think we're going to bond like sisters? Like you did with that crazy Darcy bitch on your last task?"

Molka shot Laili with a disgusted glare. "Who would ever want to be your sister?"

Molka started the car and headed for the apartment.

Laili lit a cigarette.

They drove in silence.

After five minutes, Laili flicked her cigarette out the window. "When we get home can I have some of the task money? I have to buy a new swimsuit and a wind surfboard. Time for me to get to work."

CHAPTER NINE

"We're going to die. You do realize that, right?" Donar Thorsen paced Yacht Haven Grande's private office in a white golf shirt and pleated, pressed khakis.

"Dad. Stop." Caryn Thorsen—wearing a pure Italian cashmere navy blazer and matching slacks with her long hair slicked back and pulled into a fierce ponytail—sat at the desk perusing a bridal site on a laptop.

Donor Thorsen continued pacing. "Running a little weed into Puerto Rico every couple of months is nothing to the Feds. Hell, it's almost considered polite. But this is—"

"It costs twice as much, but I think I've decided on the off-the-shoulder, tea-length-chiffon lace for my bridesmaids." Caryn spun the laptop for Donar's viewing. "Which color do you like better, dusk or dawn?"

Donar paced on.

"Dad? I asked which color you like better?"

"We're going to die."

Caryn sighed and pushed the laptop away. "Ok, let's go ahead and get the weekly nervous breakdown over with."

He stopped and braced himself over the desk. "I think we should ask them to come pick up their product and their gold and say we're not up to the job, with our deepest apologies."

"I don't think they'll let us back out now. Besides, I had to keep Paz occupied for three days and three nights while their people installed and loaded that compartment. I'm not letting that be all for nothing."

"Gus worked in Belize," Donar said. "He knows these people. He's seen what they do to partners who make even the slightest mistakes. They torture you for days with power tools and then dissolve you in a barrel of acid. It's called making soup."

Caryn sighed, annoyed. "Gus tells a lot of terrifying stories. Who knows how many are true, if any?"

Donar resumed his pacing. "We have to call this deal off."

"No, we don't. Because we promised mom."

"Don't throw your mother at me again."

"We both stood there in that ICU and promised her," she said. "Mom didn't cry. She didn't complain. All she asked is we not screw up and lose this place her father spent his life building. But we did screw up. And we will lose it unless we get a major cash influx, like soon."

"What about your modeling and acting careers? Those professions can be very high paying."

"I have no modeling and acting careers."

"Why do you say that?" he said.

"There are a billion beautiful women in the world I have to compete with, and I'm a terrible actor. And I'm not going to get any more beautiful, and I don't have time to get better at acting. This is our only choice."

"It's just too dangerous." Donar stopped and braced himself over the desk again. "Here's what's going to happen: Have Paz spend the night with you at the house the rest of the week, and I'll get the men to open that compartment, offload everything, and then—"

Caryn banged her fist on the desk and sprung up. "No! Here's what's going to happen: The product and gold stays right where it's at. And in 10 days, I'm marrying Paz and taking the product and gold to the connection. Then I'm coming back to do it again and again and again until we have enough money to pull this business disaster from bankruptcy and a lot, lot, lot more. Then you can go back to playing golf all day. And I can let my mom rest in peace, get a divorce, and live the luxury lifestyle I deserve forever."

CHAPTER 10

The day of the week, the expensive, flashy blue suit, the well-fed middle-aged paunch, the over-sprayed, thin combover, and the swagger of the walk all might have said "televangelist preacher coming straight from his studio-church" to the officer on duty in the Saint Thomas, US Virgin Islands Police Station.

But the ID next to his badge said *Special Agent Thomas Justain, National Bureau of Narcotics, US Department of Justice*.

"I'm here to see Detective Hodge," Justain said. "She's expecting me."

"She stepped out for a moment," the officer said. "She asked you to wait in her office."

Detective Lieutenant Naomi Hodge leaned cross-armed against the police station's side wall and watched 20 plus, excited, local kids swarm an ice cream truck and place their orders.

The mid-30s, thickset black woman wore a navy-blue polo featuring a USVI Police logo and black tactical-style pants. Only the gold detective badge on her belt beside her holstered Glock differentiated her from a regular patrol officer.

When all the kids had gotten what they wanted, she paid the ice cream truck vendor, accepted 20 plus loving hugs, and headed back inside the station.

Detective Hodge entered her office. "Good afternoon, Agent Justain."

Justain sat behind her desk, smiling at his phone. "Today's a milestone day."

"Is it? How so?"

"When I took over as Special Agent in Charge of the Caribbean Division—26 months and 16 days ago—their social media footprint was piddling. No, it wasn't even piddling; it was non-existent. I made that a top priority, and today we just went over 10,000 followers."

"Congratulations," Hodge said.

"My personal account is over 1,000 now as well. How many followers does this department have?"

"I really don't pay attention to those type of things."

"What about your personal accounts?"

"I don't have personal accounts," she said. "I try to keep a low profile."

"An opportunity not taken is an opportunity lost. You have to keep your name out there. It's all about branding today."

Hodge smiled polite. "I'm not a brand. I'm a police officer."

"How's your roofie problem coming along?"

"You mean the 'zombie girls,'" she said. "An NIB agent came here and interviewed the last victims. They still couldn't remember anything, so he said to let him know if there are any more cases and left."

Justain chuckled. "Sounds like a horror movie plot. 'The Zombie Girls of Saint Thomas. Who will be taken next?' That type of thing is kind of hard on the tourism, isn't it?"

"It's a lot harder on the girls. Mind if I sit down?"

He smiled and vacated her chair.

"Thank you." Hodge sat. "Your message said you had something big you wanted to discuss. What do you have for me?"

"It's not what I have for you. It's what you have for me. Which is 1,000 pounds of fentanyl and a cartel payoff in the form of 100, 400-ounce gold bars ready to ship from your island."

Hodge leaned forward. "Has that been confirmed?"

"My superstar confidential source confirmed it left Belize and arrived here at the beginning of the month and is set to leave for parts unknown within two weeks. But I'm not going to let that happen. You ever hear of a 1,000 pounds of fentanyl being seized before?"

She shook her head. "No."

"That's because no one has ever seized that outrageous amount in one shipment. The butt-kissers in the San Diego Division stumbled onto 250 pounds, and they all got bumped up two grades. Lord almighty, for 1,000 pounds they'll probably make me an assistant administrator." Justain smiled. "That means a townhouse in Arlington, country club membership, Nats season tickets, and no more scraping by in backwater divisions."

"What will your reward be for the gold bars?"

"Well, in DC these days, 100 million, or whatever that gold is worth, doesn't mean too much. That amount could be a rounding error for a smaller department's budget."

Hodge smirked. "Must be nice."

"The gold will slide down some bureaucratic sinkhole and be quickly forgotten. But the tragic scourge of fentanyl isn't going anywhere. And my astonishing record bust will generate headlines, shares, likes, and follows beyond my wildest dreams."

Hodge smiled polite again. "Sounds like you've given this a lot of thought. I appreciate the professional courtesy call. Good luck on your investigation and your promotion and…your perks. I'm sure your team will do a great job."

"No team on this case." Justain pointed at the logo on her shirt. "Just us."

"VIPD is an underfunded, overworked little department. I don't know how much help we can give a major federal investigation."

"I'm not talking about your department helping, I'm talking about you. And I could probably make sure you got the Presidential Medal of Valor for your efforts."

"That's very generous of you," she said. "But I didn't sign up for this job to get medals."

He crossed the room to a chair, slid it beside Hodge's desk, and sat. "You had a younger cousin in Orlando. Her name was Cheryl. She OD'd on heroin she didn't know was laced with fentanyl, didn't she?"

The corners of Hodge's mouth sagged. "That's right."

"Cheryl couldn't be saved. But how many other cousins and aunts and uncles and sisters and brothers and mothers and fathers might be if 1,000 pounds of that poison is taken down?"

Hodge rose and walked to the office window. Some of her ice cream kids were playing touch football in the street below, all smiles. "I would have to get authorization from the commissioner."

"I already did. You're at my disposal." Justain smiled. "Seems he's more interested in a Presidential Medal of Valor than you."

She returned to her desk. "Why did you pick me for this honor?"

"When you asked me to help you out on that little pill case you had here last year, I was impressed by your investigative skills. Namely, your rapport with the public. No one is more wired into what's happening on this island than Lieutenant Detective Naomi Hodge. The people love you here. They tell you everything bad they see happening, especially your own superstar CS, the one who broke that pill case. The one you call 'the Angel.' And that's who we need to talk to first."

"I don't talk to the Angel. The Angel talks to me. Actually, they don't talk to me. It's all hand-written messages that appear on my doorstep. I have no idea who they are or where they're located."

"Ok, we'll just have to shake the bushes and shake some tongues loose. The Angel will hear about it and get in touch." Justain stood and put the chair back where he had found it. "Your commissioner said you guys keep a usual suspects and undesirables list."

"He does," Hodge said.

"Get it, please. We'll start harassing them right now."

PROJECT MOLKA: TASK 4

PROJECT LAILI: TASK 1

DAY 2 OF 10

CHAPTER 11

"**Y**es, Giselle! That's it! You got it! You see her, Paz?"

"How could I not," Paz said. "It took me two weeks of lessons to do that."

"And you still can't do it that good."

The windsurf instructor and a trim, tanned, swimsuit-and-sunglasses-wearing Paz stood ankle deep off Sapphire Beach, watching in astonishment.

Laili—in a one-piece, red swimsuit and on a white board with a red-striped sail—cut through the turquoise waters with a model's grace and an athlete's agility.

She ended her ride, pulled her board ashore, and approached the instructor. As directed, she used a French accent to match her French passport name. "How was that?"

"Good," the instructor said. "Very good. Just keep your weight a little more on your back foot."

"Ok."

"Is windsurfing popular in France or something? Because there is no way today was your first lesson."

"I swear it is," Laili said. "I just bought the board yesterday."

The instructor let his leer fall on Laili's rear end. "You said you just got here. I have my own boat. I would love to take you on a free sightseeing tour and—"

"Don't listen to him," Paz said. "He gives that free boat tour line to every pretty girl who takes his class."

The instructor smiled. "Come on, Paz. You can't even spare one? But I have to get ready for my next lesson anyway." The instructor departed.

"Later, Terry." Paz offered Laili his hand. "Hi. I'm Paz."

Laili smiled and shook. "I'm Giselle. Yes. I thought that was you. You're Paz Davidov, leader of Team Paz. I watched you in the *Honor and Glory* League finals in Toronto four years ago. You guys dominated!"

Paz smiled. "We did. Surprised anyone remembers."

"But you had some hair then."

He ran a hand over his smooth scalp. "Well, all the men in my family go bald by age 30, so I decided to face the inevitable now."

"I think it looks handsome on you."

Paz smiled. "Thanks. You an HG player too?"

"I played," Laili said. "But I wasn't someone a legend like you would call a player."

"Terry said you're visiting from France."

"I'm actually here to work as a vet tech at a new animal hospital opening soon."

"Cool," he said. "How do you like it here? Having fun?"

"It's really nice. I don't know anyone to have fun with yet, though. That's why I joined this class."

"You don't know anyone here at all?"

"No one," she said. "Just the woman I work with. But she's a lot older."

"I don't know too many people here either. My friends came down with me, but they all went back home. Hey, you hungry?"

Laili smiled. "Starving."

"I found a place here that has a conch chowder that will make you question your faith. Want to check it out for lunch with me?"

She smiled again. "Sounds great, Paz."

"Cool. Did you drive?"

"Yes."

"Ok." Paz said. "I'll grab my board and you can follow me over."

Sapphire Beach Hotel sat on Sapphire Beach, and a pool behind the hotel fronted the beach proper.

DUAL DECEPTION

    A loner guest reclined in one of the pool's lounge chairs: a mid-20s, Hispanic man wearing a thick Cuban link gold chain over a black t-shirt and baggy jean shorts.

    He had watched Paz's, and later, Laili's, lesson. He had also watched Paz and Laili's conversation afterward. And when they left the beach together and carried their boards toward their cars, he took out his phone and videoed them. And then he walked to a motorcycle and followed them.

CHAPTER 12

Mr. Levy and his wife enjoyed their quiet Saint Croix retirement in a large, gorgeous home located high on a gorgeous point and overlooking a gorgeous stretch of Caribbean Sea.

The boat he had chartered to bring Molka over from Saint Thomas docked in Christiansted. She transferred to a cab and arrived at his cocktail party already in progress on the pool deck.

Set up on the party perimeter was a bar with two bartenders, an hors d'oeuvres station, and a great-sounding four-piece reggae band singing how "every little thing gonna be alright."

Drinking guests in the dozens mingled.

Molka spent the day shopping native and chose as her outfit a cute Tommy Bahama, sleeveless, coral sun dress. She had ponytailed her hair and accessorized with sandals and her black-framed glasses. She had planned on wearing her old pilot's watch for good luck right up until she remembered it belonged to Laili.

Mr. Levy greeted Molka. "The captain will arrive shortly. When he does, I think it's best if we wait toward the end of the evening to introduce you. He likes to make the rounds and chat up every guest. I'll bring him to you."

"Understood," Molka said.

"I have to get back to entertaining, so just feel free to make yourself at home."

"Thank you."

Molka asked the bartender to make her a whiskey sour she wouldn't drink and sat at an empty table on the pool's near side to observe the party on the far side.

The Levy's US and British Virgin Islands "elitist snob" guests presented as a late-middle ages mix of old money, new money, face lifts, neck lifts, and butt lifts. And as Mr. Levy said, they dressed casually and in an age-appropriate way, with one notable exception: a slender white man in his 60s, sipping a cocktail and sporting black-dyed hair, skinny jeans, and a hip-hop artist t-shirt.

He spotted Molka, broke from the pack, and moved toward her.

Molka glanced away to dissuade him.

He wouldn't be dissuaded.

Another New York City accent greeted her. "Good evening. I'm Jacob Weinberg. Call me Jake." He held out a hand for shaking.

Molka smiled, courteous and shook. "I'm Molka."

He helped himself to the seat across from her. "I find beautiful, unaccompanied women irresistible, but if I had my guess, you're here to hook-up with the same person we are all here to see: Captain Savanna." He ogled Molka again. "The captain never fails to disappoint with his female conquests."

"I'm no conquest," Molka said. "I just started working for Mr. Levy. He invited me. I didn't know what to expect."

"Captain Savanna and I are considered nautical neighbors—my island is two miles south of his—but we've never become real friends. He keeps close company. And he never entertains outside of his business affairs."

Jacob "call me Jake" Weinberg seemed harmless but exuded an unsettling vibe.

Bail on him.

"Do you know where the bathroom is?" Molka said.

Weinberg ignored her and continued. "I, on the other hand, love to entertain. Buying my own island was the best thing I've ever done. It made me realize who I am. What I'm free to do there is follow my own personality. I can't be totally wacko with what I do in the regular world. It affects a lot of other people who will be angry with me. But on my own island, I think the thoughts I want to think. And I'm free to explore as I see fit."

His meandering musings brutalized the brain, but since he was Mr. Levy's guest, Molka kept playing it polite.

"Interesting perspective. Well, I'm going to try and find the bathroom."

Weinberg edged his chair closer to Molka's. "You should come to one of my parties. I have them every weekend, all weekend. They're way better than these lame Levy snooze fests." He took out his phone and cracked open a creepy smile. "Give me your numbers."

An exited murmur and scattered applause spared Molka.

Weinberg popped up. "The captain has arrived. I better get in line."

He moved fast to join the adulating, mobbing guests.

Molka rose for a better view.

The captain's wonderfully quaffed, wavy, shoulder-length, dark-brown side-parted hair with the perfect bang flip matched the photos from her briefing. But he substituted all-black attire for a slim-cut white linen suit over an open-collar white silk shirt. A bright yellow trumpet-shaped flower in his lapel offered a stark but pleasant contrast.

And he arrived with an entourage.

He escorted a tall, young black beauty on his right arm and a tall, young Hispanic beauty on his left. Both glided in identical, white gowns trimmed with a yellow that matched the captain's flower.

And behind the captain, followed by far the sturdiest, fittest, tallest man at the party. Perhaps not yet 40, he styled cropped, brown hair and a full, bushy brown beard. Like the captain, he too sported a white linen suit, but he wore his over a black silk shirt. A shoulder holster bulge under his left arm wasn't hard to notice.

Molka retook her seat and kept observing her asset.

Accompanied by Mr. Levy, and with his ladies at his sides and his man in his shadow, the captain moved to each individual and couple with handshakes and hugs and broad smiles and laughs and whispers and thoughtful nods and selfies and pleasant conversation.

Mr. Levy's comment about the captain's schmooze prowess proved accurate.

After over an hour, Mr. Levy brought the captain to a well-dressed older lady sitting with a well-inebriated, older man at the table next to Molka and nodded to Molka she would be next.

The well-dressed lady glowed at the captain. "Oh, Captain Savanna, you are much more handsome in person!"

DUAL DECEPTION

The captain smiled. "And you are much too kind, my lady, and good evening." He bowed and took and kissed her hand.

The captain's accent sounded pleasant, but odd. If you were American, you might think he was English. If you were English, you might think he was Dutch. And if you were Israeli, you might think he was neither and his accent was a practiced contrivance.

The well-dressed lady continued. "Captain Savanna, my husband was just telling me your seamanship is the stuff of legend."

"Again, you are much too generous with your praise, my lady." The captain placed a hand on his man's shoulder. "My quartermaster, Mister Cutter here, is the real sailor of my crew."

Mister Cutter spoke with a genuine English accent. "The captain's just being modest, my lady. He's a first-rate sailor in his own right, to be sure."

After a bit more mindless banter from the lady, she and her husband said their goodnights and left. Mr. Levy guided the captain to Molka's table.

The captain approached with scrutiny tempered by politeness.

"Captain," Mr. Levy said, "this is Molka. She's the friend of our mutual friends. Molka, this is Captain LJ Savanna."

"A pleasure, Lady Molka." The captain smiled and kept eye contact as he took and kissed Molka's hand.

Molka smiled polite to conceal her discomfort. Hand kissing was a bit friendly for an asset. "Hello."

The captain gestured toward Mister Cutter. "May I also present my quartermaster, Mister Cutter."

His imposing man winked at Molka. "Evening, missy."

The captain continued. "And, best for last, Lady Maribeth and Lady Nina."

His ladies forced smiling nods toward Molka.

Molka returned their slights.

"Mister Cutter," the captain said. "Please escort Lady Maribeth and Lady Nina out front and call our driver. I'll join you shortly."

"Aye, captain," Mister Cutter said.

The captains' ladies frowned softly betraying a jealous-annoyance mixture.

The captain put an arm around each's waist. "Do not lament, my loves. I shall make up my absence to both of you a thousand-fold...," he kissed each on the cheek, "...later tonight."

Mister Cutter and the ladies left.

Mr. Levy smiled, somewhat embarrassed. "Well, I need to say goodnight to my guests." He departed.

The captain smiled at Molka again. "May I sit?"

"Please," Molka said.

"Oh, Captain Savanna, I must have another word!" The well-dressed older woman had broken away from her older well-inebriated husband as they exited and fast-clipped her high heels across the pool deck to Molka's table. "I almost forgot to mention that my foundation, The Greater Virgin Islands Conservation Fund, is having its annual pledge drive this week."

The captain's smile masked annoyance. "Has it been a year already?"

"Yes, it has. And I hope we can count on your very generous support, once again."

"Of course, my lady. Your office can expect it."

"Thank you so much, Captain Savanna. Good night." She held out her hand for another kiss.

The captain obliged. "Good night…once again." His smile morphed into a smirk as he watched her leave. "She said she *almost* forgot to mention that pledge drive. But they never forget to ask for more. Untold volumes have been written on the endless generosity expected from those who have means. However, no one dares publish even a small pamphlet on what damage such unchecked generosity requests do to the supply of those means." He turned back to Molka and smiled. "Still, we need to do our part to protect these beautiful islands. Do we not?"

Molka shrugged. "I suppose."

The captain scanned over each shoulder. "We seem to be all alone now. It's a magnificent evening, isn't it?"

"Yes. Ok. Everything is on schedule, as far as I know. My partner is working the inside, and I'll have her verify in the next day or two and keep you advised. Then we can make our plan for the exchange." Molka removed her phone from her purse. "You can go ahead and give me your number."

"I never speak on the phone, Lady Molka. I don't even own a phone."

"How will we make contact?"

The captain presented the slightly crooked rogue smile he had displayed in the initial briefing photo Azzur had shown Molka. It played different from his normal smile. And then he stood, moved near the pool's edge, and gazed beyond it out to the Caribbean. "Lady Molka, would you join me over here please? There's something I want to ask you."

What?

Oh no. Is he going to try and seduce the island newcomer by the moonlight on the Caribbean? Ugh. Azzur said Laili drew the honeypot duty of the task.

Alright. But the captain would be in for disappointment. She wasn't as easily impressed by male bravado as the frustrated, middle-aged, rich women he had titillated earlier.

Molka put her phone back in her purse, rose, and joined the captain poolside.

"May I see your glasses?" the captain said.

"My glasses?"

"Yes, if you please."

She removed and handed them to the captain. He folded them with care and tucked them into his jacket's breast pocket.

"Why did you do that?" Molka said.

The captain shoved her face first into the pool.

Molka plunged to the bottom, pushed off, surfaced, and swam to the shallow end. "Before I get out and get very mad, care to explain yourself?"

The captain stood with his feet spread shoulder-width apart, hands on hips, and face ablaze. "Another very pretty lady once approached me with an attractive business proposition. Later, I found out she wore a recording device for a law enforcement agency. It cost me four years of misfortune. But your listening device is now destroyed."

"I'm not wearing a listening device," Molka said. "I'm not even wearing a bra."

"Are you now, or have you ever been, affiliated in any way with the National Bureau of Narcotics of the United States?"

"No."

"Are you now, or have you ever been, affiliated in any way with the former *Policía Federal* or the current *Guardia Nacional* of Mexico?"

"Of course not."

The captain moved to the shallow end and offered Molka his hand. She took it, and he helped her out to stand dripping on the pool deck.

She rung out the hem of her dress. "You have a very unorthodox way of doing business, Captain Savanna."

"I'm in a very unorthodox business."

"Ok. I'll concede that. Now getting back to our conversation, if you don't own a phone, how can I get in touch with you?"

"You can't. But I can get in touch with you. And I will do so at my choosing." He moved to leave. "Good evening, Lady Molka."

PROJECT MOLKA: TASK 4

PROJECT LAILI: TASK 1

DAY 3 OF 10

CHAPTER 13

"**H**old up, boss lady." Gus Ramos trailed behind Caryn on her morning pre-opening inspection walk of Yacht Marina Grande's retail and leisure complex.

Caryn—exquisite in a burgundy velvet Chanel pantsuit—didn't take her eyes off a tablet checklist. "What do you need, Gus?"

Gus spoke in good, Spanish accented, English. "I have something to tell you."

"If you're going to tell me how pretty I am again, I'm really busy."

"No. I have something else to tell you."

Caryn stopped, turned, and assumed a stern face. "First I have something to tell you. I heard from the waitstaff about your little side hustle pimping whores to the tourists and for Jake Weinberg's private parties."

Gus pulled up his sagging, baggy shorts. "No. I'm not pimping whores. I am building an escort service. Nothing but classy ladies."

"You just better make sure your clown crew gets that load delivered on time this week."

He waved a dismissive hand. "I got that."

"Wait. Did you say an escort service?" She laughed. "Why would a guy like you think to build an escort service?"

Gus's face brightened. "For my future. To have something of my own. My own business. Something that's semi-legit. Something where I'm not just cleaning up the boss's messes."

Caryn sneered. "You mean like the messes me, and my dad make?"

"Hey, I just go where I'm told. And do what I'm told. For now. That's why I'm starting my own thing."

"Well, your ambitions aside, do me a favor and keep your *classy* girls away from here. We've had complaints of them working the restaurant lounge."

"Ok. My bad." Gus pulled up his shorts again.

"You know, the gun in your pocket is what keeps pulling down your pants. It's not cute. Maybe invest in a belt." She resumed her walk. "Now what did you want to tell me?"

He took out his phone. "This." He played video of Laili's windsurfing lesson and of her talking to Paz on the beach.

Caryn watched. "She's prettier than the last two little girls he played with. A lot prettier."

"And this too." Gus showed her the video of Paz and Laili's lunch date.

"He took her to Vinny's Hideout for conch soup?" she said. "I thought that was our thing."

Gus smiled. "They had a real good time too. Want me to find out who she is?"

Caryn resumed her walk. "No. I couldn't care less. I only asked you to keep an eye on Paz when he's out of my sight during the day because he's a stupid boy who doesn't believe in personal security. But if the wrong people find out who he's related to, they might take advantage of that stupidity."

Gus smiled. "I think that's already happened to him."

Caryn smirked. "Funny." She walked on a few more paces and halted again. "Find out who she is anyway and let me know."

CHAPTER 14

Molka entered the apartment to burnt food stench. "What were you cooking?" She moved to the kitchen and opened the microwave. Greasy remnants coated the inside. "Eck. What exploded in here?"

Laili wandered in wearing her sleeping tee and boxers. "I left it in too long."

"You think? What was it?"

"They're called pates. They sell them really cheap on the street here. Its deep-fried dough stuffed with beef or chicken or fish. They're amazing. I have some more in that bag on the counter, try one."

"No thank you." Molka grabbed a yogurt from the refrigerator, a spoon from the drawer, sat at the little kitchen table, and ate ravenous.

Laili dropped into the chair across from her. "Oh yes, I forgot. You're miss, 'I always eat clean and workout. That's why I have such a hot body and I'm so hot.'"

Molka smiled sarcastic. "Thanks for noticing."

"You know, I don't just call you ugly to mess with you. There's truth in it too. Because face it: You're really not that attractive."

Molka dropped her spoon. "Wow. That really hurts. Tonight, I'll hug my pillow and have myself a good long cry over your opinion of my looks."

Laili smirked. "You're soooo funny too."

"This is supposed to be a liaison meeting, not insult hour."

"Yes, and I wanted to get this over with first thing. Where have you been all morning?"

Molka finished the yogurt, rose, tossed her empty yogurt cup in the trash, and washed the spoon. "Looking at rental boats." She moved to the living room and sat in the lone chair. "You wouldn't believe how expensive they are here. I have to keep looking. How did things go with Paz?"

Laili moved to the couch, flopped down, and smiled. "Too easy. It only took me one windsurfing lesson and one lunch date to have him questioning his whole relationship with that dirty little whore, Caryn. We're going to hang out again today…" She craned her head to view a little kitchen wall clock, "…I need to call him in a few. I told you I got this. What happened with the pirate last night?"

"Captain Savanna informed me he doesn't own a phone and pushed me into the pool."

"What is he, a fucking lunatic?"

"No," Molka said. "He's just suspicious. He thought I might be undercover law enforcement trying to set him up."

Laili rose and headed for her bedroom. "Anyone that suspicious, you better be suspicious about."

Molka started to disagree. But she didn't.

CHAPTER 15

Laili lay on her bed and read to Paz from her phone on speaker mode. "The Skyride to Paradise Point whisks you 700 feet above the town of Charlotte Amalie. As one of the 'must do' attractions in the Caribbean, the Skyride carries 24 passengers every seven minutes along its eight-tower ascent of Flag Hill. Once you 'ride the view' the true meaning of limin' is revealed, high above the hustle and bustle of Saint Thomas Harbor. But what does limin' mean?"

"It's Virgin Islands-Caribbean lingo," Paz said. "Limin' basically means to chill and relax."

"Cool. So, you're down to do it?"

"Yes!" Paz said. "I've wanted to since I got here. Caryn won't though. She said it's just for the tourists. But that's what I am, right?"

"See you there!"

Laili, in a bikini top over tight, short-shorts, and Paz, in a tee shirt over swim trunks, stood alongside four jabbering, malodorous,

German cruisers in a Paradise Point Sky Ride cable car climbing to Paradise Point.

The day had matured into typical Saint Thomas in October: clear, bright, hot, humid, and magnificent.

At the ride's top, they exited the car, passed by all the inevitable gift shops, and found a spot on the crowded observation porch railing.

Paz placed his sunglasses atop his head and viewed the panorama of green islands floating on emerald water under light blue skies.

"Amazing!" Paz said. "Well worth the ride up!"

"Speak for yourself," Laili said. "Because for me, it wasn't worth those German farts funking up the cable car."

He laughed. "It has to be the constant starchy feedings on those cruise ships. Everyone's bloated and gassy."

"Uuk. So gross. I almost kicked out a window. Serious."

Paz laughed again. "You're so cute. Now what specifically did you say you wanted to show me up here?"

She pointed to the east. "Look over there; what do you see?"

"That's Saint John Island."

"And what do you see beyond that?"

"Tortola," he said. "That's part of the British Virgin Islands."

"And what do you see beyond that?"

"The Atlantic Ocean."

"And what do you see beyond that?"

Paz squinted. "You mean Africa?"

"No," Laili said. "I mean a whole big world of possibilities."

He nodded. "I know. You're right. And like you said yesterday, most people who hook up at a club don't get married."

"How did that go down anyway?"

"First night here, a messenger delivers me this invitation to a VIP room in this club. So, me and my boys go and we're having a good time, and then this big guy comes up to me, I guess he was the bouncer, and says there's a beautiful model in another VIP room who wants to meet just me. So, I'm like, take me to the other VIP room. We get back there, and there is a beautiful model in a short dress waiting. It's Caryn. And she said the big guy had told her a hot rich guy wanted to meet her in that VIP room. Not sure what was up with that happy mix-up, but we vibed anyway, and headed back to my yacht and…you know."

Laili made a gag face. "Yeah, I know."

"Next morning, she snuck out before I woke up and she ghosted me. Then six days later, I hear from her. She tells me we're in love and should get married. I'm like, 'she's super-hot, has a rich family like mine, ok, why not get married'? So, we are."

"Hear how crazy it sounds when you say it out loud like that?"

"Yes," Paz said. "But in a way I feel sorry for her too. Her mother died of breast cancer when Caryn was just 13. And her father treats her more like a business partner than a daughter. All he does is play golf all day and let her run things. She's had to grow up fast."

"She's not the only one who had to do that, and her, so-called tough life isn't your problem unless you make it your problem. And it's damn sure not a good reason to get married. And why do you even need problems like that at your age? You're in your prime partying years, Paz. Don't throw that all away for some little piece of ass."

Paz put his sunglasses back on and gazed to the east again. "My friend Joel said the same thing before he left." His phone buzzed. He checked the message. "It's Caryn. She wants to meet me for lunch at Vinny's Hideout for conch soup. Right now."

"Did you tell her you were hanging with me today?"

"No. I haven't told her about you at all."

The tourist flock had moved off and left Paz and Laili alone on the observation deck for the moment.

Paz smiled and stepped closer to Laili. "So, what's going on with us?"

Laili stepped back. "There could never be an us until there's no you and her."

After saying goodbye to Paz in the Sky Ride parking lot, Laili walked over to a late-20s Hispanic man wearing a thick Cuban link gold chain over a black t-shirt and baggy jean shorts and smoking next to a motorcycle. She knew who he was from her briefing: Gus Ramos.

He checked Laili out with no shame as she approached.

"What are you staring at?" Laili said.

Gus smiled. "I think you know, girl."

"Don't call me 'girl.' I'm not your girl, and we're not friends like that. And don't think I don't know you were watching me and my friend today. And yesterday you followed us from the beach and watched us eat lunch at the restaurant. You looked inconspicuously obvious drinking beer at the next table."

Gus pulled up his shorts. "I wasn't trying to hide from you."

"Then what were you trying to do?"

"Keep an eye on Paz."

"Paz is your boy?" Laili said.

"No."

"Then why do you care about him?"

"I don't, but his future wife does care about who he hangs out with. Lots of gold-digging whores in the world."

"She should know," Laili said. "Can I have a cigarette? And I see you're carrying a weapon, by the way."

He gave her a cigarette and lit it. "What's that lion neck tat for?"

"It's a lioness, and it's not your business. And you have a lot of gang tats. You some kind of badass gangsta?"

"You watch too many movies," Gus said. "These represent my family, my true family."

Three young, male tourists in a group walked past them. One, wearing a just purchased Cruzan Rum tank top, smiled at Laili. "Nice ass, baby!"

The trio giggled.

Laili turned to him. "What did you say?"

The trio stopped and Tank Top repeated, "Nice ass, baby."

Laili handed Gus her cigarette, approached Tank Top, and stopped a foot away. "Say it again."

He looked to his friends and smiled. His friends smiled back. "What?"

"Say it again."

He smiled. "Nice ass, baby."

Laili backhanded his face. Hard.

He recoiled and felt a red cheek mark. "Hey!"

His friends laughed.

"Say it again," Laili said.

He smiled through the pain. "Nice ass, baby."

Laili backhanded his face again. Harder.

Pain tears reddened his eyes.

"Say it again," Laili said.

"Nice ass, baby."

Laili cocked her hand.

He grabbed her wrist.

Laili used her other hand to grab his wrist and bend it into a vicious wristlock.

He screamed.

Laili made him scream again, and he dropped to his knees.

His friends stepped forward. "Let him go!"

Laili scowled at them. "Touch me, and I'll break it."

Tank Top screamed. "Get away from her!"

His friends stepped back.

Laili glared down at Tank Top. "Say it again."

He said nothing.

"Say it again."

He said nothing.

"Now don't ever say it again. Understand?"

His face agonized. "I understand."

Laili released his wrist and walked back toward Gus.

Tank Top rejoined his friends, and they fast-walked away.

Gus smiled, admiring Laili. "Whoo…you bad."

Laili took her cigarette back. "Never cut a punk-ass bitch any slack."

Gus nodded. "You can't."

"If you do, you're just a punk-ass bitch too."

Gus nodded again. "That's right." He smiled at her. "I like you. You street."

Laili smiled at Gus and straddled his motorcycle. "Nice bike."

"It's a CBR 1000. New. I have a boat too."

"What kind of boat?"

"Any kind you like," he said. "The place I work at charters them. I can use them whenever I want. You want to go for a ride?"

"On the bike or the boat?" she said.

"Both."

"Where to?"

Gus smiled. "I know a few good places."

PROJECT MOLKA: TASK 4

PROJECT LAILI: TASK 1

DAY 4 OF 10

CHAPTER 16

Molka—in another sundress and sandals combination—stood on an East End, Saint Thomas boat rental marina dock with the business's manager, well into another frustrating, boat shopping day.

"Now if it were me," the manager said, "and I wanted to do some island-hopping sightseeing, I would definitely go with the 38-foot Chris Craft. It's the best bargain in our fleet."

Molka viewed the boat he kept touting. "But the price you quoted me is over twice as much as the 28-footer I'm interested in."

"True, but Chris Craft boats are renowned for their safety. And you can't really put a price on safety, can you?"

"No," Molka said. "I guess not."

The manager smiled. "Shall I go ahead and print out the rental agreement?"

An English-accented voice from behind said: "Don't let him run to his printer, missy. He's trying to upsell you."

Molka and the manager turned to the voice's source: Mister Cutter. His light-blue form-fitting, long-sleeved fishing t-shirt accentuated a chiseled torso, and gray shorts exposed formidable legs.

Mister Cutter continued. "That 28-foot Scout you have your eye on will get you everywhere you need to get. She's easier to handle, and she's much easier on the fuel, which is quite pricey on these islands, you might have noticed."

She nodded. "Ok. Sounds good. I'll take the 28-foot Scout."

The manager frowned. "Great. I'll go print the rental agreement."

When the manager departed, Mister Cutter said, "Do you remember me, missy?"

"You're not overly easy to forget, Mister Cutter."

"How nice of you to say, missy."

"That wasn't necessarily a compliment."

"You're right," he said. "Who would compliment a rough old cuss like me, missy?"

"It's miss, not missy, or just Molka is fine."

"I apologize. You see, it's an old habit. I grew up with five younger sisters and had a hard time keeping their names straight, so I just called them all missy. They didn't seem to mind."

"Well, I do," Molka said. "Are you here to rent a boat too?"

"No, I have my own boat in the marina over on Vessup Bay. I'm a Charlotte Amalie resident myself. And you'll be asking me next what brought me here to be quietly standing behind you?"

"I wasn't going to ask, but I was thinking it."

"I'm here to give you a message from the captain."

"How did you find me?" she said.

"I followed you here from your apartment."

"And how did you know where my apartment was?"

"The captain ordered me to follow you home the other night to see where you lived, to keep an eye on your comings and goings."

"And why would he do that?"

"Well, you see, the captain has reasons for everything he does, but he doesn't share them reasons with many."

Molka cursed herself. She hadn't even thought to employ basic countermeasures to prevent being surveilled, mainly, because she hadn't expected to be surveilled on the task. But that was the first thing Azzur taught had her about surveillance security: Always assume you're being surveilled.

"What's the captain's message?" Molka said.

"The message is the captain wants to speak with you, at his home on Katelyn Island. I'm to take you over myself on my boat I spoke of. We should be leaving as soon as possible; before sundown's best. So, if it suits you, I'll pick you up at your apartment within the hour."

"Alright," she said. "See you there...I guess."

"You'll be wanting to change clothes too. Long pants and a long-sleeved shirt if you have them?"

"I do."

"Then darker colors, if you please."

"For what purpose?"

"Like I says, miss—Lady Molka, the captain has his ways."

Back at her apartment, Molka scanned her closet.

I guess when you visit a pirate's island, you're supposed to dress like a pirate?

The only clothes she had that fit Mister Cutter's suggestion was her preferred tactical outfit: a black mock turtleneck, black jeans, and her black tac boots. Again, she would have worn her old pilot's watch for luck if she hadn't gambled it away.

Getting on a boat alone with a relative stranger as intimidating a physical force as Mister Cutter concerned her. But he was Captain Savanna's man, and Captain Savanna was the Counsel's man.

Shouldn't be anything to worry about.

Molka loaded and tucked her Beretta into her purse anyway.

CHAPTER 17

Pirating must have paid well for Mister Cutter as illustrated by his newer model, very nice, 40-foot sport cruiser boat.

As they left a marina in Vessup Bay on Saint Thomas's east coast, Molka stood beside Mister Cutter on the flybridge and analyzed the navigation screen fronting the boat's controls. She found Marine GPS Chartplotters as somewhat similar to the GPS navigation systems in helicopters and learning how to read and operate them had been the easiest part of her yacht pilot training class.

"North by east to a destination point 10.5 nautical miles away," Molka said. "I assume that's Katelyn?"

"Aye, Lady Molka," Mister Cutter said. "You knows a little about navigation, do you?"

"A little. Tell me about the captain's private island. Such as, how do you even go about buying a private island?"

"Well, to be honest, and please don't be taking any offense, I'd rather the captain explained that to you his self…if he's so inclined."

"Understood," she said.

"Tell me about this tip you're working on with the captain. Such as, what's the prize?"

Molka smiled. "Well, to be honest, and please don't take any offense, I would rather the captain explained that to you himself...if he's so inclined."

Mister Cutter smiled. "Understood."

If Mister Cutter's question was legitimate, it meant the captain used standard, need-to-know basis, information compartmentalization. It also meant he was not just suspicious about outsiders; he didn't completely trust his own people either.

Interesting.

Twenty-five minutes into the cruise—in late twilight—they approached Katelyn Island.

On first assessment, it appeared much like the other small, uninhabited islands Molka had observed flying into Saint Thomas: a rocky hill protruding from the Caribbean, with a deep green vegetation covering. But when they rounded the island's far side, perception shifted.

A good-sized harbor had been notched into the island's steep coastal rocks. Upon a hill overlooking the harbor sat a huge, sprawling, three-story, white-walled, red tile roofed, luxurious, Spanish-style villa.

The captain's domain resembled an ultra-upscale resort hotel. However, the extensive, high tech, array of antennas, satellite dishes, and radar domes installed above it, indicated that it was also a military-type operations center to those who knew such things.

Mister Cutter powered down and entered the harbor. A mega yacht, bearing the name *Livorno* on its stern, was moored on the right. Space enough to moor two similar sized yachts was available on the left side. Straddling the harbor's far end—mounted on pilings—sat a large black aluminum building, with twin garage-style doors. A gap between the bottom of the doors and the water revealed that the building sheltered two other floating vessels.

A black man, dressed in all black, waited on the left side dock to secure Mister Cutter's boat.

Molka disembarked after Mister Cutter and followed him to the dock's end, where steps and landings climbed the hill to the villa's large front porch.

They entered the home through oversized, carved wood doors into a wide white, marbled entry foyer. The villa's cool, dry climate control provided a pleasant contrast to the sticky humidity of the boat ride, and a polished wood and leather bouquet chased sea scent from the nostrils.

A curved staircase with a decorative iron railing descended into the foyer and Captain Savanna descended the staircase. He styled a tailored, single-breasted white dinner jacket with a black tie and pants. Again, his long hair was quaffed to perfection, and his golden earring gleamed.

The captain greeted Molka with his regular smile and moved to kiss her hand again. "Lady Molka, welcome to Katelyn and thank you for coming." He addressed Mister Cutter. "Mister Cutter, you're needed immediately in the radar room."

"Aye, captain." Mister Cutter left to obey.

The captain addressed Molka. "Was your journey comfortable?"

"Very," she said. "Mister Cutter has a nice, comfortable boat."

"Indeed, he does. And I trust he behaved as a gentleman?"

"His behavior was fine. His pirate personality plays a little fake, though."

"Well, Lady Molka, we're all lying to the world to one extent or another. It's only when you realize you're lying to yourself that the real trouble begins."

"Hmm...I'll have to unpack that later. But he did ask me to identify the prize we were working on. You haven't told him yet?"

"Mister Cutter is a man who always enjoys a friendly talk. But he doesn't always wisely choose his friends." The captain stepped back and inspected Molka. "I must say, your choice of outfit is very apropos."

"Just don't push me in the pool again. These are new Bates tac-boots."

The captain laughed. "You brought a firearm with you. Does it come with a badge?"

"How did you know?" Molka said.

"You walked through a hidden scanner at the front door. I believe in living in an abundance of caution."

"I believe living in an abundance of caution too, which is why I'm armed. But no badge came with it."

He moved to a side door and opened it to a large walk-in closet. "If you would be so kind as to leave your purse in the coatroom. You can pick it up as you leave."

"Of course." She stepped inside, placed her purse on a shelf, and stepped back out.

The captain smiled again. "Excellent. The first plank in our bridge of trust has been laid. I was just about to say goodnight to my guests. Come, I'll introduce you."

He led Molka down a long hallway into a formal dining room decorated with dark wood paneling, royal blue carpeting, and gold drapes. Flanking a long, eight-place antique cherrywood dining table and chairs were a large pedestal displaying a model sailing ship on one end and a premium liquor stocked, bar at the other.

Beside the bar—all holding cognac glasses—stood two middle-aged men, also wearing white dinner jackets, an elegant middle-aged woman in a wine-red sequined evening gown, and a stunning young Asian woman in a white sequined evening gown. They all smiled at the captain's return.

The captain gestured to Molka. "May I present Lady Molka, recently arrived in Saint Thomas. Lady Molka, I give you Signore and Signora D'Annunzio of the *Livorno*; her captain, Captain Raggi; and last but far from least," he smiled toward the Asian woman, "Lady Constance."

Molka smiled through underdressed self-consciousness. "Nice to meet you all."

All submitted polite greetings.

Signora D'Annunzio spoke in lovely, Italian-accented English. "The captain was just about to favor us with Verdi's *Va, pensiero*, weren't you, captain?"

"Yes, my lady." The captain swept his hand toward an adjoining room on the right. "If everyone would please step into the drawing room."

All complied.

The large room provided a living room-type ambience with a huge fireplace, thick rugs, and much comfortable leather furniture. A long grand piano served as the room's focal point.

The captain sat on the piano's bench, and his Italian guests formed a semi-circle around the piano's front. Molka remained in the background, and Lady Constance dropped onto a couch facing away.

The captain began to play.

Classical music was never on Molka's playlists. When she worked out, heavy metal, electronic dance, or pop remixes filled her ear buds. But the piece the captain played, and played well, touched her as both inspirational and sentimental and triggered both emotions in a beautiful way. It took her back to the music her parents played on low volume after they had tucked her and Janetta into bed.

The signore and signora watched with tears flowing down their cheeks, and Captain Raggi wept unashamed over a broad smile.

When the captain concluded, his three guests applauded with vigor and shouted accolades.

"Bravo!"

"Bravo, captain, bravo!"

"Bravo!"

The captain arose, faced his guests, placed his hands palms flat together before him, closed his eyes, and bowed.

After another applause round, the captain smiled and said, "And now, I regret, I must excuse myself for the evening. But I leave you in the charming hands of Lady Constance."

Signora D'Annunzio's face broke disappointed. "Oh no. Must you really go, captain?"

Signore D'Annunzio gave Molka a sidelong glimpse. "Yes, my dear. He must."

Lady Constance glanced at Molka and filtered frustration through a smile. "LJ, my love, is there a problem?"

The captain smiled. "No problem, my love. Faithfully, just business."

"But captain," Signora D'Annunzio said, "you promised to tell us all about the interesting depravities of the Visigoths of Córdoba."

"And so I shall, my lady. Tomorrow at our farewell lunch on the veranda. I'll have my chef prepare fresh Swordfish Sous Vide."

Signora D'Annunzio smiled, delighted. "Sounds wonderful, captain."

As if on a cue, a side door opened, and a distinguished man in a black tuxedo entered. The captain motioned toward him. "My concierge, Cesario. When you are ready, he will show you to your accommodations and see to any other needs you may have. The spa and gymnasium are available and staffed. Also, please feel to enjoy my excellent home theater. All the latest films and popular series are available for your viewing pleasure. And Captain Raggi, my library contains a vast nautical collection, many volumes in Italian you may find of interest."

Captain Raggi bowed with respect. "Thank you, captain."

The captain smiled again. "Until tomorrow, lunch, I bid you all a pleasant evening." He moved to kiss Signora D'Annunzio's enchanted hand, Lady Constance's disappointed one, shake the gentlemen's impressed ones, and led Molka from the room and back down a long hallway.

"I assume the D'Annunzio's are paying guests?" Molka said.

"The signore is a preeminent investment banker, and the signora is an old money heiress. Their tribute promises to be substantial."

"They were very disappointed you abandoned them for the evening though."

"Couldn't be helped," the captain said. "New business awaits."

"But aren't you worried you're favoring the possible over the certain?"

"A very astute observation, Lady Molka."

"I stole it from my very astute grandfather."

"I once asked one of the world's top businessmen how much is enough. His reply: How much is there? I concur."

They stopped outside the entrance to a well-appointed study. "Lady Molka, if you will please excuse me and wait in there a moment while I change into something more suitable."

"Alright."

Molka entered the study: more dark wood paneling trimmed with hunter-green carpet and garnet-red-drapes. A large antique desk and high-back red leather desk chair anchored the room, but the wall across from it caught Molka's interest most.

She approached it. Framed mega yacht photos—in the dozens—covered the space. Each frame carried a gold plate engraved with the yacht's name, the owner's name, and a date. The photos—like stuffed game heads mounted on the wall of a hunter's lodge—showed the captain obviously took great pride in flaunting his prizes.

Ten minutes later, the captain returned wearing an open-collared, long-sleeved black silk shirt, a wide black leather belt, and black pants tucked into knee-length black leather Wellington-style boots. He had also ponytailed his hair and covered his head with a black bandana tied at the back.

"Lady Molka, our discussion will have to be postponed until after our cruise, if you're agreeable to accompany me?"

"Cruise to where?" she said.

The captain presented his rogue smile. "Fortune."

He escorted Molka from the villa, back down the stairs and landings, to the harbor dock, and over to the black aluminum shelter building at the far end. Before they even entered the rear door, the low, deep-throated grumble of powerful motors idling vibrated both the dock and the surrounding air.

The captain opened the door for Molka. She stepped onto another dock and viewed a matched pair of long sleek all-black racing-style boats moored side by side. Each mounted a radar dome and several antennas.

"Those are my hunters," the captain said. "*Betrayal* and *Vengeance*. Custom-built, 60-foot Miami Magnums. Each have specially modified twin turbo Cat diesels coupled to Arneson surface drives. They can rundown or outrun anything in these waters. What say you, Lady Molka?"

"They're gorgeous," Molka said. "Almost makes me want to take up piracy."

The captain laughed. "The night is still young enough to grant wishes."

All around each boat, well over a dozen serious-faced black, white, and Hispanic crewmen—all clad in black military-style, fatigues and black combat boots—loaded gear bags, coils of line, and various sized sealed containers. Each man wore a sidearm, and some also slung M4 carbines.

A crewman brought the captain a sweet looking, black leather double shoulder holster rig carrying a pair of nickel-plated classic M1911 .45s. And when the captain strapped them on, his all-black ensemble made an instant upgrade from hipster bland to pirate cool.

The captain gestured for Molka to follow him over to a monitor mounted on the wall. Mister Cutter stood before the screen, entering data into a tablet. He had re-outfitted like the crew—black fatigues and boots—and also carried a cross draw sidearm on his left hip, as well as a long fighting knife sheathed on his right hip. The monitor he examined displayed a luminous green radar view of the surrounding waters and focused on a moving blip.

The captain pointed to the blip. "That's the *Tranquility*. She's a stunning 220-foot Lürssen owned by billionaire industrialist Ted Halladay. We've been tracking her since she left Nassau two days ago, and we've monitored her movements for the last three months after we received the tip. And tonight, I shall have her. Mister Cutter."

Mister Cutter came to attention. "Aye, captain."

"You will take the lead with *Betrayal*. I will follow in *Vengeance* with Lady Molka."

"Aye, captain."

The captain walked to the dock's edge, faced the crewmen, and stood with boots spread shoulder width apart, hands on hips, and face ablaze. "Gentlemen!"

The crewmen stopped their activities and answered in unison: "Aye, captain!"

"All hands, man your stations! Stand-by to get underway! Our prize awaits us! To the hunt! To the hunt! To the hunt!"

The crew in unison:

"Aye, captain!"

"Aye, captain!"

"Aye, captain!"

CHAPTER 18

Betrayal led *Vengeance* by 100 yards as both ran northwest away from Katelyn at semi-high speed through medium choppy waters. Before they departed, the captain informed Molka that the legendary deep-V bottom hull design of his boats allowed them to slice through the waves as if they were, quite literally, part of the seas.

The ride did not make his boast a lie.

Molka sat beside the captain on a cushioned, high-back, three-person marine seat. Like all on board, she wore a wireless intercom headset for communications above the roaring engines and rushing wind noise.

To their front left, a crewman piloted the boat and navigated via GPS screen. To their front right, another crewman monitored a radar screen and a marine radio. Behind them, on the spacious aft deck, six other crewmen attended to their duties.

The radar operator's voice came over the intercom. "Captain, fast mover approaching from the east."

The captain rose, moved behind the radar operator, and studied his monitor. He clicked a selector on his headset that switched it from intercom only to the boat's marine radio channel. "Mister Cutter, do you copy…yes…you see her too…well, if she's a dope runner, they're badly lost…I believe she wants us…yes…she probably thinks we're two nighttime pleasure cruisers out of Tortola...no, maintain course. Out. My glasses."

A crewman handed the captain large powerful thermal imaging binoculars. He scanned east into the darkness for a few moments and said, "There she is. Thirty-foot open fisherman. Well motored. Six on board. Four hundred yards and closing fast." He lowered the binoculars. "Battle stations."

Two crewmen unbagged a pair of M60 machine guns—along with their ammo belts—attached one weapon on each side of *Vengeance,* in recessed midship mounts, and stood ready to fire. Another crewman entered the large enclosed forward cabin and popped a .50 caliber machine gun through a top-deck hatch.

"Expecting trouble, captain?" Molka said.

"Always expected, rarely encountered, superior firepower the watch word."

The boat in question came into view under the moonlight: white with big twin outboard motors, and a driver behind a covered center console. Five other dark figures crouched along the sides.

The white boat split the gap between *Betrayal* and *Vengeance,* then banked hard to her left and came head on toward *Vengeance.* Immediately, small arms fire flashes came from the occupants.

Rounds splashed on either side of *Vengeance's* hull.

"Warning shots," the captain said. "They're telling us to stop. Billy, give them our answer. Take off her top."

The crewman on the .50 caliber machinegun opened up. The fiberglass canopy over the boat's center console disintegrated.

Answer received.

The white boat ceased firing, banked hard to her left again, and raced back in the direction from which she had come.

A crewman spoke, "They're running, captain."

The captain clicked the marine radio channel switch again. "Mister Cutter, do you copy... no, all is well here...secure the *Tranquility* and hold your position...yes...we'll rejoin you shortly. Out." He tapped the pilot's shoulder, the pilot stepped aside, and the captain took over the controls. "Lady Molka and gentlemen, the only thing worse than wannabe pirates is wannabe, wannabe pirates. Let's teach these scoundrels a lesson about who to truly fear in these waters. Raise the black!"

A crewman opened a side locker and pulled out a neatly folded black flag. He carried it to the stern and flipped a switch on the bulkhead, which raised a retractable stern flagpole with an LED light atop it. He attached the flag to the pole and—under the LED's illumination—the wind unfurled the black flag to display a white Jolly Roger with the initials *LJS* in blood red below the smiling skull and crossbones.

The captain looked back at it and presented his rogue smile.

The crew cheered.

Molka heard the word "cool" escape her lips.

The captain buried the throttles, and *Vengeance* seemed to leap from the water, level off, and fly just above the waves.

Within 30 seconds, they ran parallel to the white boat at 20-yards distance.

The captain spoke. "Luis, keep their heads down."

The port side M60 gunner fired. Red tracers arced over the white boat, and its crew flattened and disappeared.

The captain pulled close alongside the white boat and rocked *Vengeance* to throw huge sheets of bow spray into her.

The white boat's crew remained flat and got soaked.

"They have no fight in them," the captain said. "The cowards. So let them crawl home on one motor. Jack, do the honors."

The crewman manning the starboard-side M60 machine gun swung around, took aim, and fired a short burst into one of the white boat's outboards. Smoke poured from it.

The captain increased speed again, made a sharp turn across the white boat's bow, gave its cowering crew a waving salute, and turned to rejoin the *Betrayal*.

When the maimed white boat disappeared back into the night, the captain returned control to the pilot and attempted to call Mister Cutter on the radio several times to no answer.

The captain spoke to the radar operator. "Danny, how far out are we?"

"Almost three miles, captain."

"Get us back there in all haste," the captain said. "Full speed ahead."

The blue and white mega yacht *Tranquility*—lit up brilliant with exterior flood lights—lay dead in the water with *Betrayal* moored along her starboard side.

A device Molka recognized as a tactical assault ladder—a black anodized, adjustable aluminum ladder with two heavy-duty hooks on one end—was fastened to *Tranquility's* aft railing. The ladder's feet rested inside *Betrayal* and had, presumably, allowed Mister Cutter and his crew to climb aboard the much taller yacht.

But no crewman, or any other person, was visible on either vessel.

Vengeance came alongside *Betrayal* and shutdown. The crewmen held the two boats together, and one spoke. "Where's the deck watch, captain?"

The captain leaned over and confirmed her deck as unwatched. "I'm going aboard. Cover me."

The side gunners and three other crewmen aimed their weapons in cover fire positions.

The captain cross drew his .45s, cocked the hammers, hopped aboard *Betrayal*, and moved to her front cabin door. He stood aside it, opened it, paused, and peered in pistols first. "Empty. This is damn strange. Any other craft in this vicinity?"

"No, captain," the radar operator said. "Nothing within 13 miles."

Another crewman spoke up. "Maybe Mister Cutter has everyone sheltering below on *Tranquility,* until all the shooting we did is confirmed to be friendly."

"Perhaps." The captain holstered his weapons, re-boarded *Vengeance*, retrieved a megaphone from a side locker, switched it on, and angled it up toward *Tranquility*. "Ahoy, Mister Cutter. All is well. Please acknowledge."

No reply except waves slapping against the three fiberglass hulls.

He hailed again.

No answer again.

"Take us around to the port side," the captain said. "Prepare to board. Full battle mode."

The crew checked, locked, and loaded their personal weapons while the pilot restarted *Vengeance*, brought her around to *Tranquility's* opposite side, shut her down again, and moved to join the others.

DUAL DECEPTION

Two crewmen secured *Vengeance* to *Tranquility's* side cleats, while two others removed another tactical ladder, from a rack running along *Vengeance's* interior side, and attached it to *Tranquility's* aft railing. Once secured, the entire crew lined up in an assault formation ready to climb.

The captain smiled at Molka. "Lady Molka, please shelter yourself in the cabin while we go aboard."

"What's going on?" Molka said.

"Another abundance of caution. Everyone's likely below decks enjoying Mr. Halladay's well-stocked bar. These types of custom yachts often have substantial soundproofing for the passenger's comfort. They probably can't hear us. But just indulge me by waiting inside the cabin and locking the door. I'll call you out shortly."

"Alright."

Molka entered the cabin and locked the door. The roomy space was finished in light polished wood. A black leather couch ran along one side and a kitchenette along the other. A table large enough to seat six fronted the couch, and an open door revealed a forward stateroom with a sizeable bed, above which was the open hatch mounting the .50-caliber machine gun.

She started to look in the refrigerator for a bottled water, but she paused at the sounds of muddled confusion, yelling, and cursing.

She moved to the cabin door, unlocking and opening it a crack to hear the captain's voice speaking from the *Tranquility's* afterdeck. "What I think is, one should die proudly when it is no longer possible to live proudly."

A gruff male voice replied, "A profundity for every occasion. You haven't changed a bit."

"And where is Mr. Halladay, true master of this vessel?"

The gruff male voice answered, "Right now, probably smoking a fine fat Cuban Cohiba, sipping 25-year-old Macallan, and sharing many laughs at your expense with his host…Señor Delgado."

"I see," the captain said. "My compliments to Señor Delgado. Well played. Although, I believe this brilliant tactical plan came from your astute mind, Captain Solomon."

"Great praise coming from you, Captain Savanna."

"And Mister Cutter and the rest of my crew?"

"Below decks and praying, if they're praying men."

"I see," the captain said. "And now what do you have in mind?"

"Before I tell you what I have in mind, I will tell you what I have in hand. I have *Betrayal,* and I have *Vengeance.* And I have your crew. And I have you. And when we get back to Katelyn, I'll have everything in your famed treasure cave. And then I will tell you what I have in mind…most especially for you."

"My treasure cave?" the captain said.

"Your old friend Jesse Denmark told me that's what you call your vault."

"How is 'ol Jesse?"

"Good. He also told us—"

THUNK!

Molka looked up.

Something had dropped onto the deck above her.

Her eyes tracked footsteps moving toward the bow. She turned to face the forward stateroom. Tennis shoes emerged through the machine-gun hatch, followed by jeans, followed by a thin, male, red-t-shirted torso and a young Hispanic male face.

The invader held a Glock.

Molka started to move.

He pointed the pistol at her. "Don't move!"

Molka complied.

"Turn around."

Molka complied.

"Now move. Walk out onto the deck."

Molka complied.

The young man looked up at *Tranquility* and shouted. "Captain Solomon! I've captured Captain Savanna's woman!"

Molka looked up at *Tranquility* too. Captain Savanna and crew were lined against the stern rail disarmed with hands on heads. Over 20 camo-wearing, bearded men covered them with AK-47s.

The biggest among them—with the biggest beard—pointed a long-barreled .357 revolver at Captain Savanna. He stared down at Molka and grinned. "Yet another rare beauty in your possession, captain. Doesn't surprise me. Bring her aboard, Jorge. She belongs to me now."

Molka didn't agree.

The young man, Jorge, prodded Molka with the Glock barrel. "Up the ladder, woman."

Molka took a step, spun blur-quick, ducked under the pistol, and came up firing a right hammer fist into Jorge's temple and smashing a right knee to his groin, bending him over in pain. Simultaneously, her left hand grabbed the pistol's barrel, pulled it down, and wrenched it from his hand into hers.

Before Jorge recovered, she pushed him back into the cabin, followed him inside, and closed the door to a crack.

Captain Solomon said, "Your woman is quite capable, captain."

"She is that, captain. Shall we discuss a truce and hostage exchange?"

Silent pause.

Captain Solomon broke it. "No. I don't believe so. That boy sacrificed his life by his own stupidity. Go ahead and kill him. I'll kill five of yours, and we'll proceed as I planned."

"Captain Solomon, wise Captain Solomon, you mean to say you will return to your boss, the notorious, ruthless Señor Hector Delgado, and inform him that his only son, his beloved Jorge, heir to his illicit empire, was personally and callously discarded for death by you?"

"Captain Savanna, clever Captain Savanna, you have called my bluff. And now I'm calling yours. I don't believe your woman—capable as she may be—will shoot that boy."

BANG!

Jorge screamed.

Silent pause.

Captain Solomon broke it. "Is he dead?"

"Not yet," Molka said from the door crack. "But he'll limp on one leg for life. Should I go ahead and put him in a permanent wheelchair next?"

Silent pause.

Captain Solomon broke it. "What are your terms, Captain Savanna?"

"Lower your weapons and release my crew. Then head north at cruising speed. When you see our flare, you can come back for Jorge."

"And where will Jorge be?"

"In a life raft with an EPRIB so you can easily relocate him. Do you accept?"

Longer silent pause.

Captain Solomon broke it. "LJ, remember that time in Maracaibo when I told you one of these nights you were going to be too smart for your own good, and it would all blow up in your face?"

"I remember, Sol," the captain said.

"Well…tonight's not that night."

CHAPTER 19

Vengeance and *Betrayal* floated side by side, lashed together.

Mister Cutter and his part of the crew stood at attention on *Betrayal*, facing the captain and his part of the crew standing at attention on *Vengeance*.

Molka observed their formations from her previous seat.

"Mister Cutter," the captain said. "You may proceed."

"Aye, captain." Mister Cutter raised his voice. "Three cheers for Lady Molka. Hip hip!"

Entire crew in unison: "Hooray!"

"Hip hip!"

"Hooray!"

"Hip hip!"

"Hooray!"

Molka gave a little wave. "Thank you."

The captain spoke up. "Gentlemen, your attention please. Not one man among you bears any responsibility for the debacle of this night. I alone, as your captain, deserve the full blame. And I humbly beg your pardons for my failings. However, that is not sufficient. Many of you have families, and all of you have financial obligations. Therefore, you will all receive your projected shares of this lost prize, paid from my personal account."

The crew exchanged smiles and high fives.

Mister Cutter raised his voice again. "Three cheers for Captain Savanna. Hip hip!"

Entire crew in unison: "Hooray!"

"Hip hip!"

"Hooray!"

"Hip hip!"

"Hooray!"

"Cut Jorge loose," the captain said. "Let's go home."

An uninjured Jorge waited behind *Vengeance* in an orange rescue raft, holding an emergency position-indicating radio beacon device.

A crewman cast off the line holding the raft while other crewmen undid the lines holding the two boats together. Within a minute, *Betrayal* and *Vengeance* rumbled to life and moved off at high speed again. Jorge faded astern into the dark Caribbean.

Five minutes later, the captain produced a flare gun from a side compartment and fired a red flare high into the night sky, signaling Captain Solomon he may come back and reclaim Jorge.

"Lady Molka," the captain said, "we'll have our talk now, and I'll have a drink. Please join me."

Molka followed the captain into the cabin and sat on the couch behind the table.

The captain removed Maker's Mark 46 bourbon and a tumbler from an overhead cabinet.

"I thought pirates drank rum," Molka said.

"They wouldn't have, if they could have gotten their hands on a fine barrel finished Kentucky straight bourbon whiskey. Join me?"

"No thanks. Well, a bottled water if you have it."

The captain opened the refrigerator, retrieved Molka a water, sat at the table across from her, filled his tumbler, and took a generous swig. "Ah…heaven."

"Great morale boost move still paying off the crew," Molka said.

The captain winced and finished his drink. "I would tell you how much that is going to cost me, but then I would ask you to shoot me." He smiled and refilled his glass. "Speaking of which, Lady Molka, I'm glad you really didn't shoot young Jorge. He has no business being out here. Shame on Señor Delgado. How did you get him to scream on cue like that?"

"I told him if he didn't, he wouldn't get the chance with the next one. But I'm sorry about the hole I put in your beautiful hunter." Molka pointed to a nine-millimeter bullet hole in the bulkhead above them.

"That's all right. Battle scars make for good tales." The captain presented his rogue smile. "And oh, the tales I could tell."

Molka took a water sip. "I'll settle for an explanation of what happened tonight."

"I got bested by a rival, Señor Hector Delgado. He's a man I once did great things with. And we became great friends. Nevertheless, we had a falling out over the one thing a man cannot ever forgive another man for."

"A woman," she said.

He smiled and took another drink. "Since then, his quest to humiliate me knows no end. Apparently, in this latest attempt, he enlisted Mr. Halladay of the *Tranquility* to work in league with him. A false tip was then fed to us. We took the bait, and Delgado put his top man, Captain Solomon, and his crew aboard her in Nassau. They were lying in wait for our boarding. And the white boat's attack was a clever diversion to separate us and take my crew in two easier pieces. And it would have worked had it not been for you." The captain toasted Molka. "My thanks, my lady."

Molka shrugged. "Don't think of it. But this Captain Solomon mentioned a conversation you had with him in Maracaibo. It almost sounded like you were friends with him too."

"We are friendly. He and I have collaborated in the past on behalf of American intelligence, and that is all I will say on that." The captain smiled. "Now tell me, where did you learn that incredible disarmament move you used on Jorge?"

"I picked it up in the military."

"No doubt you have some good and interesting tales as well."

"Some interesting. I wouldn't call any good, though."

"Lady Molka, my original intention tonight was to make you party to an act of piracy within US territorial waters, a serious crime for which someone affiliated with a US law enforcement agency would be obligated to prevent."

"So now do you believe I'm not with US law enforcement?"

"I do indeed."

"Alright," Molka said. "Now we can coordinate our plan for *Outcast*."

The captain refilled his glass and took another drink. "Paz Davidov is an extremely wealthy trust fund baby who would definitely bring a very significant tribute. However, he also presents a very significant risk. Perhaps more of a risk than I care to take."

"Sounds like you're trying to back out. I thought we had an agreement?"

"Out here, agreements are fluid things, open to further considerations. Of late, I've been reconsidering how unpleasant the taking of a nephew of a sitting head of state could get. Especially in an election year for said head of state."

Molka was ready for that. Azzur—in his brilliant shrewdness—had anticipated the captain having second thoughts about ransoming Paz. So he had included on her briefing tablet a "sweetener tale" to get his mind right again.

Molka toasted the captain with her water bottle. "You've done your homework. And in a normal risk-reward situation, what you say is true. But you haven't taken into account the full reward possibilities of this prize."

The captain's hazel eyes gleamed. "I'm listening."

"I've done my homework too. Paz's trust fund is on probationary status due to all his irresponsible behavior. He's on notice; one more incident will cause him to forfeit it. So in addition to the tribute, you demand from him for his release, you can also blackmail him to keep this irresponsible incident—traveling without security and getting captured by a pirate—confidential from his trust fund's managers. Indefinitely."

"Which could provide me with a very generous passive income. Indefinitely."

Molka smiled. "And me too."

"Which is the dream of all dreamers: financial security to live free and well for life."

She smiled again. "And mine too."

The captain presented his rogue smile. "Lady Molka, larcenous minds think alike. And with your help, that is precisely what I shall do."

"Great. Let's make our plan."

The captain stood with boots shoulder width apart, hands on hips, and face ablaze. "And a great plan we shall make. But first, I want to meet your partner."

PROJECT MOLKA: TASK 4

PROJECT LAILI: TASK 1

DAY 5 OF 10

CHAPTER 20

"I told you, we got this, Paz."

Laili in bikini and Paz in swim trunks reclined on the *Outcast*'s uppermost deck: the sundeck.

Paz rolled in a lounge chair toward Laili. "I'm just going to walk in her office and tell her the wedding is off. We haven't known each other long enough to make that kind of commitment, our relationship was just a thing, but it's over now, and I need to get home and get on with my life. Right?"

"No. That's what I'm going to say to her while you sit there quietly and agree. No offense, Paz. We're friends and everything like that, but you're not up to this. You're not an alpha. You're a beta."

Paz rolled back and laid his forearm across his eyes. "It feels a little weird taking this kind of life advice from you. I've only known you for like a week."

"And you've only known her for like five weeks and already agreed to spend the rest of your life with her. Which is weirder?"

"You're right. Ok. You've got my back, right?"

Laili stood and pulled Paz to his feet. "Come on, let's get it over with and go to our lesson."

"You think you're pretty?" Caryn said. "I'm prettier. You think you're smart? I'm smarter. You think you're stubborn? I'm stubborner."

Laili sprung from her chair in front of Caryn's desk. "Hold up! You—"

"No!" Caryn said. "You hold up. I gave you your turn to talk. It's still my turn. Sit down and listen or I'll just call security and have you trespassed off this property."

Paz side eyed Laili from his chair next to hers. "Please Giselle; I don't want you to get trespassed."

Laili sat.

Caryn composed herself and continued. "Paz and I have discussed his past fame. And we know you aren't the first, and probably won't be his last, stalker."

Laili started to stand but checked herself. "I'm not a stalker; I'm a vet tech."

"He's already told me you know all about his gamer career and how you were a huge follower of his. That's a stalking red flag."

"Hold on, Caryn," Paz said. "I didn't say she was stalking me. And I also told you we've become friends."

"And that's fine," Caryn said. "I want you to have your friends, baby."

"Well, you did tell all my friends that came here with me they weren't welcome in your marina anymore."

"That's because they spent 24/7 drunk and high on your yacht. They never left us alone."

"That's true too."

Caryn addressed Laili. "Regardless of what you may think, I'm not all bitch. Paz told me you came down here to get away from an abusive relationship. I feel you on that. Before I met Paz, all my past relationships were abusive. And if you're struggling, I can put you on as a server at one of our restaurants. Servers do very well at them."

Laili sneered. "I won't take charity for sympathy."

"And I won't take anyone interfering in Paz and I's relationship." Caryn reached under the desk and pulled up a black handbag. "Do you know what this is?"

"It's a purse."

"No, it's a Givenchy Medium Eden crocodile-embossed leather shoulder bag and it costs more than your job as a poodle groomer makes—"

Laili's face fumed. "I'm a vet tech."

"It costs more than your job as a *vet tech* makes in three months."

"So what."

"So the fact you didn't know that disqualifies you from giving Paz lifestyle advice. Paz's lifestyle is beyond what someone like you can comprehend. That's why someone like Paz needs someone like me. We wealthy people stay with our own kind. It's just how it's done. Right, Paz?"

Paz sagged. "Well…I…I don't know…"

Caryn bored in on Paz. "Paz, damn you, you promised. So is the wedding off or not?"

Paz cringed. "I…I…guess not?"

"Thank you, baby. Now both of you get out of my office. I have a beautiful bridal shower brunch to plan." Caryn addressed Laili and smiled, arrogant. "I win, you lose. And as Paz used to say, game over."

CHAPTER 21

"Thought I smelled Paco Rabanne 1 Million and bullshit," Justain said.

Gus winced in disgust and turned on his barstool at the Sapphire Beach Hotel beach bar, where he was flirting with two young girls in bikinis.

Justain and Hodge waited behind him.

"What are you doing over here, Agent Justain?" Gus said.

"That was going to be my first question for you."

"I stay here now."

"You mean here at the hotel?"

"Yeah, I stay here at the hotel now, this island too. I live here now."

Justain addressed the bikini girls. "Excuse me, young ladies. Allow me to tell you who you're spending this fine afternoon with. This is Gustavo 'Gus' Ramos. He served four years for aggravated kidnapping and is suspected of dozens of other drug cartel kidnappings before that. And before that, he worked as a cartel *sicario*. Which means he sometimes sawed people's heads off with a chainsaw while they were still alive."

Bikini Girl One said, "He told us he wanted to take us to a lit party on a private island."

Bikini Girl Two said, "We have to go."

Gus watched his nubile prey get up and walk away. "*Gracias, cerdo.*"

"Watch your mouth, *puta*," Justain said. "Because I'm half-tempted to arrest you and then figure out a charge."

"How did you know I was here?" Gus said.

"Detective Hodge has lots of friends, concerned citizens who let her know when a piece of shit criminal is posted up at one of the tourist spots macking on barely legal girls."

Hodge stepped forward. "I really hope you're not dealing on my island,"

Gus frowned at Hodge. "Why do you want to hassle me too, *mami*?"

"It's Detective Hodge. You better not be dealing on my island."

"No. I'm a businessman now. I'm trying to get a clean start. I'm building something of my own for my future."

"You better not be dealing drugs on my island."

"He's not dealing drugs," Justain said. "He's worked for many drug dealers, but drugs aren't his thing. He's one of those short-dick narcissists who gets off controlling women by turning them into whores."

"Is that right?" Hodge said.

"Tell her about that Belize escort service, Gus."

Gus glared straight ahead.

Justain continued. "Detective Hodge, talk to the bartenders at the nicer hotels and ask them about recent whore activity. Bust one of the whores, and she'll give up Gus as her pimp, and then you can bust and remove him from your island before he gets his new business established here."

"I'll just do that," Hodge said.

Justain patted Gus on the back. "Nice seeing you again, Gus."

Hodge and Justain departed.

A chunky 20-something, white man wearing a white polo with *Yacht Marina Grande Boat Charters* embroidered in the left breast, pleated, pressed, khaki shorts, and brown deck shoes, left a nearby table, approached Gus, and sat on the stool next to him. "You're not answering your messages, so I came here to talk to you. I was waiting until you got done with those girls, but then I saw that cop come in with the other guy. Who's the other guy?"

Gus kept glaring straight ahead. "Another cop."

"Shit. Trouble?"

"No."

"What's up with his hair? Dude looks like a clown."

"He's no clown," Gus said. "What do you want?"

"Like I said, I've been trying to message you. Everything's loaded. Sixty packages. You want to come and count it before we leave?"

"No," Gus said. "I have more important things to worry about right now. Leave."

"You mean leave now for Puerto Rico or leave this bar?"

"Both."

He got up and left.

Gus pulled out his phone, scrolled contacts, and dialed. "Yo, Jake, it's Gus Ramos…Right…So that other thing we talked about…Yeah…I changed my mind…Yeah… I think we can do business now."

Justain sat passenger in Hodge's USVI Police patrol SUV. "Who's next?"

Detective Hodge checked her phone. Barry Tamblyn. Pot dealer. He hangs out over in Red Hook."

"Let's go see Barry."

"You said this Gus Ramos worked with cartels in the past; you think he's involved with your case? I can bust him, like you said, and we can lean on him."

"No," Justain said. "He's devious, but not smart enough to put something that big together. Just ignore him for now."

CHAPTER 22

Molka returned from afternoon grocery shopping to an apartment air-conditioned ice-cold and overpowered with gun cleaning solvent and lubricating oil aroma. "Why is it every time I come home, you have a new, gag-inducing, odor waiting to greet me?"

She laid the grocery bags on the kitchen counter and viewed Laili at the kitchen table with her Sig pistol disassembled atop a towel. She used a toothbrush to give a tiny part a violent scrubbing.

Molka sighed. "Where to start… Ok. I really hope that's not my toothbrush you're using."

"It's not yours," Laili said. "I bought it when I got these cleaning supplies, ugly."

"Why do you have it so cold in here, brat?"

"Because I'm boiling hot right now."

Molka placed her soy milk, orange juice, grapes, lettuce, cucumber, and tomatoes in the refrigerator. "And our weapons were freshly cleaned and lubed before we got them. Why are you servicing yours again?"

"Because it's the closest way I can take out my frustrations with it. Azzur said we can't take our task weapons to the shooting range."

"Frustrations with what?" Molka cupboarded organic oats and protein bars. "Setback with Paz?"

"Nothing I can't handle." Laili started scrubbing another part with frustration.

Molka dialed back the AC control on the living room wall and sat across from Laili. "Liaison meeting. First item: We need to minimize our task expenses. Like I was telling you, it's crazy costly to rent a boat here. And they have a waiting list. So I had to pay an extra fee to get moved to the top of it."

Laili smirked. "Sucka."

"Anyway, I got my boat."

"Good for you. What's the next item? I have to get ready to go out tonight."

"Tonight is the next item," Molka said. "Cancel your plans. Captain Savanna wants to meet you."

"He's your asset. Why does he want to meet me?"

"Because you're working with me. It's part of his vetting process. In his mind, everyone is undercover law enforcement trying to set him up until they prove to him otherwise."

"That man's not dumb," Laili said. "Where are we meeting him?"

"At a marina."

"He's taking us out boating?"

"No," Molka said. "He's taking us out pirating."

CHAPTER 23

"When you meet him, he may kiss your hand," Molka said. "But don't freak out. That, and the way he talks, is all part of his…character. So just go with it."

"Yeah, ok," Laili said.

At 10PM, Molka and Laili—both outfitted in their black tactical wear—arrived at the Saint Thomas, Vessup Bay marina where Mister Cutter kept his private boat. But they wouldn't be riding that night on his sport cruiser.

Instead, *Vengeance* awaited them in all her menacing beauty.

As they walked down the dock approaching her, Mister Cutter—dressed again for pirating, including his fighting knife—could be seen loading gear as the lone crew member.

And strolling toward them from the dock's opposite direction—also clad in his full pirating regalia—was Captain Savanna with a gorgeous young redhead in a red dress on his arm.

Molka and Laili arrived aside *Vengeance* at the same moment as the captain and his latest lady.

The captain grasped her shoulders. "I shall endeavor not to be all night. But if I am, be prepared for an epic morning."

He kissed her, and she departed biting her lower lip under lustful eyes.

The captain turned and presented Molka and Laili his rogue smile. "The true gentleman wants two things: danger and play. For that reason, he wants woman…the most dangerous plaything."

Laili's wide eyes walked *Vengeance*'s length stern to bow and back. "This is the chillingly coolest boat I've ever seen!"

"I'm happy you approve of her," the captain said. "Please come aboard, my ladies."

Molka and Laili boarded, and the captain joined them.

"Captain Savanna," Molka said. "This is my partner, Giselle. Giselle, this is Captain LJ Savanna."

The captain kissed Laili's hand. "A pleasure, Lady Giselle."

Molka gestured at Mister Cutter. "And this is the captain's quartermaster, Mister Cutter."

Mister Cutter smiled at Laili. "Hello, missy, or Lady Giselle, I should say."

"What's a quartermaster?" Laili said.

"Lady Giselle," the captain said. "The quartermaster is the heart, the soul, the conscience, the confessor, the absolver, the enforcer, the healer, the mother, the father, the brother, the sinner, and the saint, of the crew. And they come none better, on all accounts, than that man you see before you."

Laili nodded. "He's carrying a badass fighting knife too."

The captain laughed. "Mister Cutter."

"Aye captain."

"Get us underway."

"Aye captain."

With Mister Cutter piloting, the captain invited Molka and Laili into the cabin to sit and be briefed on the night's prize.

"Here's the tale," the captain said. "A friend of mine controls the marijuana trade in the British Virgin Islands. He's an honest crook who provides a highly desired—and mostly harmless, in my view—commodity at a reasonable price. However, on occasion, an upstart seeks to infringe on my friend's trade. Tonight, one such upstart will attempt to make a product drop on an isolated part of Tortola's north coast. My friend has employed me to seize their cargo and make a strong impression on them to permanently end their intrusions. In exchange for this service, I will receive a fee equaling 75 percent of the booty's current retail value."

"How can we help?" Molka said.

"By assisting in a support capacity. Lady Molka, you said you served in the military; are you able to operate an M60 machine gun?"

Molka nodded. "I've fired that weapon several times."

"Good."

Laili bounced on her seat. "What weapon do you want me to operate, captain?"

"Were you in the military too, Lady Giselle?"

"Yes…well…not really. They kicked me out after a month. But I'm a better shot then her and have the trophies to prove it. Just ask her."

Molka addressed the captain. "She outscored me by less than a 10th of a second in a practical shooting match and it seems to be the greatest accomplishment of her life."

Laili sneered. "Shut up, ugly."

Molka sneered. "Behave yourself, brat."

"As if you could make me."

"Can and will."

"You're not my boss." Laili looked to the captain. "Captain, she's not my boss."

The captain raised calming hands. "Now ladies, we can't have disharmony on the crew. And on my ship, my decisions are sacrosanct. Lady Molka will operate the M60. However, Lady Giselle, I have something else in mind for you. Something equally—if not even more—vital to our quest tonight. Let's go topside, and I'll teach you."

Twenty-five minutes into their run, the captain checked the radar screen. "Right where she was supposed to be and right on time. Mister Cutter, you may close on the target."

"Aye, captain."

DUAL DECEPTION

The captain faced Molka and Laili sitting in the rearmost seats and addressed all over their wireless headsets. "Now hear this, crew: For security reasons, from this point on, we will not refer to one another by formal names. I will be referred to only as captain, Mister Cutter as quartermaster, Lady Molka as gunner, and Lady Giselle as chief mate. Is that clear?"

The crew in unison: "Aye, captain."

Mister Cutter spoke. "I have a visual, captain. Thirty-foot sport fisher off the port bow."

The captain stepped into the cabin and returned wearing his double shoulder holster rig with the matching .45s.

Laili's eyes devoured his gear.

"Gunner," the captain said.

"Aye, captain," Molka said.

"Make ready on your weapon."

"Aye, captain." Molka moved behind and cocked the port-mounted M60.

"Chief mate," the captain said.

Laili jumped to attention. "Aye, captain."

"Are you ready to take our prize?"

"Aye, captain!"

"Then show them the black!"

"Aye, captain!"

Laili removed the captain's personally monogrammed Jolly Roger from a side locker, raised the LED-illuminated stern flagpole, and attached the black. As it flapped free, her face broke into a grin of unbridled delight.

The captain assumed control of *Vengeance* and brought her on a parallel course with the sport fisher.

"Gunner," the captain said.

"Aye, captain," Molka said.

"Tell her to stop. Put tracers across her bow."

"Aye, captain." Molka took aim and fired. A red tracer line arced over the sport fisher's bow.

Messaged received; the prize cut her engines.

The captain brought *Vengeance* alongside the drifting boat and Mister Cutter secured the vessels together.

Two terrified men, barefoot in t-shirts and shorts, stood with their hands up. Both were in their late 20s—one tall, one short—and they appeared and smelled like they had been at sea a few days.

The tall one spoke with an English accent. "Please don't shoot. We're British citizens. We're not armed."

"Quartermaster," the captain said, "prepare to board."

"Aye, captain." Mister Cutter strapped on and drew his sidearm.

"Gunner," the captain said, "keep him covered."

"Aye, captain." Molka swung the M60 onto the Brits.

Laili moved next to Molka to observe.

"Quartermaster," the captain said. "Board."

"Aye, captain." Mister Cutter vaulted onto the sport fisher's aft deck and backed the two men to its far side.

The tall Brit spoke again. "What are you going to do with us?"

The captain moved to *Vengeance*'s side and stood with boots shoulder width apart, hands on hips, and face ablaze. "First, I'll have your cargo."

"What cargo?" the short Brit said. "We're just fishermen."

"Insult my intelligence again, sir, and I'll have my gunner cut you into fish bait."

"Yes," the tall Brit said. "Yes, please take it. It's in the livewell. Please take it."

Mister Cutter moved back to the transom and lifted the lid on a large gray rectangular fiberglass container. The inside was filled with shoebox-sized marijuana cubes tightly wrapped in vacuum-sealed, green plastic.

"Is that all of it?" the captain said.

"Yes," the tall Brit said. "I swear, sir."

"Give the quartermaster a hand making the transfer. Now!"

A cargo transfer line formed, with the short Brit removing the marijuana cubes from the box and tossing them to the tall Brit standing near the sport fisher's side, who tossed them over to Mister Cutter back on *Vengeance*.

The captain observed and kept count.

Molka maintained her covering position.

Laili moved closer to *Vengeance*'s side and watched the short Brit with intensity.

"How much more?" the captain said.

"Just one more," the short Brit said. "Way down deep here." He kept eye contact with the captain, bent, and reached his arm all the way into the livewell.

Laili leapt into the sport fisher and crushed the short Brit to the deck with a flying side kick.

The captain yelled: "Chief mate! Stand down!"

Laili reached into the livewell, removed a black machine pistol with an attached sling, and held it up. "PTR 9KT, captain. It's sweet. Always wanted one of these."

"Confiscate it for me," the captain said.

"Aye, captain." Laili slung the weapon on her back.

The captain glowered at the prisoners. "That was a serious mistake, gentlemen. Mister Cutter, secure the prisoners and prepare to get their vessel underway."

"Aye, captain." Mister Cutter vaulted back into the sport fisher, used flex-cuffs to bind the Brit's hands, laid them face down on the deck, removed the lines holding the two vessels together, and re-started the sport fisher's engines.

The captain re-started *Vengeance* and led the sport fisher north into the night.

Ahead in the distance, lightning reflected off low clouds.

"Where are we taking the prisoners, captain?" Laili said.

The captain's face reflected stonelike in the control panel's glow. "Where bad men go to tell no more tales."

Twenty minutes later, the two boats approached a small flat jungle covered island. More lightning flashed on the distant clouds and a cooling wind arose and shuffled the island's trees.

The captain came in slow and beached *Vengeance*'s nose on soft white sand. From a side locker, he removed a long, galvanized steel spike, a mallet, and rolled line. He jumped over the side into shin-deep water, splashed ashore, and used the mallet to drive the spike deep into the ground 15 feet inland. He attached one end of the line to it, and the other end to *Vengeance*'s bow, securing her in place.

"Please come ashore, ladies," the captain said.

Molka and Laili hopped over the side and joined the captain on the beach. Laili still carried the confiscated machine pistol slung across her back.

Mister Cutter arrived, beached the sport fisher beside *Vengeance*, and likewise secured her with her shore anchor.

The captain addressed Mister Cutter. "Bring out the prisoners."

"Aye, captain."

Mister Cutter ordered the bewildered Brits to stand, picked each one up, and dropped them over the sport fisher's side, feet first, into the shallows. He dropped behind them, walked them onto the beach, and ordered them to sit.

"Make ready, quartermaster," the captain said.

"Aye, captain." Mister Cutter boarded *Vengeance*.

"Chief mate," the captain said.

"Aye, captain," Laili said.

"Keep watch on the prisoners with their own treachery."

"Aye, captain." Laili unslung the machine pistol and moved behind the Brits.

Mister Cutter recovered a shovel and an LED lantern from *Vengeance* and headed into the jungle on a narrow path.

"Where's he going?" the tall Brit said.

The captain moved before the Brits and crouched to face them. "This place is called Forgotten Cay. Many problems have been forgotten here. But there's always room for a couple more."

The Brits broke into a whimpering, crying plea for their lives.

The captain walked back to *Vengeance*, returned with duct tape, and sealed the Brits' mouths. "The pleadings of cowards sicken me. Don't you agree, chief mate?"

Laili narrowed her eyes. "Aye, captain."

The captain paced.

Laili guarded.

Molka dropped on the sand and did sets of wide and close grip pushups. She missed the fitness center in Galveston, so close and convenient.

Thirty minutes or so later, Mister Cutter emerged from the jungle, glistening with sweat. "All ready, captain. The usual spot." He handed the lantern to the captain.

"Very well," the captain said. "Let's finish our work." He pointed the lantern toward the same jungle path Mister Cutter had taken and moved down it.

Mister Cutter drew his sidearm and ordered the Brits to stand and follow the captain.

They complied in dazed terror.

Mister Cutter trailed behind the Brits, and Molka and Laili trailed behind Mister Cutter.

Fifty yards into the jungle, Laili held Molka up and whispered. "Do you think we should stop this?"

Molka's eyes went cold. "No."

Laili beamed. "Good. Neither do I."

They reached a small, sandy clearing. The captain hung the lantern on a low tree branch and illuminated two fresh dug graves.

Mister Cutter made each terrified man kneel at the end of a hole facing their grave.

The captain drew his .45s.

The Brits muffled cries and screams became heartbreaking and pathetic.

Molka almost pitied them.

Laili didn't. "Don't cry like little fucking bitches! Die like fucking men!"

The captain moved behind his victims, placed a barrel against each bowed, whimpering head, and cocked the hammers. "Go with this final thought, gentlemen: One should part from life as Odysseus parted from Nausicaa—blessing it rather than in love with it."

Mister Cutter bounded forward and pushed the captain aside. "Hold fast, captain!"

The captain recovered his balance and yelled, "What is this insolence?"

Mister Cutter raised his hands. "I ask for mercy for the prisoners."

"Mercy?"

"Aye, captain. I think they've learned their lessons."

"Perhaps tonight they've learned a lesson. But what about tomorrow? And the next day and the next? Dead men never need to be retaught."

"That's sure to be true, captain. So I guess I'm making this a personal matter between you and me."

The captain raised his .45s to a barrels-up ready position. "Choose your next words carefully, quartermaster. Disloyalty is a fine shovel for digging another grave."

"Aye, captain. And my words are these: Now you've said yourself you owe me the favor of saving your life that night off Martinique. I'll be calling in that favor now."

The captain's face fell incredulous. "You would waste such a priceless favor on such unworthy bilge scum as these two?"

"Aye, captain."

The captain smiled, annoyed. "I think I know what's going on here. As an ex-British subject, yourself, maybe you have some sentimental sympathy for these monarchists?"

"Well, I'd be lying if I said otherwise, captain. But I can assure you, we'll never see or hear from these two again." Mister Cutter ripped off their gags. "Isn't that right, lads?"

"YES, WE SWEAR!"

"YES, WE SWEAR!"

The tall Brit added, "We swear by all the angels and saints you'll never see or hear from us again!"

Mister Cutter unsheathed his fearsome fighting knife and put it to each of their throats in turn. "All the angels and saints won't be enough to save you if I ever do hear tell of you back in these waters. Because I'll personally hunt you down and slice you deep and wide, from your noses to your nuts."

After 2AM, back at the Vessup Bay marina in Saint Thomas, Molka stood alone with the captain dockside of *Vengeance*.

He had relieved Mister Cutter, who had headed back to his home in Charlotte Amalie.

And Laili had run to the car to smoke a cigarette safely away from the marina's gas fumes.

"I'm convinced your partner is also not a cop," the captain said. "Truth be told, she might be more pirate than any of us. She really believed I was about to execute those two men and had absolutely no problem with it."

Molka exhaled for effect. "And for a moment there, I thought you were about to execute them too. They're both fine actors. Where did you find them?"

"I imported them from a London based thespian troupe." The captain smiled. "You played along with my little drama, brilliantly. You're quite the actress yourself."

"Comes with the job. But I thought Mister Cutter's performance stole the show."

"Lady Molka, Mister Cutter—like Lady Giselle—was not privy to our play. His reactions were genuine as well."

"Interesting. I'm not sure whether to admire his compassion or worry about his insubordination."

"Both would probably be the judicious choice."

"Noted," Molka said. "Now can we make our plans?"

"We're on the precipice of doing that. However, I need you to run a quick errand for me first."

"What kind of errand?"

"I just need you to pick up something for me."

"What, where, when?"

"I'll have Mister Cutter contact you and explain the details tomorrow."

Laili returned, hyped. "That was wildly crazy fun tonight." Her eyes admired the captain's sidearms again. "I love your classic .45s, and that double shoulder holster is beautiful."

"You have a fine eye," the captain said. "I had this rig custom made in Mexico, home of the finest leather smiths in the world."

Laili smiled. "I know what I'm asking daddy to get me for my birthday."

"Lady Giselle, I would be negligent if didn't acknowledge you may have saved our lives tonight. My thanks."

"You're welcome, captain. You too, ugly."

"The captain's just being polite, brat," Molka said. "I had him covered the whole time. Before that weapon even cleared the livewell halfway, I would have put the whole belt through him."

"She never gives me any credit, captain," Laili said. "She's very jealous of me."

"Ha." Molka folded her arms across her chest. "That will be the day."

The captain smiled. "But how did you know that man had the concealed weapon in the livewell?"

"I watched his eyes," Laili said. "The eyes are the killer's tell. His were darting toward that livewell as soon as we arrived and even more while the tall one talked and quickly gave up the cargo. The smaller one was obviously the boss and responsible for the product. So he wanted to make a move to try and save it and probably save his ass too."

The captain smiled. "Lady Giselle, you have a pirate's eye and a pirate's head."

Laili smiled. "I do?"

"Indeed. And as you are French, you are worthy of one of the greatest pirates who ever sailed: your countryman, Olivier Levasseur. He was known as *La Buse* due to the speed and ruthlessness with which he always attacked his enemies."

"Cool," Laili said. "I'm going to check him out."

The captain retrieved the confiscated machine pistol from where Laili had left it on her seat. "Lady Giselle, as a token of my thanks for your service tonight, I would like to present you with this brand new, just out of the box," he sniffed the barrel, "lightly fired, PTR Industries 9KT machine pistol, which currently retails, I believe, for just under 2,000 dollars." He passed the weapon to Laili.

Laili's face lit up with glee. "Awesome! Thank you, captain!"

The captain bowed. "And now, my ladies, I must say goodnight." He presented his rogue smile. "I still have a man's work ahead of me before I sleep."

Laili hopped in place. "Captain, please captain, do you have a few more minutes? I have a problem I want to ask your advice on."

PROJECT MOLKA: TASK 4

PROJECT LAILI: TASK 1

DAY 6 OF 10

CHAPTER 24

Molka stepped from the small, chartered helicopter and followed Mister Cutter across the apron of a heliport in San Juan, Puerto Rico. A much larger twin-engine passenger helicopter waited on the heliport's opposite side.

The late afternoon flight had taken less than an hour from Saint Thomas and—with no wardrobe recommendation given to her—she had come dressed neutral in a green polo, jeans, and running shoes.

Mister Cutter—carrying a laptop—led Molka into a small terminal building and back to a small office where a table with two chairs waited. "Friend of the captain runs this place, so we'll have privacy in here. Have a seat, Lady Molka, and I'll get right to it."

Molka joined him at the table, and he opened the laptop and swiped to a photo of Captain Savanna standing and smiling with his arm around a 40-something lanky white man styling a platinum mullet without shame.

"That's Jesse Denmark," Mister Cutter said. "At least that's the name he goes by. He's what they call an arbitrator in the drug cartel world. They use him to peacefully settle disputes amongst themselves because he's trusted and respected by all. He also used to be the captain's trusty crooked accountant before Señor Delgado hired him away to be his trusty crooked accountant."

"The same Señor Delgado who sent men to attack us the other night?" Molka said.

"The same. And now the captain wants 'ol Jesse back."

"Ok. How can I help with this little errand?"

Mister Cutter swiped to a small island's satellite view. "Señor Delgado is having a party tonight on his private island—Delgado Island—which is located 12 miles off the city of Luquillo on Puerto Rico's northeast coast. That big helicopter you saw outside is going to fly you over. Señor Delgado hosts these parties once a month for his employees." He zoomed in to a pair of houses, one huge, the other big, located on twin hills. "You're to mingle at the party here in the main villa, then slip away and go fetch Jesse here in the guesthouse, where he lives, and tell him the watch words."

"What are the watch words?" Molka said.

"Alissa and Jason."

"What does that mean?" she said.

"It's a personal thing between him and the captain. Jesse'll understand, and afterwards, he'll do whatever you tell him to." He zoomed back out to a full island view. "Without being noticed, bring Jesse to this rocky outcrop on the island's north beach called Smuggler's Point. You can't miss it. The only road leading away from the villa goes straight to it. I'll be waiting and watching for you just offshore in an inflatable boat and come in and pick you two up."

Molka traced the route with her eyes. "Alright. How will I signal you?"

"You won't need to, and it's better if you don't. And don't be worrying, I won't miss you. We've done this more than a few times."

She raised sarcastic eyebrows. "Ok. If you say so."

Mister Cutter zoomed the map out further. "After the extraction, we'll make a straight run for this unoccupied beach north of Luquillo." His powerful forefinger tapped a spot. "We keep a little safehouse here for the transfer of booty and such. Our ride will meet us at the safehouse and bring us back here for our return flight to Saint Thomas." He sat back and smiled. "And we'll all be home and happy before Señor Delgado ever realizes 'ol Jesse's gone."

"Question," Molka said. "Why does the captain think a stranger like me can just show up at this party and go unnoticed?"

"Another friend of the captain will be providing entertainers for the party. They aren't known either. So, you'll blend in with them. Should be easy for you."

"Easy is a dangerous word. What kind of entertainers?"

Mister Cutter rose. "I had something brought here that's more appropriate for you to wear to the party. Señor Delgado has sort of a dress code, you see. It should be waiting for you in the bathroom." He pointed to a small bathroom on the left and checked his watch. "You're scheduled to leave in fifteen minutes, best get changed now."

Ten minutes later, Molka emerged from the bathroom squeezed into a tight, shiny silver short-short dress, and silver high-high heels.

Mister Cutter inspected her and smiled. "If I may be so bold, you look like a priceless goddess, Lady Molka."

"I look like a cheap hooker."

"Time for you to go."

He led her back out of the terminal toward the large passenger helicopter. Just before they reached it, a shuttle bus arrived and opened its doors. Twenty-four young Puerto Rican ladies—all with big boobs, thin waists, and big butts; squeezed into tight short-short dresses; and walking on high-high heels—stepped out and headed to the helicopter.

"Who are they?" Molka said.

"That would be your crew for this evening."

"My crew?"

"Yes. Those are the entertainers for the party I told you about."

"Entertainers?" Molka stopped and watched them board the chopper. They look more like—"

"Yes, Lady Molka, that's what they are, one and all. And when you get to Delgado Island, as far as everyone knows, you're to be one too."

CHAPTER 25

"For those of you who've never met me, my name is Jacob Weinberg—call me Jake—and this is my island. I love beautiful girls, I love to live free, and I love to party. I hope you do too! Welcome to Candyland!"

Weinberg handed the wireless microphone he used to a thick security man, pulled off his t-shirt, and ran in swim trunks to join several dozen other partiers spilling from his mansion, across the pool deck, and down to the beach for the night's festivities.

His guests were a perfectly balanced mix: young, hard-bodied girls in bikinis and out-of-shape, middle-aged men in swim trunks.

Several years prior, a Saint Thomas reporter had been given an interview and a personal tour of the 75-acre island by Weinberg himself. This had occurred after Weinberg's young girlfriend had died from a prescription drug overdose there. The death was ruled accidental, but rumors of bizarre happenings on the island—which Weinberg had renamed from Little Saint Paul to Candyland—began to flow and would not abate. Weinberg needed a PR win.

The article described a gorgeous 20,000-square foot main residence on the island's north coast and a 10,000-square foot guesthouse on its west coast. A smaller, plain-looking home in its south coast, obscured within planted palms, the reporter was told, was used for housing security and staff members. And a just started tunneling system would be an extensive wine cellar for Weinberg's immense collection.

The island also featured a helipad, a small harbor, a manufactured beach, a tennis court, and on a hill in the dead center, a large playground with swings, slides, teeter totters, and monkey bars.

The article concluded that while eccentric and somewhat juvenile for a middle-aged billionaire, "Jake" came across as friendly and pleasant, and his island exhibited nothing overly nefarious.

Two months after the article's publication, the reporter accepted a position in the Weinberg organization and relocated to Manhattan.

Gus—wearing his usual thick Cuban link gold chain over black t-shirt and baggy shorts—and his guest for the evening, Laili—in a bikini under a crop top and short-shorts—listened to Weinberg's greeting and stayed behind in a poolside, wooden smoker's gazebo smoking while everyone else got crazy down on the beach.

"That Weinberg guy's a weird freak," Laili said.

"Nah, Jake's alright," Gus said. "He just likes to party with younger people is all."

"Why?"

"Doesn't want to grow up, I guess."

Laili blew smoke. "I heard someone say all his security guys are gay."

"That's true. He only hires gay security men because he doesn't want them sexually harassing his female guests."

"What about all those other fat old men slobbering on and groping the girls?"

"Those are Jake's friends," Gus said. "Other super rich dudes. Some famous ones too. He has a lot of rich and famous friends into the same thing he is."

"You mean pedophilia fantasies?"

Gus laughed. "You need to stop, girl." He picked up her cigarette pack from the bench. "Why you smoke those menthols? That's so ghetto."

"Because I like them, and in the ghetto, I grew up in, that's what we smoked." Laili rubbed Gus's right arm sleeve tattoo. "Are you going to tell me about your gang tats or not?"

Gus flipped away his cigarette butt. "Because we get along so well, you probably think I'm street too. But I didn't grow up down and dirty in the hood like you. I come from a good family in Miami with money. I even went to private schools and got a good education."

"Then why aren't you living the rich boy lifestyle like your boy, Paz?"

"I messed up."

"How?" Laili said.

Gus lit another cigarette. "It don't matter. You don't need to know."

"No; tell me. I told you personal shit about my past."

Gus gazed past Laili toward the beach fun. "When I was 16, I went to stay with my cousin Miguel in El Paso. He was 18 and like the older brother I didn't have. His family was poor and had nothing. So he looked up to the local cartel soldiers who had lots of money, nice clothes, fast cars, pretty girls, and respect from fear. My cousin wanted that too, so he joined. I joined too because I wanted to do anything he did. I was just a stupid kid like that."

"They sent us to what they said was a training camp. I thought since we were training to be soldiers it would be like the real military: running, marching, obstacle courses, learning discipline and all that. The first day we get there, they lined us up with 100 other boys. Then they bring this guy out of the back of a truck. He's tied up and crying and begging and they put him on his knees in front of us. The instructor takes out a pistol and hands it to the first boy in line and says, 'You want to be a soldier? Kill the enemy.' The boy's face was panicked, and he froze. So the instructor shot the boy in the head, bang, just like that. Then he hands me the pistol and tells me the same thing he told the dead boy. I didn't hesitate. It was like someone else was controlling me. I shot the begging man in the face. The instructor liked that. Then I puked, and he laughed."

"Damn," Laili said. "That's messed up."

"The training went on for a few weeks, but I couldn't stop thinking about that man I killed, and I felt sick about it all the time."

"Then one day the instructor comes to me, and my cousin carrying an AK and says it's time for us to graduate and go to work.

We can't be happier or more excited. We just have to pass one final test. He takes us out to this small one-room concrete block house in the desert. It has a steel door and no windows. We followed the instructor inside. There's nothing inside but a cement floor. The instructor says me and my cousin have to stay in there while he goes back outside, closes the door, and smokes a cigarette. When he's done smoking, he's going to come back in and shoot us both with his AK. But while he's smoking, one of us is allowed to walk out and go to work. Just one. If we both come out, we'll both be shot. Then he tosses a hunting knife in the middle of the floor and leaves."

"Oh fuck," Laili said.

"I walked out by myself with the knife before the instructor finished the cigarette. My cousin wasn't dead yet. He was moaning for his mother, my auntie. The instructor handed me his AK, and I went inside and finished it." Gus flipped away his cigarette. "After that, I didn't feel sick about killing that other guy anymore. I didn't feel anything. I still don't."

Laili laid her head on Gus's shoulder. "That's hardcore, Gus."

Weinberg approached Gus and Laili's position from the beach with his arm around a barely 18-year-old girl in bikini bottoms only. Upon arrival at the gazebo, all his focus shifted to Laili. "Yo, Gus! Is this one of your girls or your girl?"

Gus smiled. "Come on, Jake. Don't tell all my secrets. This is my road dog for now, Giselle."

"Hello, Giselle; are you having a good time at Candyland?"

Laili diss-faced him. "I'm having *a* time."

Weinberg addressed Gus. "Let me holler at you a second." He turned to the barely 18. "Go wait upstairs for me." She complied.

Gus looked to Laili. "I'll be right back."

Laili shrugged and lit another menthol.

Gus followed Weinberg out of eavesdropping distance from the gazebo.

Weinberg stopped and said, "You know I have serious royalty visiting in a couple of days. I need some more fresh candy, homie."

"I'm working on it. Don't sweat it. I got you."

Weinberg leered back at Laili. "What about that sweet little piece of French pastry. I REALLY like her."

"No. She's not that sweet."

"What the hell are you talking about?"

"She's not that innocent," Gus said. "She not the classy, type of girl you like. She's a hood rat. Probably a ho back in France. I was just working her to recruit her for my escort agency. But now I'm about done with her."

Weinberg leered at Laili again. "I'm still interested."

CHAPTER 26

Mister Cutter cut the twin outboards on the 19-foot, inflatable boat and let its momentum carry it onto the small, darkened private beach north of Luquillo, Puerto Rico.

Molka, and the one she had helped escape Delgado Island an hour before, rode in the boat's open bow and would be the first to exit. She left the island no longer wearing the silver tight-tight "cheap hooker" dress and the silver high-high heels. A cutoff olive-green tank top, camo pants—with the right leg ripped away at the knee, exposing a nasty abrasion on her shin—and two sizes too big black combat boots served as her new garb.

The escapee next to her wore nothing but a blood-stained yellow sundress.

Earlier that night, Molka arrived at Señor Delgado's party with her "crew" incident free. And her extraction by Mister Cutter and two of his crewmen several hours later from Delgado Island's Smuggler's Point was eventful, but successful.

However, she hadn't brought out the captain's former trusty crooked accountant, Jesse Denmark. Instead, she had rescued a petite, early-20s, barefoot Hispanic girl with a badly beaten face.

Molka helped the girl from the boat and waited for Mister Cutter and his crewmen to lead the way off the beach and up a narrow rising path through thick mangroves.

Molka took the girl's hand and followed them.

At the top of the hill, the trail ended at a clearing, which cradled a modest two-story home mounted on stilts. No other structures could be seen in any immediate direction, and the absolute 2AM-ish blackness didn't allow longer range views. And if you paid attention to it, the massive, incessant, buzzing of insects might have driven you insane.

The crewmen dropped on a bench in the open space under the raised home—which probably served as a carport—and lit cigarettes.

Molka and the girl continued up the side stairs to the front door after Mister Cutter. He unlocked the door, and they followed him into a darkened kitchen. The musty scent created by prolonged closed windows in a humid climate permeated the air.

Mister Cutter flipped on the kitchen light to illuminate a table and four mismatched chairs. The attached living room contained no furniture.

Overall, as far as safehouses go, you could do much worse.

Mister Cutter sat at the table and motioned for the women to do the same. The girl didn't move.

Molka smiled at the girl. "It's ok."

The girl sat, and Molka sat close beside her.

Mister Cutter checked his watch. "We have a few minutes yet before our ride gets here." He exhaled heavy. "You said when 'ol Jesse got himself shot in the head it was during a firefight you got into with Señor Delgado's security team. Did I hear you right on that?"

Molka tugged at the base of her ponytail. "Yes. That's what happened."

Mister Cutter pointed at the girl. "What are you going to do with the little *chiquita?*"

"Her name is Salvia," Molka said. "I'm sending her back to her family in the Dominican Republic. She was being used as a sex slave by Delgado's vaunted 100-man security force. Well...not quite 100 anymore."

"I hate to be pressing you," Mister Cutter said, "but you still haven't said exactly how you managed to get away alive from those 100 and make it to the extraction point with your new friend."

Molka shrugged. "The only way I knew how: Load, shoot, run, repeat."

"And what does that—"
POP! POP! POP! POP!
POP! POP! POP! POP!

Two AR-15 bursts, followed by heavy steps running up the stairs, followed by the two crewmen bursting inside.

One said, "They're everywhere!"

The other said, "We're surrounded!"

Mister Cutter hopped up. "Everyone down!"

All complied.

Mister Cutter killed the light, drew his sidearm, peeked through the front window's thin curtains, and crouched aside the widow.

"At least 16 by my count. All with assault rifles. They're standing in the open because they're not afraid of us, because they know our numbers."

"How could they?" Molka said.

"Likely, they're local *vaqueros* Señor Delgado has contracted to come after us. Not the best of soldiers, but in those numbers good enough."

"How did they find us?" Molka said.

"Tracked us here, no doubt. His island has radar too. Just as good as we have on Katelyn."

"You didn't account for that in your plan?"

"Well, what I didn't account for was you starting a running firefight with his men that ran all the way to the extraction point, which exposed us and gave him the chance to track us."

"They didn't give me a choice," Molka said. "Now what?"

"We can't fight them with three Glocks between us."

Molka grimaced "And I threw away two perfectly good M4 carbines before I got on the boat."

"Maybe we can parlay?" Mister Cutter said.

A Spanish-accented male voice called from outside, "Cutter! Cutter! You hear me?"

Mister Cutter reached over and raised the window a crack. "I hear you. What can I do for you?"

"Nothing for me. Just confirming you there. Jorge's on the way to talk to you. Don't try to go nowhere."

Mister Cutter addressed his crewmen lying flat on the kitchen floor next to Salvia. "We're done, boys. As a crew, we embarrassed Jorge's manhood on the *Tranquility* job, and he'll have his revenge now. If you want to make a break for it, every man for his self. I'd never hold it against you, and the best of luck to you. But you won't make it."

Crewman One said, "What are you going to do?"

"I'm going to stay and take as many of them shore rats out as I can, and save the last round for myself, if I live that long."

Crewman Two said, "I'll do the same."

Crewman One said, "I'm staying too."

Molka crawled over to Mister Cutter, sat beside him, and lowered her voice. "If Jorge's mad at you for his major manhood fail, what do you think he's going to do to me? I started that emasculation."

"Not even mentioning what you also did to his daddy's pride tonight. Jorge wants to please his daddy in the worst of ways."

"I guess I'm going down with you."

"Well, Lady Molka, I don't want to alarm you, although, you don't alarm easy from what I've seen, but he won't let you die here if he can help it. He'll take you and the little *chiquita* back to Señor Delgado's alive. And that's all I'll say on the subject as your mind's filling in the rest right now."

Molka put her hand on Mister Cutter's shoulder. "Please don't tell Salvia this."

Mister Cutter checked the mag on his pistol, racked it, and laid it aside his thigh. In a powerful whisper he said, "My only regret is I won't get a sea burial. Always wanted a sea burial. Nothing more noble, in my books. Probably toss the three of us in a shallow mass grave behind the house here, the bloody bastards. But all in all, I've had a good run these years with the captain. Made and spent more than any 10 men of my low born birth could make and spend in 10 lifetimes."

"How long have you been with the captain?" Molka said.

"Over seven years."

Molka wanted him to keep talking while she considered her escape options. His voice gave a calming effect as no options became apparent. "How did you and the captain meet?"

"To tell you that right and proper, I'll have to tell you this: I used blues, oxycodone, for the first time in Jakarta. I was a First Mate in the Merchant Navy back then. There was trouble with payment for the cargo and we had a four-day layover. In Indonesia vendors sell blues right out in the street alongside the food stalls. At least they did back in them days."

"A lady of the evening I went home with showed me how to snort them. It was an epiphany, if you'll pardon my blasphemy. I've never felt so perfect before or since. We snorted them for three days and three nights straight until my pay was gone. Then I went into a coma-type sleep. She thought I was dead and went and told some of my shipmates. They got me back aboard just in time to leave port. That's when my pitiful, pill-head junkie nightmare started."

"I got kicked out of the Merchant Navy and kicked off a half-dozen other good ships before I finally kicked. But by then it was too late. No decent captain would have me. I was doing petty jobs with petty crooks and ready to start using again till it killed me off from my misery."

"Then one night, I'm in a bar in Bridgetown, and this long-haired gentleman sits down next to me and says I look like a seafaring man. I says, 'Aye, that I am.' He buys me a shot or 12 and we talk all manner of things. Then he comes out and says, 'Mister Cutter'—and mind you we hadn't introduced ourselves yet—but 'Mister Cutter,' he says, 'I'm putting together the best crew the West Indies will ever see to do great things, and I need the best quartermaster in the West Indies to do them.' So I suggests Diego Hernandez or Caleb Trunbull. Course, I didn't know poor Caleb had gone missing in a hurricane by that time. Then he says to me, 'Mister Cutter, you don't understand; I wasn't asking you for a recommendation, I was offering you a job.'"

"He saved my life in that moment. I've been with the captain ever since."

"How long have you been clean?" Molka said.

"Eight years next June. But I still think about getting high every day, all day. And even more so at this very moment, if I'm being completely honest."

Another voice from outside called, "Hey, yo, Mister Cutter!"

Molka had heard the young male Spanish-accented voice before: Jorge Delgado.

Mister Cutter turned his face toward the window crack. "What can I do for you, lad?"

"Don't call me lad. I'm not a kid."

"My apologies. What can I do for you, Jorge?"

"I just wanted you to know we ran into your ride up the road. He decided he can't take you back to San Juan tonight."

"That's very considerate of you to mention, Jorge."

"I also wanted you to know we brought 30 gallons of gas and we're going to soak the stilts, light this bitch up, and shoot anyone who tries to get out to keep from burning alive."

"That's very compassionate of you, Jorge."

"Or we can make another deal."

"My ears are all yours, Jorge."

"Give us the bitch, Molka. I'm making a gift of her to the men she didn't kill tonight. When they're done using her, she's going into the woodchipper. The little whore with her is coming back too."

Mister Cutter had called it.

Jorge continued. "But you can live if you join us. My father says Captain Savanna took Jesse away from him but taking the world's best quartermaster away from Savanna would more than make up for it."

Mister Cutter turned away from the window and contemplated.

Jorge called out, "You hear me, Mister Cutter?"

Mister Cutter turned back to the window. "Your father's praise is much appreciated, but I know of his employment policy: Once with Delgado, always with Delgado."

"Yeah, it's a lifetime position."

"What about my men?" Mister Cutter said.

"Same deal. Join, burn, or bullets."

"Can I have a few moments to put your offer to them?"

"Yeah, I guess," Jorge said. "But don't take too many moments. The mosquitoes are bad out here. A nice big bonfire might scare them off though."

Mister Cutter closed the window. "Lady Molka, would you be so kind as to accompany me to the window upstairs where you can take a better vantage point and offer me your military expertise on picking off the bastard who's promised to put you through a woodchipper?"

"My pleasure," Molka said. "And good call. Take the leader out and break the followers' morale." Molka smiled, relieved. "For a second there, I thought you were going to give us up."

"And bring your friend along," Mister Cutter said. "Poor thing can't stop shaking. She'll feel safer in the comfortable confines of the secure room up there, surely."

Molka called to her. "Come with me, Salvia."

They followed Mister Cutter upstairs and down a short hall to an open door. He moved aside. "Right in here, ladies. We use this room to store spoils in."

Molka and Salvia entered the dark space.

Mister Cutter fast-stepped out and slammed the heavy door shut. Before Molka could move, a sliding metal bar and padlock click sounded outside.

Molka spun and side kicked the door.

Unmoving.

She backed up and thudded a running double front kick into the door.

Unyielding.

"It's no use, Lady Molka," Mister Cutter said. "This lock bar has kept stronger ones than you from opening it."

"So we're your prisoners now?" Molka said.

"We're all prisoners now. It's just that some might get pardons, and some might not."

"And you're going to buy a better pardon for you with us."

"Don't be taking it personal now," Mister Cutter said. "You have to remember, a pirate's always a pirate."

His footsteps headed back downstairs.

Salvia moved to a corner and sat. The blank expression under her bruised face had not changed since Molka found her hiding in Jesse Denmark's guesthouse: hopelessness.

The room featured three small windows. One each faced the front, side, and back of the house. Molka moved to the front facing window and looked down. Delgado's men stood and squatted in a rough skirmish line across the driveway facing the front door, many smoking, most chatting. One played loud salsa on their phone. Unlike the Delgado Island security men, they wore civilian clothes. And by the way they held their weapons, they showed no signs of formal training.

Mister Cutter was right again: undisciplined local cowboys.

Opportunity.

Jorge paced behind them with his hand on the grip of his pants-tucked Glock. And directly behind him was the edge of the small forest surrounding the house.

Molka examined the windows again: no bars, not sealed shut. The room was designed to keep people from entering and stealing the stolen goods. And the stolen goods, once secured inside, weren't going anywhere. But she would have to if they had a chance to survive.

Molka knelt before Salvia. "Mister Cutter will give us to them when he makes his best deal. I'm going to have to try and grab Jorge—again—and make a better deal. Come over here." She took Salvia's hand, pulled her up, and led her to the front- facing window. "Look down. You know who Jorge is, right?"

Salvia nodded meekly.

"You see the big, beautiful poinsettia tree behind him?"

She nodded meekly again.

"Keep your eye on that tree. When you see me behind it, I want you to open this window and start screaming. Scream loud, as loud as you can. Scream for all the things that have happened to you. Scream for all the things they did to you. Can you do that?"

"Yes, I can do that."

"Good. I'll wave to you when to stop."

Molka moved to the rear-facing window, pushed it open, and viewed the sandy, grassy ground below. She could hang on the windowsill and lower her legs to make the drop a bit shorter, but impact from 30 feet still wouldn't be fun.

On the plus side, she wore thick-soled Danner combat boots, which would give her ankles some support. And she had learned how to do the PLF—parachute landing fall—in the week of paratroop training she had done with the Unit. The Major had made her quit before an actual jump though. He had said she was too valuable a pilot to be jumping from perfectly good aircraft.

Molka glanced back to Salvia. "Ok. Here I go."

Salvia turned to watch the poinsettia tree.

Molka put her right leg out the window, straddled the windowsill, grabbed the lower frame as hard as she could, swung her left leg out, hung for a two count, and let go.

She impacted and rolled through the PLF five points of body contact:

Balls of the feet.
Side of the calf.
Side of the thigh.
Side of the butt.
Side of the back.
MMMPH!
It still hurt.

Molka popped up and moved into the trees. The long grass crunching under her boots sounded deafening, but the fool's blasting salsa music masked it. She looped through the trees past the side of the house and around to the front, right behind Jorge and his men's backs.

She wiped the sweat from her face on her shirt, took some deep, heart-rate-slowing breaths, and eased behind the poinsettia tree.

Salvia SCREAMED!

Everyone froze, and every face focused on her screaming face in the window.

Jorge included.

Molka burst from cover and spun a crushing roundhouse into Jorge's temple.

He collapsed.

She took his Glock and dragged his lightweight frame back behind the poinsettia tree.

Salvia kept SCREAMING!

She screamed words in Spanish Molka didn't understand, but she knew they must have been the angriest curse words the language provided.

No one looked back.

Molka slapped Jorge awake.

Jorge's eyes burned with surprised anger.

Molka pointed the Glock at his forehead. "Rollover. Face down. Do it now."

Jorge complied.

Salvia kept SCREAMING!

Some of the men screamed back at her.

"Jorge," Molka said, "last time I didn't shoot you and you might think I won't shoot you this time either. You're wrong."

She moved the barrel close to his outer right thigh.

BANG!

The round tore a nasty blackened red gash in the thigh flesh.

Jorge screamed: "YOU SHOT ME! IT BURNS!"

"Because you're burned, bad." Molka pulled off his t-shirt and tied it around the wound tight. "And that will get infected fast in this humidity, and you'll lose that leg if you don't get to a hospital soon. I'm going to take you to the hospital. You're leaving with me. Where are your vehicles?"

"Parked at the end of the drive."

"Types, colors, and where are the keys?"

"Blue SUV and a tan pickup truck. Keys are inside."

"Ok," Molka said. "Before we leave, I need your help. Do any of your men speak English?"

Jorge winced "Yes. It hurts so bad."

"When I tell you, speak only English to them. Tell them you're shot and I'm about to kill you—which I am—if they don't follow my instructions. Do you understand?"

"Yes."

Molka stood, showed herself to Salvia from behind the tree, and waved to her.

Salvia stopped screaming. After what she had been through, Molka was surprised she did. Maybe they had broken her body, but her mind still had the strength to show discipline.

Molka moved back behind the tree. "Ok. Call him now."

Jorge took a deep breath. "Benny! Benny!"

A man answered in English. "Boss? Where are you, boss?"

"I'm shot. Savanna's woman got out and shot me. She's got a gun to my head. She's going to kill me. Do what she says."

"Benny," Molka said. "I'm putting you in charge out there. I know there are 16 of you with 16 assault rifles. How many sidearms? And if I even suspect you're lying by one, I'll cap Jorge off right now."

"Then you die," Benny said.

"I already consider myself dead. But I want you to think about, and tell all of them to think about, what Señor Delgado will do to all of you if his baby boy Jorge gets killed while you were with him on a job."

"Five pistols," Benny said.

Molka smiled and whispered to Jorge. "Worked again. Fear of your father cuts both ways for you, doesn't it?"

"It hurts so bad. I need a doctor."

"Benny," Molka said, "collect all the weapons and line them up on the driveway where I can see and count them. And tell the other 15 to go lie under the house face down where I can see and count them too. Do it now. Remind them, Jorge."

Jorge yelled, "Benny do it now! Do what she says! Fast! I need a doctor!"

Benny spoke to them in Spanish, and all complied quickly.

"Done," Benny said.

"Benny, go lay beside your friends."
Benny complied.
Molka yelled. "Mister Cutter!"
Mister Cutter answered. "Aye, Lady Molka!"
"I'm in control of the situation."
"So, I see."
"Let Salvia out and tell her to come down here to me and then bring your men out."
"Aye!"
During the pause, Molka ran over to the weapon line, retrieved an AR-15, and returned to cover.

Salvia barefooted down the stairs, followed by Mister Cutter and the two crewmen.

"Salvia," Molka said. "Go down the driveway and get in the blue SUV. I'll be right there. You did great, sweetie."

Salvia complied.

Mister Cutter flashed a broad smile toward Molka's position. "Lady Molka, you've done it again! We'll take Jorge with us in one vehicle as our hostage and disable the others. Then we'll drop him at the hospital right before we get to our ride back home." He turned to his men. "Gather up all their weapons and phones, boys. They won't be needing them any more tonight."

Molka kept the Glock pointed at Jorge's head with her right hand and used her left to aim the AR-15 around the tree at the mutineers. "Mister Cutter, I'll need you and your men to remove your pistol belts and toss them with the other weapons. Do it now."

Mister Cutter frowned. "After serving together as we have, I'm sorry you feel this way."

"And I'm sorry you decided to join crew Delgado."

"Well, Lady Molka, when it comes to who I crew with, I'm a pragmatist, if nothing else."

"A pirate's always a pirate. And a pirate's also a pragmatist? What's the Caribbean coming to?"

"A fortune to the bold, like you, Lady Molka."

"Drop your weapons."

"I'm appealing to your better angels, Lady Molka. If you leave us behind, we'll die for sure."

Molka sighed. Azzur had told her difficult decisions are the curse of success. "Considering Jorge has passed out, and I'm too tired to carry him, and I don't know where I'm at…you and your men can come with me as my prisoners. Get me and Salvia safely on the helicopter home, and I'll pardon you."

PROJECT MOLKA: TASK 4

PROJECT LAILI: TASK 1

DAY 7 OF 10

CHAPTER 27

A more beautiful day for a beautiful bridal shower brunch could not have been scheduled by the Saint Thomas Council's Committee on Tourism had they so desired.

The beautiful *Outcast*'s sundeck, upper deck, and main deck were filled with beautiful guests enjoying a beautiful catered brunch. And a beautiful local singer sang beautiful songs with beautiful verve.

And the most beautiful sight of all—in a beautiful haute couture pink-coral dress—was the beautiful bride to be, the beautiful Caryn Thorsen.

Only a small black boat speeding into the marina toward *Outcast* threatened to interrupt all the beautiful perfection. The boat featured a tinted window cabin, which concealed the pilot.

Donar Thorsen spotted the imminent catastrophe first and his worry lines deepened a little more. "What the hell?"

He climbed to the yacht's second level, entered the bridge, and activated its PA system. "Attention, black boat: This is a private marina and a no wake zone. Please reduce speed and leave this marina."

The black boat kept coming.

"Black boat, this is a private marina and a no wake zone. Reduce speed and leave this marina."

The black boat kept coming.
Donar blasted the yacht's warning air horns.
The black boat kept coming.
Donar warned all on board. "Everyone, brace for a collision!"

Confused questions and a few gasps rippled through the assembly. But at the last possible moment, the black boat slowed and eased alongside *Outcast*.

Before anyone could look down upon the boat, a tactical ladder was raised from it and hooked on the *Outcast*'s stern railing, followed by a small, black object tossed onto *Outcast*'s deck.

Bright FLASH.

Loud BANG!

The flashbang grenade's detonation caused no injuries but scattered the guests into a screaming panic.

Up the ladder, over the rail, and onto the deck came Laili. She wore her all-black outfit from the previous night with a black bandana addition.

Two of Captain Savanna's crewmen, dressed for pirating, followed her aboard. Each had a pistol tucked in their belts.

Laili stood with boots spread shoulder width apart, hands on hips, and face ablaze. "Nobody move, and shut your mouths, or they'll draw those weapons and commence firing!"

The beautiful guests fell into stupefied silence.

One of her crewmen took out a phone and began to video the scene.

Laili addressed the assembled. "I'm Captain Giselle, proud adopted descendant of the French pirate Olivier Levasseur, known as *La Buse*, and you are all my prisoners! You can beg for your pathetic lives but expect no mercy unless you heed what I've come to say."

The guests laughed and clapped in relief. Some offered Caryn praise for her choice of entertainment.

Laili continued. "Everyone shut up! I have a proclamation to make!"

The guests went quiet, happy to play along.

"The proclamation is this: Pick up all your shit and get the fuck off this boat! The wedding is cancelled!"

The guests laughed and clapped again.

Caryn descended rapidly from the sundeck, mortified. "This is not a show! She's Paz's crazy stalker!"

Laili pointed at Caryn. "Hold your tongue, wench, or I'll cut it out!"

The guests laughed and clapped again.

Caryn freaked. "Stop clapping! This is not a show! She's crazy! Dad!"

Donar descended from the bridge. "What do you want?"

Laili turned to the other crewman. "Bring up the counselor."

The crewman climbed back down the ladder.

Laili yelled, "Paz, come out here!"

Caryn freaked again. "Dad! Call the police!"

"For what?" Laili said. "I'm welcome here. Right, Paz?"

Paz emerged from the cabin. "Yes, you're my friend. Who set off fireworks? Cool bandana. What's up?"

The crewman returned, followed by a middle-aged man in an expensive gray suit.

Laili addressed him. "Identify yourself, counselor."

"I'm Seth Morgan, an attorney from Miami, Florida specializing in bankruptcy proceedings."

"Do you know Donar and Caryn Thorsen?"

"I do."

"Did they approach you several months ago about their business?"

"This is outrageous!" Caryn said. "I want these trespassers to leave now!"

Paz raised his hand. "Hold on. I want to hear this."

Laili smiled slyly. "Objection overruled, wench. Counselor, did the Thorsens hit you up several months ago about their fancy-ass business?"

"They did," Morgan said.

"And you examined the financial records?"

"I did. In great depth."

"And what did you find out and what did you tell them?"

"The business is insolvent, and the Thorsens should file for bankruptcy protection."

Laili smiled at Caryn. "Thank you, counselor. Now get the fuck out of here so I don't have to pay you for another five-hundred-dollar hour."

Morgan climbed down the ladder.

Paz glared at Caryn. "So that's what this was all about? Marry me to save your business?"

Caryn moved toward him. "Paz, what are you talking about, baby?"

Paz backed away.

Laili stepped between him and Caryn. "He's talking about a gold-digging little whore and her pimp daddy old man wanting to scam a wealthy young gentleman to save their broke asses."

Caryn ran to her father. "Dad! Call the police and report these trespassers!"

Laili smiled again. "Fuck your trespassers. Paz already told you we're welcome on his yacht."

"Dad!"

"But you're not welcome in my marina," Donar said.

"Fine. Then we'll just move *Outcast* to another marina. Right, Paz?"

Paz sagged. "I guess so..."

Laili smiled. "And this party is over, and everyone needs to leave. Right, Paz?"

"Probably be best if they did."

"You heard him," Laili said. "Everybody, get the fuck off!"

The appalled guests all moved to leave.

Caryn bowed up before Paz. "Paz isn't leaving. He and I are going to talk privately and get this straightened out. Aren't we, Paz?"

Laili bowed up before Paz. "Don't listen to her, Paz. She's just using you. I proved that."

Paz closed his eyes and sighed. "We definitely need to talk. About a lot of things. And the wedding is definitely on hold until we do." He turned and moved back into the cabin.

Caryn moved close to a smiling Laili. "You disgusting piece of street trash. Who do you think you are?"

Laili slapped her across the face. HARD. "That's who the fuck I think I am. And now you'll never forget it."

CHAPTER 28

"What a fantastic tale!" the captain said. "You swear, every word true?"

"Aye, captain," Mister Cutter said. "My source confirmed the massacre she left behind while trying to get 'ol Jesse out."

The captain—wearing only white silk pajama bottoms—took a late breakfast on his veranda with a stunning young East Indian woman wearing only white silk lingerie.

Mister Cutter stood table-side, dirty and exhausted from his harrowing night in Puerto Rico.

The captain continued his debriefing. "And you're also being truthful about your shameful actions at the safehouse that Lady Molka thwarted?"

"Aye, captain. But in my defense, accounting for the dire alternatives I was offered—those being join, burn, or bullets—I looked to make the best deal for myself as I saw fit at the time."

The captain sipped his mimosa and considered. "Well, I suppose we all strive to make the best deal for ourselves in any given moment." He presented his rogue smile to the girl and winked. "It's aspirational. So I can't really fault you, Mister Cutter. Consider yourself reprimanded though."

"Aye, captain."

"And consider yourself fortunate Lady Molka didn't leave you to those Delgado cutthroats, which she was within her rights to do."

"Aye, captain."

The captain rose, moved to the veranda's rail, and gazed out beyond Katelyn's harbor to tranquil Caribbean waters. "A real shame about Jesse. This was not what I wanted for him. At least he knew I found his children before he died."

"Aye, captain."

"And seeing they're taken care of will be how I mourn him."

"A fine tribute, captain."

"Lady Molka is extraordinarily formidable. Even for someone working for an organization that has a reputation for extreme formidability. And her partner is equally impressive…in her own unpolished way."

"Aye, captain."

"I'll wager, no matter the circumstances—desperate and hopeless included—those two would find a way to adapt, improvise, lie, cheat, or steal to get the job done."

"Aye, captain. I wouldn't put much past either of them."

"Indeed. Get yourself refreshed and rested, quartermaster. We shall speak more on this later."

"Aye, captain." Mister Cutter moved to leave.

"Oh, one moment, Mister Cutter, if you please."

"Mister Cutter stopped. "Aye, captain?"

"Wasn't crewman Jonas a locksmith in his old life?"

Laili paused at the kitchen table in mid-pates bite at Molka and Salvia's afternoon apartment entrance.

Molka—carrying a plastic bag from a drug store—pointed Salvia toward the bathroom. "Take a shower. Use whatever products you want in there. I'll bring you some clean clothes in a minute."

Salvia complied.

Molka sat on the couch's edge, unlaced and removed the Danner combat boots, pulled off the double pairs of socks she wore on each foot, stood, undid the belt and button on her camo pants, removed them, and sat back down.

Laili fired rapid questions:
"What the hell are you wearing?"
"Who is she?"
"What happened to your leg?"
"Where were you last night?"
Molka fired rapid answers:
"Borrowed clothes."
"She's a friend. Her name is Salvia."
"A jeep hit my leg."
"I was in, and near, Puerto Rico running an errand for the captain."
"Oh," Laili said.

Molka removed alcohol wipes, antiseptic gel, and bandages from the bag, and cleaned and dressed her leg abrasion.

"Can we have our liaison meeting now?" Laili said. "Because I want to hang out with my friend tonight."

"You've made a friend here?"

"Yeah. Gus."

"Gus Ramos?" Molka said.

"Yeah."

"Gus Ramos is not your friend. Your instructions were to recruit him as an asset, if possible, to get information on the Thorsens and their drug trafficking operation as it pertains to our task. And to use caution when doing so because he is a dangerous criminal."

"I know," Laili said. "I read those instructions 10 times."

"Then you need to follow them."

"He had to kill his own cousin, who he loved like an older brother, or they would've killed him. Do you know how fucked up that is? Do you know how fucked up that would make you?"

"Very," Molka said. "So don't trust him. Don't believe anything he says. Verify everything and be careful."

Laili smirked. "Yes, *Azzur*."

Molka stood, removed the torn, stained olive-green cut off t-shirt, and tossed it into the kitchen trash. "Salvia is more your size, so let her borrow something to wear and some shoes. We're taking her to the airport. Then we're going out drinking."

CHAPTER 29

"*Vive la France!*" Donar danced across his living room with a half empty champagne bottle he had pirated from the morning's aborted bridal shower brunch.

"Dad." Caryn slouched on a couch, still in her bridal shower dress. "I just finished my talk with Paz. He told me to get all my things off his yacht while he thinks things over."

Donar danced on. "Bless that girl! She's delivered us from death!"

"Dad. Please. But how did a little French ghetto slut find out we talked to that the low-life, lawyer Morgan? And what happened to client-attorney confidentiality?"

Donar danced, ecstatic. "It's a blessing in disguise. With the wedding canceled, the cartel cannot expect further trips. This load can be a one-off, and we have fulfilled our obligation. We're free!"

"Dad. Stop. The wedding is not cancelled yet. She's insane, but she's also smart, and that makes her very dangerous. I need to get her out of my way, and once I do, it will take me all of five minutes to get Paz back under my power."

Donar stopped dancing. "Are you insane too? You can't get rid of her. That spectacle was witnessed by over 50 of the most prominent residents in the USVI, not to mention Father McKenzie,

Rabbi Silverman, and the police commissioner's wife. She gets killed, we're going to be suspects one and two."

"I'm not going to kill her. I just need her to disappear for a few days."

Donar held up his palms and backed away. "No. Absolutely not."

"Dad. Leave. Wait. I saw Gus skulking around the garage waiting to talk to you. Go tell him to come in here. Now leave."

CHAPTER 30

Hodge herded her little helpers from the baseball field under construction to a large open tent set up with tables and chairs. Drinks and snacks awaited them, and they ploughed right in.

Justain sat at the table's end checking his social media.

Hodge approached him. "Thanks for meeting me out here."

"I thought you said today was your day off."

"It is," Hodge said.

"Teaching kids to lay sod is how you relax?"

"I'm teaching them that when you help to build something with your own hands and sweat, you appreciate it more and take care of it better."

Justain went back to his social media. "And you're a better person than me."

Hodge took a soda from the table and motioned for Justain to follow her outside the tent. "I heard from the Angel."

Justain's face alit. "Yes? And?"

"The Angel is sending a crew over here tomorrow to build a backstop and dugouts for our field." Hodge viewed her kids with affection. "This will be the first real baseball diamond these children have ever played on. And that will mean more to them and me than anyone knows."

Justain's face slumped. "That's it?"

"The Angel also said they know why you're here and what you're looking for."

Justain's face alit again. "Yes? And?"

"And very soon, they're going to give you what you want, and something you'll never forget."

Justain triple fist pumped the air.

"I guess you take that as good news?"

"In South America I worked with some great cops—not just good—I mean some truly great cops. And we did some great—not just good—I mean some truly great work. But 99 percent of it got flushed because we had to share it with local law enforcement who were almost always bought off. And the one percent that did get used and got results, our superiors stepped in and grabbed all the credit for themselves."

Justain closed his eyes and balled his fists. "The futility of it all broke the minds and hearts of those great cops. And one by one they left the service or retired early. It was a crying, damn shame and a real loss to the profession."

Justain opened his eyes and gritted his jaw. "But I hung on. Just for spite. I hung on. And it cost me most of my hair and all of two marriages. But I hung on. And finally, after 10 brutal years, I shamed them into admitting an agent of my experience and tenure should be in charge of a division. But they screwed me on that too. Don't get me wrong, the Caribbean Division has fine people and does fine work, but it's far from the front lines and far from where I should be."

"And now…I was a great cop in Marion, Indiana and a great cop in Guadalajara and a great cop in Bogota and a great cop in Brownsville, and I'm still a great cop, and soon the whole world will recognize it." Justain smiled and raised his face and arms to the sky. "Lord almighty! My time has finally come!"

CHAPTER 31

"**F**ifty-four?" Laili said.

"Fifty-four," Molka said.

Molka worked on her second strawberry margarita and Laili had almost finished her third Painkiller and second menthol at the same table in the same dive bar they had visited on their arrival day.

"Wait," Laili said. "That's not including probables or badly wounded?"

"Just the confirmed kills."

Laili beamed, impressed. "What a fucking blood bath!"

Molka grimaced. "Shhh!"

Laili leaned forward and lowered her voice. "What did you use?"

"A standard AK-47 and four mags."

"No optics, no night vision?"

"None," Molka said.

"It wouldn't have taken me four mags to take out 54 security men, but still not too bad. I wish I would have been there."

"No, you don't. And this is not a happy day."

Laili's sneered, agitated. "What do you care about them? They wanted to rape you and toss you into a woodchipper."

"I don't care about them. But it's still not a happy day, ok?"

Laili sat back. "Ok, fuck me then. But that made you good with the captain. He's going to do the job for you, right?"

"Yes," Molka said. "What's the update with Paz?"

Laili inhaled her cigarette, tipped her head, and blew smoke at the ceiling. "It's done. I did it."

"The captain's bridal shower brunch assault worked?"

"It worked perfectly flawless. You have to give the captain much respect. The man really knows how to spring a surprise. Check this out."

Laili showed Molka video of Captain Giselle on *Outcast* making her declaration, the damning presentation of the counselor, and the sudden ending to the bridal shower brunch.

"Wow," Molka said. "You really laid in the parting slap on Caryn. I've never seen such a pleasant face look so unpleasant. But maybe too much. The captain told you to make her the victim of a farce, not a fight."

Laili shrugged. "Hey, I had to make the plan my own."

"And then Paz broke up with her on the spot?"

"More or less. He's agreed to talk to her about things. But it's basically over. I mean, the whole thing between them was a joke to start with. They got introduced by a bouncer in a club, went and fucked on his yacht that night, and then she ghosted him. But then her daddy found out Paz was rich, and they dreamed up the marrying scam to save their business. But even that wasn't enough for them. So they got him involved with their fucking drug trafficking too. Poor Paz."

Molka straw-poked the ice down in her drink. "Do you realize if Paz would have traveled with his government assigned security detail, we wouldn't be here. They're trained to spot and prevent those very situations."

"Anyway, he kicked Caryn off *Outcast* and asked me to stay over tonight."

Molka raised her eyebrows. "TMI."

"No; it's not like that with me and Paz. We're just friends. We're going to our windsurfing lesson together tomorrow when we wake up. There's another boy I'm talking to anyway."

"Gus Ramos?"

"Yes. And I did fuck him."

Molka covered her ears. "TMI. TMI. TMI."

Laili smiled. "Very funny." She raised her glass for Molka to clink. "Glass me. We did it. This task is ending, and our vacation is about to begin."

"Nothing is decided until it's decided. But things look good."

They clinked glasses.

"My first task almost completed," Laili said. "Really wasn't as hard as I thought."

"You never told me how many tasks you have."

"Twenty."

Molka finished her drink. "That's rough."

The server brought them another round, right on time.

Molka exhaled hard. "Whew."

"Don't bitch," Laili said. "You told her to keep them coming."

"I mean, whew, I haven't drank like this since college."

Laili started on Painkiller four. "I wish I would've had a chance to go to college."

"You can still go."

Laili looked away and shook her head. "No. It's too late for me."

"It's never too late," Molka said. "I went back to school after five years in the military."

"I meant it's too late for me to have what people call…the college experience. You know, when you're an 18-year-old freshman leaving home for the first time, and everything is new and exciting as you enter the adult world."

"You're only a year older than the 18-year-old freshmen."

"But I've already seen and done a lot of adult things," Laili said. "Too many. Most people my age look ridiculous to me. I wouldn't fit in. I missed my chance."

"If you want to go to college, go. Don't worry about what other people call the college experience. Have your own experience."

"Maybe." Laili ate the cherry from her drink. "You haven't told me why you wanted to have our liaison meeting here. I love it. But you were the one who said no partying."

"I'm not partying." Molka said. "I'm memorializing."

"Memorializing what?"

"Today is my little sister Janetta's birthday."

"Azzur told me about what happened to her. And to your parents. He said you came from an exceptional family."

"Azzur needs to stop telling so much."

Laili blew smoke. "Did he tell you anything about my fucked-up family?"

Molka fanned Laili's smoke away. "Nothing."

"You didn't miss much. The only one who turned out decent was my little brother, Eitan. That kid is so cute it's sickening. I didn't see him all that much though. I spent as little time at home as possible, and if you saw the shit show they called my home, you wouldn't blame me."

"How old is Eitan?" Molka said.

"Seven."

"Where is he now?"

"I don't know," Laili said. "In my mom's suicide note, she said she gave him to a nice rich family in Nahariya. She didn't say who they were or how she knew them. She just said she didn't want any of our relatives to have him."

Molka sighed. "That's really sad."

"No. She was probably right. But when I finish the program, I'm thinking about going up there and find him. You know, just to see how his life is going. Maybe we could even hang out and get to know each other."

"I have clients in Nahariya who know a lot of people there. Call my office. I can give you some numbers."

Laili shrugged. "He's probably better off if I just leave him alone." She stubbed out and lit another cigarette. "How old would she have been today, your little sister, Janetta?"

"Nineteen."

"Then we were born the same year."

"Yes. I always visit her grave on her birthday." Molka laid her arms on the table and laid her head on her arms. "This is the first one I've missed."

Laili sprung up and turned to the bar. "Hey! Wake up over there! She needs another drink—I mean—my partner needs another drink." She sat back down and looked at Molka. "Anything else you want, let me know. Tonight, I got you."

"Thanks...partner."

Molka swallowed back more than a few tears.

CHAPTER 32

"I truly appreciate you doing this for me, lad," Mister Cutter said. "I wouldn't begin to know where to look or who else to ask."

"You're just lucky I need to pick something up too." Gus entered the passenger side of Mister Cutter's SUV at the Sapphire Beach Hotel front entrance. "Turn left and keep going until I tell you to turn right."

Mister Cutter drove on. "How's Jorge?"

"Hurting and very pissed. He's partly blaming you for getting shot."

"Why?"

"Because you didn't agree to his deal sooner."

"I can't say he's wrong about that. And I'm sure his daddy blames me too."

"No; check this out," Gus said. "Jorge wants to take an army after the Bitch of Death, but—"

"Who's the bitch of death?"

"That's the name Señor Delgado's soldiers gave the bitch after she took out over half of them. But check this out. Jorge wants to take an army after the Bitch of Death, but Señor Delgado said no. He said it's over. He said they took two big swings at her and missed, and she's had two easy chances to kill Jorge and passed. In his mind, that evens things out."

Mister Cutter nodded, thoughtful. "There's some sense to that."

"Turn right on the next street. Tell me about the Bitch of Death, this captain's woman, his assassin machine."

"She's not one of the captain's women or his assassin. She's working with him on a tip."

"What's the tip?" Gus said. "Hey, turn left here. What's the tip? Maybe we can do some more business."

"Maybe. Maybe not."

"Maybe not? Our mutual information exchange deal means we exchange information mutually beneficial to each. And my man on Delgado Island pays big benefits for anything on Captain Savanna."

"As you've said many times, lad."

"And I know you liked the money I got you for *Tranquility*."

"I would've got a lot more if Jorge didn't muck it up."

"Why do you want to rip off your boss, anyway? I heard Captain Savanna treats you guys like kings. Big shares."

"Because, lad," Mister Cutter said, "the biggest shares are ones you don't share."

Gus laughed. "Ok. Now I know."

"Know what?"

"Since that night you rolled up on me in the bar and said you knew of my reputation and we could do some business together, I haven't been able to decide if you were a snitch, crazy, or gay. But now I know you're just a plain old thief."

"No, lad; I'm a pirate. And a pirate's always a pirate. But I've long suspected the captain has been undercounting the hauls for his own personal enrichment. By more than just a little, I'm saying. So, I'll take back what's rightfully mine, as any good pirate would. You get me now?"

Gus waved a dismissive hand. "I don't even care about all that. I just want to know about this new tip?"

Mister Cutter stopped at a traffic light and turned to Gus. "The captain's keeping close mouthed on this prize until right before we go after it, even from me. That means it's something big. Maybe more than big. How much can you get me tonight?"

"You said 20, but he's only got 10 right now. Can you find out about that tip sooner?"

"But can you get me more? Like tomorrow first thing."

Gus laughed. "When you jump back in, you plunge deep, don't you? You sure you want to do this?"

"Yes, lad. I'm sure."

"It's the guilt, isn't it? That's why you want to fuck up again."

"What guilt?" Mister Cutter said.

"I know guilt too." Gus turned his face toward the window and focused on the darkness. "You've betrayed your captain and your friend. There's no coming back from that. There's no forgiveness for it."

Mister Cutter focused straight ahead. "Aye."

Gus turned back and pointed at the traffic light. "Hey. Green. Let's go. I don't have all night. I have to run some fresh candy over to Candyland."

"Candyland, you say? Not that your personal business is any of my business—"

"It's not," Gus said.

"But if I had to make a list of the top one million individuals, I would never consider in one million years to ever do personal business with, Jake Weinberg would—"

"Jake's personal business is his personal business too. But the business we're doing together is setting my shit up for the future like you wouldn't believe. Next right and slow down. It's the pink house on the left. There it is. Stop. Park."

Mister Cutter stopped and parked.

Gus exited, pulled up his baggy shorts, strolled to the pink house, and knocked. The door opened, Gus entered, and the door closed.

Mister Cutter drummed his fingers on the steering wheel, looked at the house, checked his watch, looked at the house, rolled down the window and spit, looked at the house, rolled the window back up, looked at the house, drummed his fingers on the steering wheel again, looked at the house…

The pink house's door reopened, Gus stepped out, the door shut, and Gus strolled back to the SUV and got in.

"Everything go alright, lad?" Mister Cutter said.

"Sweet as candy."

Mister Cutter held out an open palm to Gus.

"Look at you," Gus said. "You're already sweating." He smiled. "You can taste it, can't you?"

"Let me have it, lad."

"Where's my money?"

Mister Cutter passed Gus some cash.

Gus reached into the front pocket of his shorts, removed a small packet with blue pills, and tossed it in Mister Cutter's lap.

Mister Cutter restarted his SUV and drove away fast. "So, can you get me more tomorrow? First thing tomorrow, I mean?"

"I don't know yet. Can you find out about this big tip Captain Savanna and the Bitch of Death are working?"

"Ok, lad. I see how this is going to work. I'll find out something."

PROJECT MOLKA: TASK 4

PROJECT LAILI: TASK 1

DAY 8 OF 10

CHAPTER 33

Muted voices woke her.

Laili strained against restraints securing her to a small bed in a darkened bedroom. Daylight from a crack in the window curtains revealed another girl restrained on a bed across from her, sleeping or passed out.

The muted voices spoke again, and the bedroom door opened.

A man entered. He wore a red polo, khakis, and a white bunny mask. He carried a small black medical bag.

Laili's discipline used her Giselle voice. "Where the fuck am I? What are you doing to me? Who are you, you fucking freak?"

"I'm the doctor," the bunny man said in an obvious fake voice. He opened the bag and removed a syringe.

Laili thrashed but moved little. "Don't fucking stick me with that needle! I hate fucking needles! I hate fucking drugs!"

"You'll feel much better very soon."

"NO! FUCK YOU!"

"Just stay still…here it comes…"

"NOOOOOOOOO!"

CHAPTER 34

The run in the late morning humidity sweated out some of the previous night's alcohol. And the extended post-run cold shower and two ibuprofen made her head feel better. But Molka reminded herself that hangovers were a good incentive not to get drunk more than once a year.

Molka sat in the living room chair in a towel brushing out her hair. *Ugh.* Split ends. She needed a trim. Vacation was coming. A nice long day at the spa would be her first self-treat.

Knock.
Knock.
Knock.

Someone was knocking on the door of the future home of the Saint Thomas Animal Hospital.

She rose, peeked out the front curtains, and looked down upon the knocker's bald head. It had happened two other times—people inquiring about a job despite the *no hiring* sign in the window. She took time to politely thank them anyway because they had made the effort. But this applicant didn't seem as serious showing up in a t-shirt, board shorts, and flip-flops.

Ignore him.
Knock.
Knock.

Knock.

Molka took a second glance at the knocker and identified the bald head: Paz Davidov.

What was he doing there? Looking for Laili? But she had said she was spending the night on his yacht. Was there an accident or something?

Molka pulled on shorts and a t-shirt, descended the interior stairs into the hospital, opened the door to him, and played it unaware. "Sorry, sir, the hospital won't be open for a few more weeks."

"I don't need a veterinarian," Paz said. "Is Giselle here? She told me she worked at the new animal hospital off Veterans Drive near downtown. I've been driving around this area for an hour, and this is the only one I've seen."

"She works here. But she's not here right now."

"Are you the lady she works with?"

"Yes; I'm the veterinarian. My name is Molka."

"Do you know where she is?"

"Who are you?" Molka said.

"I'm her friend, Paz."

"Oh. Ok. She's mentioned you. She said she was spending the night on your boat."

"She did," Paz said. "And we were supposed to do a windsurfing lesson this morning but..."

"But?"

"But I think you better come look at something."

CHAPTER 35

"**S**he and I had our differences over her odd friendship with Paz," Caryn said. "But I know now she's a very disturbed girl. We're all very concerned about her."

Molka stood with Caryn and Paz in the cabin Laili had used on the *Outcast*. Caryn was all business in a black Prada business suit.

Laili's purse and phone sat on the nightstand. Her sandals from the previous night lay on the floor by the bed. And when she arrived, Molka found Laili's car was in the marina parking lot, locked with a cool engine compartment.

Molka ignored Caryn's faux concern and turned to Paz. "Giselle and I left the bar last night separately at about 11:30PM. What time did she show up here?"

"Just before midnight," Paz said. "I heard her come down the passageway and shut the door. My stateroom is two doors down. I was still awake watching movies."

"Anyone else stay onboard last night?"

"No."

"This is a huge boat," Molka said. "Does it have a captain and crew?"

"I have a captain, but he's been staying in a condo over on Saint John. He's actually coming back aboard this evening to start getting her ready to go home. But I haven't seen him in weeks."

Molka addressed Caryn. "Does that security guard I saw picking his nose in the parking lot work for you?"

Caryn suppressed a smirk. "Yes."

"Was he working last night?"

"No. We have a night man. He didn't report anything suspicious." Caryn turned to Paz and fanned herself. "It's stuffy in here, baby."

Molka folded her arms across her chest. "I didn't ask you if he reported anything suspicious. Why did you say that? Do you think something suspicious might have happened to Giselle?"

Caryn shrugged. "I don't know. I just—I mean, I hope not. We're all very concerned about her."

"What about security cameras?" Molka said.

"We don't have any covering the actual mooring slips. Our yacht clients are quite adamant about their privacy." Caryn smiled. "You understand. What goes on aboard, stays aboard."

Molka faked a smiled. "Yes. I'm sure. Where's her friend Gus this morning?"

Caryn looked down and smoothed nothing on her immaculate fitted blazer. "Gus?"

"Gus Ramos," Molka said. "Giselle said he works here."

"Oh, Gustavo. Yes, he works here. I didn't know they were friends."

"Is he here?"

"Uh, no. He's off this week." Caryn turned to Paz again. "It's really stuffy in here. You should adjust the climate control, baby."

Molka pressed on. "Can you give Gus a call and ask if he's seen her?"

Caryn reinstated her insincere-concern face. "I will."

"Never mind," Molka said. "I'll call him. Can you give me his number?"

Caryn furrowed her brow. "I think I have it on file somewhere in the office. I'll send it to you when I find it. Are you going to report her missing to the police?"

Molka checked the time on her phone. "She's technically only been missing 11 hours. She's an adult—no obvious signs of foul play—so they'll probably wait at least 24 hours before they take an official report and start looking. But I would appreciate it if you don't touch anything in here until then, just in case."

"Absolutely." Caryn put her arm around Paz. "We're leaving on our honeymoon in two days, but I'm sure she'll turn up before then."

Molka moved to the nightstand and checked Laili's purse. Her keys and passport were inside. She picked up the purse and dropped Laili's phone into it. "I am going to take this and go through her contacts. Maybe she met another guy or something. And here." She took a pen and an old receipt from her purse, jotted down her number, and handed it to Paz. "Please call or message me if she shows back up here or if you hear from her."

"We will," Caryn said. "Paz has asked me to stay on board with him. So, I'll be right here watching everything." She smiled. "Thanks for coming."

"Yes," Paz said. "Thanks for coming. I really hope she's ok."

Molka left the *Outcast* and headed back toward the marina's retail and leisure complex and her car. Of course, Caryn Thorsen was lying. She knew what had happened to Laili. Because she had made it happen. And she had the motive—Laili's extreme interference—and the means—convicted kidnapper Gus Ramos—and the opportunity—Laili passed out after four Painkillers on *Outcast* the previous night.

It was Laili's own fault though. She had pushed the captain's clever plan one slap too far. So she also got herself abducted and possibly killed. And it seemed to have had the opposite effect of what she had intended by drawing Paz and Caryn together again.

But was Paz in on it too? Not likely. His concern over Laili was genuine.

The situation exposed a dangerous flaw in the Projects Program that Azzur often had lamented. He pointed out how in normal times, before the Traitors changed everything, operatives would never be allowed to work in a legend until they could forget their legend and just live it. It might take some people years to master the technique. Some people could never do it. But the projects didn't get that safety margin. And the conscious effort required—because of their inexperience—just to maintain their legend's lies sometimes didn't allow for the recognition of dangerous "non-threatening" threats closing in on them. At least not in time to stop them.

As Molka knew only too well.

But what should she do? Contact Azzur? No. He would be livid if his communication security policy was broken: *Always assume all electronic communications are being monitored and deciphered, including when using the latest encrypted devices. In other words, while on a task, never contact me.*

And even if she did contact him, he would just say, "Don't worry about Laili. Adjust and finish the task at all costs." He sometimes talked about a Japanese corporate technique he admired, in which right after someone committed a major foul up, they put all efforts into solving the problem first and then went back and assigned the blame later.

And he would be right. She should finish the task first and worry about Laili later.

Molka reached her car in the parking lot, got in, and started it.

But still…

Laili is your partner. And even if she doesn't like you and maybe you don't really like her, she's still your partner. And if something happens to your partner, you're supposed to do something about it.

Right?

Molka removed Laili's phone from her purse, scrolled through the contacts, and found Gus. She read through their messages. Nothing telling, mostly, short "wassup" and "let's hang out" exchanges. But it did reveal Gus lived in the Sapphire Beach Hotel, room 177.

She sent Gus a message as Giselle: *where u at?*

Two minutes later, Gus answered back: *where u been hiding girl???*

i had a bad night. I need to come see you.

ok. i'm at my place. come on girl.

CHAPTER 36

"**H**ey? Are you awake? Are you ok? Are you awake?"

Laili rolled her head to the girl strapped to the bed next to her. "No. I don't know." She looked down to view she was clad only in a long t-shirt with a teddy bear on the front. "Who took my clothes?"

"I don't know. I just woke up."

"My hair's wet. Smells like it was washed."

"Mine too."

"Where are we?" Laili said. "Is this real?"

"I don't know."

"How long have you been here?"

"I can't remember," the girl said. "That stuff they're giving us…it's hard to remember. But someone poked me with something at a party. A beach party…at night, I think. I can almost see their face." She started weeping. "It's almost there. But I…I just can't quite see it yet."

"Crying won't help us," Laili said. "Somebody poked me with something too. But I can't remember them either. Not yet. But I fucking will. What have they been doing to you?"

"I don't know. I don't know. I don't know." She wept harder. "I think they've been raping me."

"What's your name?" Laili said.

"Krista."

"I'm Giselle."

The door opened, and doctor Bunny Head and his bag returned trailed by a well-tanned, middle-aged man wearing a hip-hop t-shirt and skinny jeans: Jake Weinberg.

Weinberg smiled at Laili. "Welcome back to Candyland."

Laili fought her restraints. "Fuck you! You might as well kill me now. Because if I live, you die."

Weinberg addressed Bunny Head. "Proceed, doctor."

The doctor opened his bag and prepared a syringe.

Laili thrashed again. "I guess you didn't hear me, motherfucker. I said you're dead if I live."

"I've been told that before." Weinberg smiled. "Yet, nothing bad has ever happened to me. Why do you think that is?"

"The zombie girls," Laili said. "The zombie girls. You're the…we're the…fuck you, you sick fuck!"

Bunny Head injected the girl next to Laili and prepared a second syringe.

Weinberg smiled at Laili. "Go heavy on this one, doctor, as heavy as possible. I want her nice and docile for this evening. The prince is here visiting. But before he tastes her, I want a nice sweet, juicy sample myself."

Laili screamed. "NOOOOOO!"

CHAPTER 37

The door to room 177 at the Sapphire Beach Hotel opened on the second knock to Gus's contrived grin. "Wassup, gir—"

Molka greeted his shocked face with a thudding right cross to the chin.

He stumbled back into the room and tried not to fall.

Molka followed him in, shut the door behind her, and punished his chin further with a robust front kick.

He hit the floor, unconscious.

Molka—outfitted in her black tactical ensemble, including contacts in, high-ponytailed hair, and latex gloves over leather tac gloves—pulled several sets of flex-cuffs from her pockets. She bound Gus at the ankles and wrists, dragged him close to the bed, sat him up, and strapped his neck to the bedpost.

Molka surveyed the nice room which was trashed with empty fast-food paraphernalia. A Glock 17 lay on the nightstand. She moved to it, removed the mag and tossed it under the bed, ejected the round in the chamber and tossed it across the room, and dropped the weapon into an empty wastebasket. On the floor beside it, lay an empty drink cup. She took the cup to the bathroom, filled it with water, came back into the room, stood over Gus, and reviewed the tale she was about to tell him.

Ok. Sounds good. I almost believe it, so he will.

She removed her phone from her back pocket, turned on the recorder, repocketed the phone, and tossed the water in Gus's face.

Gus snorted, spit, and blinked awake. "What the fuck, *mami*!"

Molka retrieved a chair from the workstation, rolled it in front of Gus, sat, and leaned forward. "Now you know I'm not afraid of you. And I know you're not afraid of me. So we can talk on equal terms. I also know you're not afraid of anyone, and you're not afraid to die either."

"Who the fuck are you? And what the fuck do you know about me?" Gus closed his eyes and winced. "Fuck, my fucking jaw. You broke it!"

"Not yet," Molka said. "I know you're not afraid to die because that's how you've been trained. But I've seen stronger willed men than you beg not to be put in a lifetime cage, which is where you're going."

"Who's gonna put me in a cage for life? You?"

"No. The man Giselle and I work for, Mr. Levy."

"You that old lady she said she works with? You ain't that old."

Molka ignored Laili's mischaracterization. "Mr. Levy's a retired judge, and he's friends with all the law enforcement around here. He loves Giselle like a granddaughter, and she loves him like a grandfather. She tells him everything. He's freaked out worrying about her, and he's calling all his cop friends for help. They've asked him who she's been hanging out with. He said she mentioned your name."

"Who's the cops he's talking to? That *pendejo* Justain?"

"I just told you, he's talking to every cop here. They're all looking for you right now. But you're lucky I found you first. I can make this easier for you."

"How?" he said.

"I know Giselle's been causing problems between Paz and Caryn. So Caryn asked you to take her somewhere to get her out of the way until after the wedding. Right?"

"Maybe."

"Is she alive?" Molka said.

"Maybe."

"You know where she's at?"

"Maybe."

Molka rose and pushed the chair back to the workstation. "Alright. I'll leave you to the cops. Giselle was wrong about you though."

"About what?"

"She told me you were a sharp guy. No one's fool. But you're going to let your boss, a silly little rich girl, Caryn Thorsen, take you down by taking the fall for her."

"Yes, Giselle is alive, and I know where she's at."

"Because you took her?" Molka said.

"Yes. Now how can you make this easier for me? I know you want something. How much do you want?"

"I want you to tell me where she's at. Now." Molka removed her phone from her pocket, showed him the recorder recording and clicked it off. "Otherwise, I'll call the cops to this room and play your confession for them."

"If I tell you, you might do that anyway."

"It's the best deal you're going to get. I just want her to come home and ease Mr. Levy's poor mind. But for personal reasons, I would prefer not to involve cops either. So if she's unharmed when I find her, we won't have to."

Gus grinned. "You have something to hide too, *mami*?"

"Tell me where she's at." Molka dialed 911 and showed Gus the call ringing. "Last chance."

CHAPTER 38

Three Hispanic men—all under 30, dressed like cruise ship passengers, and wearing backpacks—stood in a line on *Outcast*'s aft deck, admiring her.

A lean, gray-haired, middle-aged man—attired in a short-sleeved white dress shirt and navy-blue pants—inspected the yacht's second level. He noticed the admirers and called down to them. "Hello; can I help you men?"

The man in the middle called up to him. "Is this your boat? It's beautiful. We want one like this for ourselves."

"No, I'm the captain, Captain Fletcher. Can I help you?"

"You're the captain?" the middle man said. "I'm Rafa." He put his hand on the shoulder of the man to his right. "This is Felix." He put his hand on the shoulder of the man to his left. "And this is Ernesto. Ernesto is a captain too. Well, he's training to be a captain."

Captain Fletcher pointed to the open security gate on the boarding stairs. "Did you men break the lock on that gate?"

The middle man shook his head. "No. We got the key from that guy in the office. We want to take a tour."

"A tour?" Captain Fletcher said. "This yacht is privately owned. It's not available for chartering."

"Oh really?" Rafa said. "Our boss told us it could be taken away from here with easy terms."

The three men laughed.

"Where did you hear that?" Captain Fletcher said.

"Hey, since you're the captain, maybe you can show Ernesto how to drive it. He needs more practice. A lot more."

The three men laughed.

"The owner and his fiancée are aboard," Captain Fletcher said. "And I'm very busy. So, I'm going to have to ask you men to leave."

The three men took off their backpacks.

"No," Rafa said. "This will just take a second.

CHAPTER 39

Two massive, sidearm wearing Candyland security men carried Laili back into the bedroom. She was handcuffed, shackled at the ankles, and muted with a ball gag.

She offered weak resistance.

They laid her on the bed and re-secured her with the leather restraints before removing the cuffs, ankle shackles, and gag.

"Thank you, Craig; thank you, Jason," Laili said. "Yeah, I know your names now. Your freak fuck boss talks loud. And next week or maybe 20 years from now, you're each going to hear me say your name again. Right before I cut your fucking throat. See ya."

Craig and Jason left and shut the door without comment.

Laili rolled her head to Krista in the next bed. "I saw two other girls. They're in another room down the hall, tied to the beds like us."

"Did they hurt you?" Krista said. "You weren't gone very long."

"It was only Weinberg. I couldn't fight him. That shit they gave me... He still had those two fuck-heads watching to make sure. They laughed. The guy waiting his turn watched and laughed too. It's all a big joke to them."

Krista's voice lowered. "He laughed when he raped me too."

"Sick fuck," Laili said. "But when Weinberg finished, another one of his guy's told him something, quietly. Then everyone stopped laughing. The guy who was waiting left quick. They brought me right back. Something's up."

"The other zombie girls got to leave," Krista said. "But I don't think we're ever going home."

The door opened and Weinberg entered.

"Please let us go," Krista said. "Please, Jake. Please. Please."

"Don't beg the fuck!" Laili said. "He loves that."

Weinberg stood between the girl's beds and double fondled them "I just wanted to say goodbye, my sweets. I'm leaving Candyland and will never return." He looked to Laili. "Thanks to you. So I've sold my beautiful island and you girls too. The new owner also employs his own security men who will be here very soon. But unfortunately for you, unlike my men—who were disinterested in raping and torturing women—your new keepers very much enjoy it. As a matter of fact, they live for it. They won't make sweet love to you as I just did."

"Fuck you!" Laili tried to spit at him, but her mouth was too dry.

Weinberg smiled and continued. "I once witnessed how they treat young girls at a private party. Too much for me to stomach. And when they're done with a girl, they promptly say goodnight to her. They say goodnight with a nine-millimeter Glock round to the back of their heads."

Weinberg inserted a final, vile violation into Laili and moved to leave.

"Hey Weinberg," Laili said, "I have one last thing to say to you."

"I know…if you live through this, you're going to kill me. Fortunately, you're not going to live through this."

"Wrong. I already knew I was going to die young. I accepted that a long time ago. I just wanted you to know I'm the badass little bitch who's going to be waiting for you at the front gate of hell to fuck you up before you even enter."

CHAPTER 40

"One of my drones took these about a month ago," Captain Savanna said. "Out of an abundance of caution, I keep a watch on my neighbor's activities."

Molka stood with the captain in his media room. He sported a gray herringbone smoking jacket—although Molka had never seen him smoke—over claret velour pants and black silk slippers.

Molka was still geared up for tactical ops.

They viewed super high-res overhead photos of Candyland Island on the captain's theater-sized screen. The island's various structures and topographical features were comprehensively labeled with white lettering. And if she had mentioned that his briefing setup was on par with many she had received with the Unit, it wouldn't have been an exaggeration.

"That's the complete overview, Lady Molka. Now how may I be of assistance in Lady Giselle's possible recovery? Did you need the use of a boat?"

"I can use my own boat," Molka said. "I just want two men to accompany me: one to watch the boat, and one to watch my back while I get Giselle. Steady and reliable is what's most important, and from what I've seen, you have an entire crew of such quality individuals."

"I thank you on their behalf, and you shall have the men you ask for, and, with your permission, some observations from one who has visited Candyland twice."

"Please," she said.

The captain removed a laser pointer from his jacket pocket and dotted the screen. "The main house, mansion more accurately, is here on the north coast. I doubt she would be held there. Here on the island's west coast is the guesthouse. I also doubt she'll be there, but right next to it is the dock. I would advise making your landing there, as the rest of the island's coastline—besides the too obvious manufactured beach fronting the mansion—is rocky and impassable."

"Understood," Molka said.

"Also of note, Weinberg had just started some type of tunneling project when I was there." The captain used the laser to point out four small openings, one on each coast. "These, I believe, are tunnel entrances or exits. He didn't explain what the purpose of the tunnels would be. However, if I had to guess, it would be to move things, or people, around the island hidden from airborne surveillance. But getting back to the location of the captives, here on the more isolated south coast is my best guess. This unremarkable-looking single-story home with palm tree concealment is the security housing, I was told. If I was looking for sex slave holding cells, that's where I would start."

"Makes sense," she said. "How many security men do you estimate he has?"

"I saw about 10 on my visits."

"All armed?"

"All with sidearms. Some also carried AR-15s."

Molka winced. "Might be a problem."

Mister Cutter entered carrying a tablet.

The captain viewed him with concern. "You feeling ok, Mister Cutter? You look quite tired."

"I'm fine, captain. Just had a little trouble sleeping these past couple of nights. It's my old shoulder injury that's been flaring up again." He handed the captain the tablet. "I just received this."

The captain read the screen for over a minute and addressed Mister Cutter. "Is this confirmed by your source?"

"Aye, captain."

DUAL DECEPTION

The captain addressed Molka. "Lady Molka, I apologize, as I somewhat doubted the veracity of your claims about Jake Weinberg, odd as he may seem. However, the tale this Ramos swine told about him and his island must be accurate because Weinberg is panicked and fleeing, with the assistance of Señor Delgado, no less."

"Where is he fleeing to?" she said.

"Delgado will be providing him safe passage to one of his haciendas in Caracas. This location was chosen, of course, as Venezuela's response to US and UK extradition requests are very slow and complicated, if they are even honored at all these days. In return, Delgado received all Weinberg's personal holdings in the BVI, including Candyland and the houses and buildings therein, all their contents, and sadly, four unfortunate girls being held there." The captain handed the tablet back to Mister Cutter and nodded. "Jake's a cunning one, isn't he? He knew Delgado would leap at the chance to gain a new island stronghold just two miles south of us here. A base he can use for unlimited harassment."

"Aye, captain."

Molka viewed Candyland's south coast house again. "And Giselle is definitely one of them?"

"They didn't say, I'm afraid," the captain said. "Only that the girls are all alive—at the moment."

"There's more to it, captain," Mister Cutter said. "Señor Delgado has already sent 25 of his jungle soldiers by chopper to Candyland. They'll land within the hour, and they're to secure his new property before Weinberg's security people can loot the place on their way out."

The captain clicked off his laser pointer. "Lady Molka, it seems your simple request for assistance is evolving into something much more serious."

"Well, I have no problem at all taking out more Delgado men. I've seen how those animals treat a woman."

"Indeed. How is poor little Señorita Salvia?"

"Back home with her family in the Dominican Republic...traumatized for life." Molka tapped her Beretta in its behind-the-back holster. "As I'm sure you know, I brought my sidearm again. May I also trouble you for an assault weapon and plenty of ammo?"

The captain jumped up on a leather couch and stood with feet spread shoulder width apart, hands on hips, and face ablaze. "I believe I can do better for you—much better. I'm still stinging over the *Tranquility*. One good ambush deserves another. Mister Cutter."

"Aye, captain."

"Get another drone over Candyland. I want live feed of Delgado's men's arrival, their strength, armaments, and disposition."

"Aye, captain."

"And tell the crew to make ready for a shore raid. Full combat arms and body armor."

"Aye, captain."

The captain presented his rogue smile. "We shall go in like enraged, marauding marines, smash all opposition, fetch our ladies' in distress, and then plunder the place to the bare pillars."

CHAPTER 41

"If I didn't know better, I would think this was written with a feathered quill," Justain said. "What type of script is this, Old English?"

Hodge sat at her desk and observed Justain standing near the light of the window, reading a message handwritten in ink on rolled parchment.

Hodge smiled. "I think the Angel's style is kind of charming in a way. And to answer your next question, yes, I've submitted a handwriting sample to the national database. No hits."

"And this simply appeared on your door overnight?"

"Yes, just like always. Two messages appeared actually. One for me and one for you."

"What did yours say?" Justain said.

"Nothing pertaining to your big, exciting case. Just boring little local issues, the Angel is concerned about." She nodded at Justain's message. "Is yours everything you wanted?"

"It's a little less than I hoped, but not in a terrible way. The Angel wants me to work for it a little more. I respect that." Justain lowered the message and gazed out the window. "I'll need to get a warrant. I'll have to go back to San Juan to expedite it, but I should have it within 48 hours. Do you think you could get me a couple of patrol officers to back me up when I execute it?"

"You'll need to talk to the commissioner about that. You seem to have his ear though."

Justain read over the message again. "Yes, right. I'll talk to the, um…commissioner."

Hodge stood. "So, are you done with me now?"

"Huh? Yes. Yes, I am. Thank you."

She moved toward the door. "Good luck, Agent Justain."

"Hold up. Come with me to the commissioner's office. I'll put in a good word for you and talk you up."

"No thank you," Hodge said. "I have a very important meeting to get to."

"Remember what I said about branding?" Justain smiled. "Let's go brand your name in his mind."

"Thanks again. But this meeting is much more important to me."

Hodge departed.

Justain took out his phone, booked his flight to San Juan, and checked his social media. Excited kid commotion on the street below drew his attention.

Detective Lieutenant Naomi Hodge leaned cross-armed against the police station's side wall and watched 20 plus excited local kids swarm an ice cream truck and place their orders.

When all the kids had gotten what they wanted, she paid the ice cream truck vendor, accepted 20 plus loving hugs, and headed back inside the station.

CHAPTER 42

"We're all dead," was the consensus opinion among three bearded, AK-47-armed, camo-wearing Delgado jungle soldiers at Candyland.

Moments before, they had left the main house—because they didn't like the music choice—and continued their drinking on Candyland's playground hill. That's when they had observed *Betrayal* and *Vengeance* docking outside the west coast guesthouse to disgorge 30 heavily armed and body-armored combatants who knew exactly where to attack. Half assaulted the guesthouse, and the other half moved toward the main house.

The third of the three jungle soldiers, who dared a closer recon, rejoined his comrades even more dismayed. "It's definitely Captain Savanna. And the Bitch of Death is with him."

Jungle Soldier One said, "Are you sure it was her?"

Jungle Soldier Three said, "Yes, I was face-to-face with her when Señor Delgado ordered her put into the woodchipper."

The consensus was reaffirmed: "We're all dead."

Jungle Soldier Two said, "The Bitch put Papi into a woodchipper instead. I had to clean his guts out of it."

Jungle Soldier One said, "She's come to free the whores here, just as she freed the whore Salvia from us."

Jungle Soldier Three said, "Papi was a good friend to me. But we can deny the Bitch her victory here. Let's go to the whore's house and kill them and ambush the Bitch when she comes."

Jungle Soldier One said, "We'll never make it. There's no cover between here and there. They'll spot us and cut us down."

Jungle Soldier Three said: "Maybe we can make it. We can use the tunnels. I was in them earlier. They run in every direction under the whole island." He pointed behind the playground. "The cistern entrance is just over there. The tunnels intersect through it. Maybe we can find one that leads to the south coast."

Jungle Soldier Two said, "Ok. We move."

The lone Delgado sentry outside Candyland's main house—fully alit and expelling deafening hip-hop music—lay wounded and disarmed on the front lawn in the moonless darkness. "Fuck you, Savanna. Just finish me."

"Maybe I won't have to," the captain said. "Let's parlay."

The captain held a suppressed .22 and knelt beside the sentry, along with Molka. And behind them, crouched along a hedge line, waited 12 crewmen, who like the captain and Molka, all wore radio headsets, black ballistic helmets, and black body armor over their black fatigues. They also carried M4 carbines in addition to sidearms.

"How many are inside the main house?" the captain said.

"Fuck you, Savanna." the sentry said.

"Sounds like they're partying hard in there, true?"

"Fuck you, Savanna."

"Are there any in the house on the south coast?"

"Fuck you, Savanna."

"Where are the girls?"

"Fuck you, Savanna."

"He's not going to talk," the captain said. "He's a tough veteran jungle soldier. These guys are unbreakable. How long have you been a loyal Señor Delgado killer, my friend?"

"Over five years," the sentry said. "Proudly."

"Five years. So, you were on that Cramer Island medical school raid and mass rape attack four years ago?"

The sentry smiled. "Fuck you, Savanna."

The captain stood, cross drew his .45s, cocked the hammers, and obliterated the sentry's face. "No, sir. Fuck you."

Molka was glad the hip-hop blare covered the execution roar.

The captain re-holstered his weapons and turned to Molka. "You said you have extensive tactical experience. I assume that includes close quarters combat?"

"Yes," Molka said.

"We'll form two teams. I'll take six men and enter the front. You take six and enter the rear. After we suppress any initial resistance, take your team and clear the second floor. My team will clear the first."

Molka nodded. "Understood."

The captain gathered the force together, assigned the teams, and reemphasized "stacking up" and their own particular technique for room clearing they had trained for and used to secure mega yachts.

Everyone knew their role.

They moved out.

Molka led her team to the gigantic house's rear. The massive pool deck surrounding the Olympic-sized pool contained dozens of lounge chairs. One held a face down, passed-out Delgado man. His AK-47 lay on the deck to one side, and an almost empty Don Julio bottle lay on the other. Molka's team flex-cuffed his hands and ankles and taped his mouth without him awakening.

They moved toward the house.

A tall sliding glass door in a row of tall windows waited open, and the thumping hip-hop poured out. Molka's team stacked up and approached the door for entry.

Molka, in the number one position, raised her weapon, quick stepped to the door's threshold, and did a fast pie off scan of the family-room-type area for center threats. Seeing none, she quick stepped left across the threshold to clear the corner, while her number two man quick stepped right across the threshold to clear that corner. The rest of the team followed.

Room clear.

CRAAAAAAACK!

Multiple small arms fire bursts erupted ahead.

The captain engaged in a firefight.

Molka's team moved to assist.

The firing ceased.

The captain and his team appeared across the room. "Clear?"

"Clear."

The captain pointed upstairs.

Molka acknowledged the message with a hand signal.

The captain moved his team to the next room.

Molka moved hers toward the stairs.

The hip-hop music coming from the first floor cut off when Molka's team was about three quarters of the way into clearing over two dozen rooms, bathrooms, and closets.

The captain's voice came over Molka's headset. "First floor clear. Lady Molka?"

Molka answered, "Almost there." She moved her team forward down the hallway.

Three doors down, a Delgado soldier stepped into the hallway and faced Molka. He wore earbuds and carried an armload of expensive leather men's shoes.

Molka raised her weapon and smiled at the caught looter.

He dropped the shoes and smiled at her.

"Hands on your head!" Molka said. "Do it now!"

He didn't move. He kept smiling.

Molka repeated, "Hands on your head! Do it now!"

He removed his earbuds and spoke, "The Bitch of Death has come for me."

Molka ordered for a third time, "Hands on your head! Do it now!"

"The Bitch of Death has come for me." The man's hand moved for his sidearm.

Molka fired—three chest shots, center mass.

The man fell onto his back.

Molka moved to the man, removed his weapon, and stood over him.

He mumbled his dying words, "The Bitch of Death has come for me. The Bitch of Death has come for me. The Bitch of Death has come…"

Molka turned back to her number two man. "The Bitch of Death? Is that some kind of local superstition or myth?"

The number two shrugged.

The team moved forward.

Molka's team finished clearing the second floor, and she descended the stairs with them following.

A piano played a classical piece from somewhere in the house.

Molka followed the music and entered a room featuring a large black grand piano. The captain's helmet and weapon rested atop it, and he sat at the bench playing.

His team covered seven Delgado men flex-cuffed face down on the floor.

The captain ceased playing when Molka approached. "I couldn't resist. Bach on a Steinway epitomizes superior taste, culture, and style."

Molka reported, "One dead. One secured: passed out on the pool deck."

"Very well." The captain's face became wistful. "This is a magnificent instrument." He gazed up and around. "And this house is spectacular. The artwork, sculptures, tapestries, and antique rugs we'll take are worth at least 10 million on the legitimate market. Perhaps a quarter of that on the black, but a great prize none the less. Jake has impeccable taste. He's a genius too, you know. He built a multi-billion-dollar financial juggernaut by his late 20s. In my late 20s I was…unfocused, to say the least. If I would have had just a quarter of his talent, I could have…" The captain's face became stern. "Of course, the man is a contemptible monster. By this time tomorrow, all his life's achievements will be forever forgotten, and he'll only be remembered for his repulsive crimes."

Mister Cutter entered with two crewmen. "The guesthouse is secure, captain. Nothing but Delgado men drinking. We killed six, and six surrendered. The prisoners were taken to the dock."

"And I've killed two, and seven surrendered." The captain's eyes counted figures on the ceiling. "Which means…three are unaccounted for. They're either in the south coast house or down in the tunnels."

"What about the girls?" Molka said.

Mister Cutter tapped his fighting knife. "I interrogated my prisoners. The four girls are in the south coast house, as the captain reckoned. And I have all their assigned guards. Discipline is right out the window. They've been having a party since they got here tonight. They had no idea anyone knew they were here."

The captain stood and picked up his weapon. "Mister Cutter, take charge of these prisoners and the one out on the pool deck."

"Aye, captain."

"And bag the deceased for sea burials."

"Aye, captain."

"And then have your men start the plunder."

"Aye, captain." Mister Cutter ran to obey.

"Lady Molka, my team will cover the four tunnel entrances and trap the rats if they're in there. Your face tells me what you and your team will do. I hope she's alive. Good hunting."

CHAPTER 43

POP!
POP!
POP!
POP!
BANG!
BANG!
BANG!
BANG!
POP!
POP!
POP!
POP!
BANG!
BANG!
BANG!
BANG!
"What's that?" Krista said.
"AR-15s and AK-47s," Laili said. "Sounds like a firefight."
"Oh my god. They're coming to say goodnight. They're killing the other girls! We're about to die!"
POP!
POP!

POP!
POP!
BANG!
BANG!
BANG!
BANG!
Female screaming and crying reverberated from the next room.
POP!
POP!
POP!
POP!
BANG!
BANG!
BANG!
BANG!

Laili arched her back against the restraints. "Stop crying! Don't give them the fucking satisfaction! If we're going to fucking die, let's die like fucking badass bitches!

BOOM!
BOOM!

Laili froze. "Listen! That wasn't an AR or an AK."
BOOM!
BOOM!
"That's not a Glock either."
BOOM!
BOOM!

Laili's face lit with excitement. "Did you fucking hear that?"
"Hear what?" Krista said.
"Oh fuck, yeah! That's a Beretta 96A1, .40 caliber!"
"What's that mean?"
Laili beamed "It means my partner's here!"

CHAPTER 44

Laili inspected three dead Delgado men in the south coast house's front yard while Molka and her team helped the other three freed captives into a commandeered Candyland maintenance pickup truck they found parked there.

Molka joined Laili beside the bodies and said, "They were just waiting in those prone positions. Their idea of an ambush, I guess. We spotted them easily. They left the porchlight on behind them. Silhouetted themselves. My team pinned them in place, and I flanked them for the kill shots. Delgado seems to like his men long on guts, short on brains."

"Did you kill the rest of them too?" Laili said.

"No. Most surrendered. We caught them in mid-party."

Laili kick-rolled the last body over to view the face. "None of these are the ones. Where's Weinberg?"

"Probably in Venezuela by now." Molka viewed with pity Laili's sole covering: the long teddy bear sleepshirt. "Sorry I didn't bring some clothes for you."

"Where are the prisoners?" Laili said.

"Waiting on the dock. Everyone is there. Waiting on us. We're leaving right away."

Laili walked to the truck and addressed the girls. "Don't be scared now. They can't hurt you anymore. I promise. Ok?"

The girls nodded timidly.

Laili headed back into the house.

Molka followed her.

Laili entered the kitchen and searched inside every cupboard and cabinet. She did the same in the bathroom. She walked out onto a small back patio which held a BBQ grill. From under the grill, she grabbed a lighter fluid bottle and a butane grill lighter.

She moved back into the house and squirted lighter fluid on all the beds in the four bedrooms, then moved through the house spraying carpet and walls. She used the fluid's final squirts to leave a trail from the front room carpeting, out the door, and onto the porch.

Satisfied, she tossed the empty bottle back inside, clicked on the butane lighter, ignited the fluid trail, and moved well back.

A short blue flame ran into the house and burst into huge orange flames. Thick smoke followed.

Molka joined Laili and watched the house burn.

"Are you sure you're alright?" Molka said.

"They've been drugging me," Laili said. "I can't remember coming here or much else. I don't want to talk about it right now. Ok?"

Memory flashes from South Florida tore free from the vault in Molka's mind. The nausea from the GHB O'Donnell gave her that night and his laugh behind the camera nearly made her vomit and scream aloud.

Laili repeated. "Ok?"

Molka took a deep breath. "Yes. Ok. Let's not talk about it right now."

Laili moved to a dead Delgado man in the yard, removed his AK-47, checked the mag status, and slung it over shoulder. "Come on. We have a task to go finish."

At the lighted dock near the west coast guesthouse, *Betrayal* and *Vengeance* sat well laden with booty, and the crew rushed to fill Weinberg's confiscated 30-foot race boat with more.

Mister Cutter hurried things along, and another crewman kept a weapon pointed at the 14 Delgado men kneeling in a line on the dock with their hands flex-cuffed behind them.

Molka stopped the truck alongside the dock. Laili remained in the passenger seat while Molka and her team assisted the three captives from the back, onto the dock, and toward the waiting captain.

The captain addressed the lead crewman. "Make them comfortable in the cabin aboard *Betrayal*."

"Aye, captain."

They moved off.

Molka remained with the captain. "What's your plan for those poor girls?"

"We'll take them over to the RVIP in Road Town, on Tortola," the captain said.

"What's the RVIP?"

"Royal Virgin Islands Police. This is the BVI's jurisdiction."

"They should be taken to the hospital first."

"Of course. I'll see to it. And congratulations, Lady Molka. You've solved the 'zombie girls' mystery. You're about to be a local legend."

"Well, I would appreciate my name being kept out of this legend."

"Enough said. And Lady Giselle?"

"They were drugging the girls, and Giselle was a little woozy. But she has a freakishly strong system and seems to be quickly shaking off whatever they gave her, and she has no visible injuries. I'm taking her to the hospital to get checked out anyway. She's said she's alright and doesn't remember much. But…"

"Enough said."

Laili exited the truck with the AK-47 still slung on her back and approached Molka and the captain.

The captain greeted her with kind compassion. "Lady Giselle, I'm overjoyed to see you alive and well, or as well as can be hoped, considering the circumstances. I apologize for our tardiness. We just this afternoon heard of your distress."

Laili viewed the kneeling prisoners. "What are you going to do with them, give them to the cops?"

"No. Pirate's creed. We handle our own disputes. I'll ransom them back to Señor Delgado. If he refuses to pay, they'll be allowed to join my crew and work off their ransoms."

Laili moved to the prisoners.
Walked down the line.
Viewed each face in the dock lights.
Walked back down the line.
Viewed each face in the dock lights again.
Centered herself facing the prisoners.
Took two steps back.
Unslung the AK-47.
Cocked it.
And in quick succession:
Executed man number three with a headshot.
Executed man number seven with a headshot.
Executed man number ten with a headshot.
The crewman guarding the prisoners lurched back.
The surviving prisoners cowered, and some begged.
Mister Cutter jumped from *Betrayal* with his sidearm drawn.
The captain waved Mister Cutter off.
Molka gave no reply. She understood.

Laili lowered the weapon, made it safe, and returned to Molka and the captain. "I'm sorry, captain. Those three won't be able to bring you any ransom. They took turns with us for hours before you arrived. Hope you understand."

The captain closed his eyes and spoke with a soft seriousness. "I understand, Lady Giselle. And I understand it is impossible to suffer without making someone pay for it; every violation already contains revenge."

Laili handed the weapon to Molka. "I'm cold and tired, captain. Can I go lay down inside *Vengeance*?"

PROJECT MOLKA: TASK 4

PROJECT LAILI: TASK 1

DAY 10 OF 10

CHAPTER 45

Laili pounded the dash. "If I had just one more day, I could have gotten Paz away from her. It's your fault that stupid doctor kept me 24 hours for tests. I'm totally good. I didn't even want to get checked out in the first place. Thanks a lot, ugly."

Molka smiled. "You're welcome, brat."

Laili rode passenger in Molka's car and vented after Molka informed her that the Davidov-Thorsen wedding was still on. She had just received a 6AM hospital discharge, and they drove to Yacht Marina Grande to retrieve her car.

Molka brought her a clean crop top, jean shorts, and her tennis shoes. Molka wore a white polo and khaki shorts.

For task security, Molka and Laili didn't disclose to the doctor and nurses the circumstances behind her drugging. If they had, their recommendations would have been contacting law enforcement and years of counseling.

The former was not possible, and Laili didn't want to discuss the latter. She chose suppression and anger as her follow-up treatment and made Molka promise not to tell Azzur.

Molka interrupted Laili's vent. "What time is their ceremony today?"

"They're having two ceremonies. One o'clock at the temple and then two o'clock at the church. Then the reception will be held on

Outcast from four until seven, when the happy couple will sail off into the sunset on their new life together." Laili's lips curled into a sarcastic grimace. "How fucking romantic is that?"

Molka shrugged. "Actually…very."

"When we get there, I want to say hi to Paz. I mean goodbye. I'll probably never see him again."

"Ok. He was really happy when I told him I found you."

"What did you tell him?" Laili said.

"Just that you went to a party with some strangers and passed out."

"I really hope Gus is there too." Laili checked her phone. "He's not answering my messages. I want to show him I'm alive."

Gus wouldn't be there. If he was smart, he would be in Caracas with his fellow predator friend, Weinberg.

Maybe Molka would tell Laili one day what her good friend Gus had done to her. But not that day.

"Azzur's going to kill me for failing," Laili said.

"Probably. But he'll also find a way to get them divorced before they get back home. And speaking of which, if Caryn is there, don't start anything with her."

"She starts shit with me, I'm going to finish it."

"I'm going with you to make sure that doesn't happen."

Laili pounded the dash again. "I just can't believe she won, and I lost."

"You lost? She and her dad are about to lose 1,000 pounds of pharmaceutical grade fentanyl and 100 million in gold bullion fronted to them by a notorious cartel. You couldn't lose that bad if you tried."

A small smile parted Laili's lips. "Ok. I just started feeling a little less fucking angry."

"And you should also be happy to know I have the rest of the task all handled."

Laili smirked. "Well, excuse me for not having an awesome asset to work with like Captain Savanna."

"I want you to come with me tonight as back-up."

"What's your plan?"

"I deliver the flash drive to the captain at 5PM. Wait for him to take Paz. Wait for Flotilla 15 to take Paz back. And deliver the *Outcast* to the contractors. Task complete."

"Then we collect our bonuses. And start our vacations."

"Exactly," Molka said. "Feeling even a little more less angry now?"

Laili allowed a larger smile. "A little."

"Take a look in the glove box."

Laili opened it and removed a large envelope filled thick with US currency. "What's this, the rest of our task money?"

"No. That's from the captain. My share of the Weinberg booty."

Laili flipped through it. "How much is it?"

"Forty thousand."

"Shit, for one prize? Fuck the program. I want to be a pirate."

"Half is yours."

Laili tossed the envelope back in the glove compartment and slammed it shut. "I don't need charity for sympathy."

Molka lied. "That's not how I mean it."

"How did you mean it?"

"If things were the other way around, would you have joined the captain's raid on Candyland and got me out?"

"No question."

"And I believe you," Molka said. "But I still want to buy some insurance from you in case things are ever the other way around."

"Like on another task you get in trouble, and they send me to bail you out?"

"Exactly."

Laili nodded. "Yeah, ok. I can live with that."

"That gives us 35,000 dollars play money each." Molka smiled. "I know a girl who's going hardcore shopping first day of vacation tomorrow. What about you?"

Laili shrugged. "I haven't decided yet."

"And day two, a day at the spa. Full treatments and pampering. Throw everything they have at me."

"I'm definitely getting drunk the first day," Laili said.

"And then?"

"And then…I'm sure you're going to laugh at me, but the island next door, Saint John, is mostly a national park. And I was reading online where they have all these different hiking trails where you can really get into some serious nature sights, and even one where you can see some ancient petroglyphs. When I was a kid, no one ever took me hiking or camping or anything like that. I mean, I know it sounds lame as fuck."

"Not at all," Molka said. "It sounds interesting."

Laili smiled. "And then, of course, I'm going to hit downtown Charlotte Amalie and shop my ass off."

"Of course," Molka said. "But you know what the very best part of these eight vacation days will be?"

"Fuck yeah, I do."

"No Azzur!" they exclaimed in unison, erupting in genuine laughter.

Laili radiated. "Ok. Now I'm feeling a whole lot less fucking angry." She flipped on the radio. A newer pop song played. "I love this song!"

"I do too!" Molka said. "Turn it up!"

Laili turned it up, and they bopped their heads and sang along and smiled and laughed more.

Molka parked next to Laili's car. Yacht Marina Grande's retail and leisure complex didn't open until 9AM, so they cut around to a separate outside marina entrance.

Walking through the gate, Molka tripped, stumbled, and recovered.

Laili laughed. "Hey, watch your step."

Laili trailed behind Molka for a few paces and playfully tripped her.

Molka stumbled and recovered again.

Laili laughed again, harder. "Hey, walk much?"

Molka crinkled her nose. "Hilarious."

They proceeded down the long dock—past numerous lesser yachts—toward the marina's biggest mooring slip at the far end, home to Yacht Marina Grande's largest ever hosted mega yacht: the soon to be departing *Outcast*.

They reached the dock's end.

They stopped suddenly.

Molka gaped at Laili.

Laili gaped at Molka.

They both gaped at a big area of empty water.

The big area of empty water where *Outcast* should have been floating.

FREDRICK L. STAFFORD

CHAPTER 46

Molka gaped at Laili again.

Laili gaped at Molka again.

"Wait," Laili said. "A 200-foot yacht doesn't just get up and walk away."

"No," Molka said. "They start up and cruise away."

"No. Wedding this afternoon, reception this evening, leaving tonight, remember?"

"Maybe they eloped and left early."

"If they did that, we're—"

"Both dead."

"Now what?" Laili said.

"Now you're going to wait here while I go to the marina office and hopefully find Caryn there, but if not her, whoever is managing the place right now, and ask."

Molka left, and Laili lit a cigarette.

A portly, 60-ish man appeared on the deck of the yacht moored behind where *Outcast* had been. "Good morning, young lady. You're very pretty."

"Yeah, I know," Laili said. "Do you know what happened to the big boat that was parked here?"

"You're talking about the *Outcast*, owned by playboy Paz."

"Yeah."

"It left yesterday without so much as hosting a sendoff party, which is tradition in this marina. I mean Paz brought a party onboard, but I wasn't invited."

"What party?"

Marina Office
Private

Molka found the office door, with an identifying gold plate, next to Yacht Marina Grande's main entrance. Lowered blinds covered a large window on the door's right side, but a bent slat allowed a small peek in. She peeked in.

A youngish red-shirted Hispanic man with a moustache sat at the desk viewing porn on a laptop.

Classy. An employee playing around. Bosses must be out. Ask him where they are.

Molka knocked once and tried the door handle. Unlocked. She opened the door to find a haggard Donar Thorsen sitting in a chair against the wall and another youngish, Hispanic man, in a blue shirt, sleeping face down on the couch. A pistol butt protruded from his jeans' back waistband.

Molka's situational awareness redlined.

Trouble; use caution.

"Excuse me," Molka said. "I'm looking for the marina manager." She flashed a disarming smile. "And good morning, everyone, by the way."

Donar's eyes moved from Molka to the red shirt guy at the desk and back to Molka. He answered in a monotone. "I'm the owner-manager."

Molka smiled disarming again. "Great. I'm actually looking for a yacht that was berthed here named *Outcast*. I'm an old friend of its owner, Paz Davidov. We know each other from back home. I heard he was here and would love to say hello."

Again, Donar's eyes moved from Molka to the red shirt guy and back to Molka. And again, he answered in monotone. "I'm sorry, miss. There's no yacht here by that name."

"Yes. I know it's not here now. But maybe you can tell me where he moved it to?"

Once again, Donar's eyes moved from Molka to the red shirt guy and back to Molka. Same monotone. "I'm sorry, miss. There's no yacht here by that name."

"Ok, thank you." Molka offered a parting disarming smile. "I must be at the wrong marina. Sorry."

Molka rushed over to Laili, who still waited on the dock.

"It left yesterday," Laili said. "Three Hispanic males with backpacks boarded it an hour before. What did you find out?"

Molka came close to Laili and whispered, "We need to go home and get our weapons."

CHAPTER 47

"**D**addy Thorsen signaled you with his eyes and voice that he was in a hostage situation," Laili said. "Are you positively definite?"

"Absolutely," Molka said.

Molka—with Laili riding passenger again—sped toward their apartment.

"Why would he be held hostage in his own marina?" Laili said.

"I would guess it has something to do with *Outcast* being gone. Either way, we'll find out when we rescue him. What time is it?"

Laili checked her phone. "6:32."

"We need to get this done before the marina's mall part opens."

"What gear do we need and what's your plan?"

"We need our weapons with their suppressors," Molka said. "How many flashbang grenades did the captain give you for that bridal shower op?"

"A bandolier of six. I still have five left."

"Good. We'll need one, and you'll need to get into your smallest bikini."

DUAL DECEPTION

Laili stood outside the Yacht Marina Grande office door scarcely covered in a miniscule gold bikini and standing statuesque on platform sandals. A large floral beach bag hung from her left shoulder.

Molka stood to her left, back pressed against the wall with her suppressor attached Beretta held in a barrel-up ready position.

Molka nodded.

Laili knocked.

A finger parted the door side blinds and a sleepy brown eye peered out. The sleepy eye awoke on Laili's taunt, young, perfect body and the door unlocked and opened.

Laili stepped into the office.

Red Shirt smile-gawked.

Blue Shirt, awake on the couch, smile-gawked.

Laili smiled seductively. "Oooo…three handsome men! One of you has to know where the pool is?" She let the beach bag slip from her shoulder and land behind her. "Ooops…" She turned and bent at the waist to retrieve it.

Her move had the desired distraction effect.

Laili's right hand went into the bag and came out with a flashbang grenade, and with blur-quick coordination, she tossed it into the far corner of the room, ducked, and drew her suppressor attached Sig.

Bright FLASH.

Loud BANG!

Molka vaulted into the room with weapon ready to fire. "NOBODY MOVE!"

Blue Shirt and Red Shirt, both stun-crouched on the floor, moved—to draw their pistols.

Molka shot Red Shirt in the head.

Laili shot Blue Shirt in the head.

Molka shut and locked the door.

Laili stood and opened a rear window to vent the smoke.

Donar glanced up from his position on the carpet, where he had been lying face down with his hands covering his head.

"Stand up," Molka said. "You're safe now." She viewed Red Shirt and Blue shirt. "They saw we had them covered. It was suicide."

Donar rose and addressed Molka. "That's because they're sworn to die before being arrested. You did the right thing killing them, officer." He smiled, relieved. "I hoped you caught my signals and called the police. But I had no idea you WERE the police." He addressed Laili. "And I knew there was something special about you, officer. That crazy act was just an act. I assume you were sent to keep an eye on Paz because of who he is?"

"Where is the *Outcast* and Paz?" Molka said.

"They left yesterday."

"We know that."

Donar paced.

Molka repeated. "Where's the *Outcast* and Paz Davidov?"

Donar paced.

"I had a very bad last few days," Laili said. "So I'm in no mood for shit today." She bowed up on Donar. "Where's Paz and the fucking boat, fuck-face!"

Donar stopped pacing and sighed. "I may as well tell you everything."

"You better," Laili said.

Donar pointed angrily at the dead men. "Friends of theirs, three of them, took *Outcast*, along with Paz, his captain, and…" His eyes teared over. "My daughter. They gave me until tomorrow morning to transfer ownership of this marina to their boss."

"Who's their boss?" Molka said.

"He runs a drug cartel. Horribly dangerous man."

"Do they know who Paz is related to?"

"I don't know. If they do, they didn't say."

"You going to pay the ransom?"

"I can't." Donar pointed to Laili. "As she knows, the business is in bankruptcy proceedings. I tried to explain that to them. But they won't listen."

"Where did they take *Outcast*?" Molka said.

"They moved her to a small unoccupied bay on the remote northwest coast of the island. They're holding everyone onboard."

"Ok." Molka tucked her weapon behind her back and took out her phone. "We'll go free them too."

Donar sobbed with joy. "Thank you, officers. Thank you, thank you."

"What's the name of the small bay?" Molka said.

"Pennington Bay."

Molka tapped the info into a map search.

Laili removed short-shorts and a crop top from her bag and pulled them on over her bikini. "Is Gus around?"

"No," Donar said. "I haven't seen him in a few days."

Molka held her phone for Donar to view. "Is that the place?"

Donar squinted. "Yes, that's it."

"If it's not, we'll be back for you." Molka pointed down to Red Shirt and Blue Shirt. "Until we recover the hostages, it's better if no one sees, or even knows about, these bodies. Ever."

Donar wiped his eyes. "You don't need them for your investigation?"

"Not really," Molka said.

"Then don't worry about them. I have people to take out that kind of garbage."

"Perfect." Molka looked to Laili. "Let's go."

They moved to leave.

"Hold on," Donar said. "What should I do in the meantime, officers?"

"You may want to postpone the wedding," Molka said. "Then wait and worry. If your daughter doesn't come back by tonight it means…we all died."

CHAPTER 48

Molka and Laili decided to leave Laili's car at Yacht Marina Grande since they would finish the task as a team. Mr. Levy could pick it up later. However, Laili did grab her binoculars and a half pack of cigarettes from it.

They drove to Saint Thomas's lower populated northwest coast and followed a twisting narrow side road, which ended at a locked yellow gate. The beginning of a dirt path leading into dense vegetation waited on the other side.

Molka checked her satellite map view again. "That goes straight to Pennington Bay."

They exited with their binoculars, jumped the gate, and headed down the long sandy trail.

"Thorsen better not be lying about *Outcast* being way the hell out here," Laili said.

"I don't think he lied to us," Molka said.

"He's already lied to us when he said he would tell us everything but didn't mention the drugs and gold, he's smuggling on her."

"Would you have mentioned that? We're the police, remember?"

"Azzur said leaving out key facts of a situation is the same as lying."

"True. But I'm sure Thorsen's not lying about *Outcast* being here."

"How are you sure?" Laili said.

"Because of a father's love."

Laili laughed sarcastically. "I wouldn't know about that."

The path broke from the trees and ended on a hill overlooking the small gorgeous, pristine emerald-watered Pennington Bay.

Molka and Laili raised their binoculars. Anchored 50 yards off the bay's curved white sand beach, *Outcast* presented an advertisement-quality image. Three shirtless men lounged on her sundeck.

"My map said this entire area is a nature preserve," Molka said. "Some would call it a tremendous waste of prime real estate. But it is an excellent place to conceal a 200-foot mega yacht from tourist eyes and cameras."

"Those three cartel guys are drinking beer for breakfast," Laili said. "They look half-drunk already."

"They're not expecting any trouble in this peaceful setting."

"Good. Then it should be easy."

"Don't say that."

"Got an assault plan?" Laili said. "You're the badass former special forces warrior."

"Well, all my experience was in helicopter—not seaborne—assaults. But right after dark, we can use the inflatable life raft from my boat for a stealth approach to *Outcast*, board her, and neutralize the three combatants."

Laili lowered her binoculars. "You mean kill them, right?"

Molka lowered her binoculars. "We don't have the time or means to take and detain prisoners. And like Thorsen said, they're not going to surrender anyway. They sacrificed their lives when they became cartel soldiers."

"Damn, you sound just like Azzur."

"Don't say that either."

Laili yawned. "We'll use our suppressors and flashbangs again?"

"Yes. Sure you're up for this?"

"I'm good. Just a little tired. I want to eat and catch a nap before the op."

"Alright," Molka said. "Me too."

They backtracked on the path toward Molka's car.

"We got this, right?" Laili said.

"We got this. Because when we work together, we're a pretty effective team."

Laili turned her head back to Molka and rolled her eyes. "Whatever, ugly."

"Grow up, brat."

CHAPTER 49

Mister Cutter jogged down Katelyn's harbor dock to his 40-foot sport cruiser moored at the end, hopped aboard, and ducked into the forward cabin.

Gus waited at the small galley table.

"Let me have it, lad," Mister Cutter said.

"You got my money?"

"Letting you hide out on my boat is all the pay you'll be getting from me."

"Don't forget," Gus said, "I only asked to hide out here because you fucked me over with my Delgado Island connection."

"How you figure that?"

"I told you about Señor Delgado buying Candyland as a courtesy, so you wouldn't wake up surprised he moved into your backyard out here. Not so you guys could go on a kill crazy rampage, take down all his men, steal everything you could steal, and set a fire that burned half the island down."

Mister Cutter shrugged. "Well, the captain has his ways."

"Fuck the captain and fuck you too. You weren't the only one I was trading Delgado info. And when Señor Delgado finds out my man there was his leaker and puts the blowtorch to his nuts, he's going to give me up, and then Señor Delgado will put an open contract out on my ass."

"That's what happens to snitches, lad."

"Fuck that! You're a snitch too."

Mister Cutter unsheathed his fighting knife and put the point to Gus's throat. "I knows what I am. What are you? Because if I find out you had anything to do with those poor abused girls we found as prisoners there, I'll execute the contract on you myself—no charge."

Gus tipped his head back. "Easy bro, easy bro, we're cool. I told you, I just brought young girls to Jake's parties and then took them home after. I had nothing to do with all that other shit he was doing."

"Give it to me."

Gus took a small packet of blue pills from his short's pocket and placed it on the table.

Mister Cutter lowered and re-sheathed his knife, opened the packet, dumped two pills on the table, retrieved a hammer and straw from a galley cabinet, crushed the pills with skilled hammer strikes, and used his thick fingers to form two tight, equal-length powder lines.

Gus chuckled. "Looks like you've done that a few times."

Mister Cutter put one end of the straw in his right nostril, bent over the table, snorted the lines in rapid sequence, sat down, leaned back, and rubbed his nose. "The captain wants me for a briefing about tonight's prize in 10 minutes. It's the big prize he's been working on with the two ladies."

"Did he finally tell you? What's this big prize?"

Mister Cutter exhaled deeply and rocked his head back. "When you worked for your now former employer, you remember a big beauty named *Outcast*?"

Gus smiled and then laughed. "You serious? Captain Savanna's going to take *Outcast*? You serious, because that's—you serious?"

"That's right, lad. Then we're going to take *Outcast* away from him. And she's worth at least 40 million if she's worth a penny. And then you're going to use all your famous connections to make us both—fuck the captain—rich."

CHAPTER 50

The three shirtless cartel soldiers—Felix, Rafa, and Ernesto—drinking beer on *Outcast's* sundeck, watched a charter boat enter Pennington Bay behind them. Nine men, plus the charter pilot, filled the open boat. Two huge coolers and three large bulging gear bags sat stacked on the boat's deck.

The charter pilot brought the boat alongside *Outcast*'s sizeable stern-mounted, retractable swim platform, which had been lowered to just above water level. The nine men used the platform to board *Outcast* and unload their gear.

Rafa removed his sunglasses and looked down on them. "Hey Manny, I see you brought your boyfriend with you."

Manny looked back up to him. "Fuck you, Rafa."

All the men laughed.

"Get your ass up here," Rafa said.

Manny climbed the two levels to the sundeck. "The boss said you needed his best men to guard his shit and his new yacht on the way home."

"Yeah," Rafa said. "Do you know when they're getting here?"

Manny laughed. "Fuck you, bitch. What's up Felix?"

Drunk Felix toasted him with a beer.

Manny addressed Ernesto. "They tell me you're a fucking yacht pilot now. Sure you can handle this big motherfucker?"

Ernesto nodded. "Just like a handled your girl."

All the men laughed.

Manny surveyed the yacht. "This thing is fucking gorgeous! What's the plan?"

"Play before work," Rafa said. "You bring my pig?"

"No, I left your wife at home. But I brought your roasting hog."

Rafa pulled a Glock from his shorts and pointed it Manny. "That's it, pussy. You die now."

Manny smiled, side stepped, and pulled Rafa's shooting arm down. "Come on, Rafa. Quit fucking around, man."

Rafa laughed and re-tucked his Glock.

"So, we party tonight," Manny said. "What's up for tomorrow?"

"The boss is waiting for old man Thorsen to come through with his papers by tomorrow morning. Carlos and Luis are babysitting him. But whether he does or doesn't, he and the two dudes downstairs get smoked. Easy job." Rafa raised his beer. "That's why we're chilling."

"What about the girl? I heard she's fucking gorgeous too."

Rafa put his sunglasses back on. "She is. But I'm keeping her for a while."

CHAPTER 51

Right before they got home, at Laili's insistence, Molka stopped at a pates truck. And Molka didn't admit it to Laili, but the deep fried, beef-filled dough made her stomach growl. She stopped at a café and ordered a fresh seafood salad to-go for herself.

Early lunches secured, the debate that had begun on the drive back from Pennington Bay resumed.

"Why are you lecturing me?" Laili said. "Better lecture yourself. I'm the better shot, remember?"

"Yes," Molka said. "But you said this will be your first live, night tactical op. And we need exceptional fire discipline. One shot, one kill. So a stray round doesn't hit Paz or his yacht captain. Or Caryn."

Laili grinned. "Hey, stray rounds happen."

Molka glared at her. "Don't even joke like that. She's a civilian. She's off limits."

"What are we going to do with the dirty little whore, anyway?"

"Tell her to go home, grab her dad, and start running."

Laili laughed. "Fuck yeah, they better. But you know, this op will burn our cover stories with Paz."

"Can't be helped," Molka said. "Azzur will have to find something to keep him quiet about us. Get his mind right, as he likes to say."

Laili stared out the side window. "Azzur's definitely good at that."

Five minutes later, Molka parked at the curb outside their apartment. The door to the animal hospital stood open.

"You leave that unlocked?" Molka said.

"I haven't touched it," Laili said.

"And why is the paper covering that window missing?"

Laili shrugged. "I don't know."

"Hope we haven't had a break in."

"Maybe someone is still in there," Laili said. "Take our weapons with us?"

Molka pushed the trunk release. "Yes."

Molka and Laili exited and moved to the trunk.

Two USVI Police vehicles sped toward them from opposite directions and blocked in the car. The driving officers leapt out with Glocks drawn and aimed them at Molka and Laili.

One officer yelled, "Get on the ground!"

Molka and Laili laid face down on the dirty street.

The officers cuffed them.

A smiling, black suit wearing Agent Justain exited the animal hospital doorway holding a police radio and a white document. He swagger-walked to Molka and Laili's prone positions and crouched before them. "Good morning, ladies. What's left of it, I should say. This is your copy." He held the document for Molka to read.

Molka bent her head back and scanned it. "A search warrant?" She gazed mystified at Justain. "What is this?"

Laili bent her head back and scowled at Justain. "And who the hell are you?"

Justain showed Molka and Laili his badge and ID. "This is who I am." He smiled again. "And as to the previous question, you're both under arrest."

CHAPTER 52

Molka and Laili sat side by side in an interrogation room inside the USVI Police station wrist-shackled to a metal ring bolted atop a bolted-down table.

Justain entered, sat across from them, and tossed their passports on the tabletop. "Told you it wouldn't take long. Our new system is a beautiful thing. And I also took a closer look at those pistols found in your car. Besides the serial numbers being removed—quite professionally, I might add—every other manufacturing mark was removed, making them untraceable. Hmm…I wonder why you would also have such highly illegal weapons in your possession. But where were we?"

Molka spoke. "You were about to tell us your theory on why a veterinarian and a vet tech would have vacuum-sealed packages of marijuana totaling 200 pounds stored in our workplace under our apartment."

"Right," Justain said. "I would theorize you were going to use it to top off the load of fentanyl and gold bullion on the yacht I'm looking for."

"Wrong," Laili said. "We were obviously set up. Someone else put that shit on us."

"Why did you have cause to search our workplace?" Molka said.

"A confidential source gave me a tip there was a huge quantity of marijuana sitting in plain sight inside an old bakery. And this bakery was supposedly being converted into an animal hospital by two young women who lived above it. I went over there and looked through its street facing display window, and sure enough, there sat a huge quantity of marijuana in plain sight. I took some photos, and I got the warrant. Oh, thanks for reminding me. Bit of bureaucratic red tape. I'm waiting on a separate warrant to search your apartment. Two different addresses at the location caused the snafu. I tried to contact the property owner, but he's away, so you wouldn't want to give me consent to search, would you?"

Molka thought about the task cash, night vision goggles, and flashbang grenades in their closets she would have to account for. Deflect the question. "What exactly are we being charged with?"

"Besides the illegal weapons, I can easily build a tidy trafficking case. I'm also going to seize the 40,000 dollars in your glove compartment. But that's just for starters. Unless you decide to cooperate."

Laili snorted. "We're not snitches, cop."

"Giselle, please be quiet," Molka said. "Agent Justain, we're innocent of your charges, so we want to cooperate. What do you want from us?"

"I want the name and present location of the yacht. I want the names and present locations of your co-conspirators. And I want the names of your contacts in the yacht's destination port."

Laili turned her cuffed hands palms up. "Well, you can want in one hand and shit in the other and see which one fills up first."

"Shut up, Giselle," Molka said.

Justain chuckled. "Giselle's funny, isn't she." He picked up and opened Laili's passport. "Giselle Binoche is funny, funny. But you know who doesn't think she's funny, funny? The real Giselle Binoche this passport was issued to in France. She had no idea a stranger was using it down here in the commission of crimes."

He picked up and opened Molka's passport. "Yours isn't quite as humorous, Miss Molka…I'm not even going to try and pronounce your last name. Your Canadian passport comes back as applied for but not yet issued. Yet, you have it anyway. Or a very good forgery." He put down Molka's passport and smiled. "See what happens, ladies, when you leave loose ends? Eventually you trip over them."

Molka and Laili exchanged looks, and Molka said, "I don't think we should answer any more questions at this time."

Justain winked. "I don't blame you."

"So what happens next?" Molka said. "We bond out of jail and get a court date?"

"No. What happens next is I take you back to my division office in San Juan and lock you up in a dungeon they call a jail there until your real identities are confirmed. Might take me weeks. Or you could tell me everything now."

Molka and Laili replied with silence.

"Need some time to discuss it?"

More silence.

Justain smiled. "Not a problem." He rose, opened the door, and called down the hall. "Officer, I'm going to get some lunch and make some calls. Do you have a holding cell for my prisoners?"

Molka sat at the top bunk's head and Laili sat at the bottom bunk's foot in the third-floor, old-fashioned, barred holding cell.

Their whispered argument began when Molka made a suggestion to Laili right after the officer escorting them locked the door and moved away.

Laili whispered, "Are you fucking crazy? We'll get in trouble."

Molka whispered, "Trouble? We've been arrested by a US federal agent who caught us in possession of a stolen and a forged passport and illegal weapons, and who found 200 pounds of weed, basically under our beds. Trouble? I would kill to *only* be in trouble right now. We have to tell him."

"But we were set up."

"Yes, but we can't prove that. Which is why we need to tell him."

"No way we can tell him," Laili said. "No way. We can't tell him. That's a stupidly idiotic idea. He'll still take us down for it."

"Obviously there's been a major security breach. We were probably burned before we arrived, so this wasn't our fault. But if we don't tell him, we can't work a deal, and the US authorities will go public and make an example out of us. We don't want to be responsible for embarrassing our country like that."

Laili sneered. "You always say *our country*. It's not my country. Maybe I was born there, but I don't claim it, and I'm leaving it soon as I can. I only care about the country of *Laililand*. We can't tell him."

Molka dropped to the floor. "I'm going to tell him."

Laili whispered through gritted teeth, "Don't do it."

Molka walked to the bars.

Laili whispered louder, "Don't fucking do it."

Molka put her face through the bars. "Officer."

Laili vaulted to her feet. "Don't tell him!"

CHAPTER 53

Justain stopped chuckling. "Thanks for telling me. But I must say, in my 22 years of law enforcement, that's the wildest, craziest story I've ever heard. And trust me, I've heard some crazy wild ones. Ok, now indulge me a moment. I'm going to repeat your story back to you, to make sure I heard it correctly. But I'll tell it like an espionage movie plot. Because that's what it really sounds like to me."

"So, it begins when two attractive young women, one a veterinarian, one a vet tech, come to an exotic Caribbean Island to help open an animal hospital. But they're not there to open an animal hospital. That's just a cover story."

"And they're also both using fraudulent passports. And even though they've been strongly implicated, they're not involved in a major narcotics trafficking conspiracy either. They were just framed for that by some unknown entity. They are—in fact—covert foreign operatives."

"And they've been sent to break up the engagement of their prime minister's wayward nephew to a local drug lord's daughter. And also—and most importantly—stop the nephew from inadvertently smuggling, when he cruises home, a huge quantity of cartel fentanyl and payoff gold bullion into their country, which were put on the nephew's yacht clandestinely by the cartel."

"And to assist them, the young women will use an infamous pirate, Captain LJ Savanna, to seize the nephew and his yacht and demand a ransom."

"But before the ransom will be paid, a special forces unit from the young women's country will rescue the nephew. Which will cause the wayward nephew to be so grateful to the prime minister, he'll stop being an embarrassment to them and also—and this is the biggie—allow the young women themselves to steal the nephew's yacht during the rescue operation's confusion, so the fentanyl and gold can be secretly offloaded and used by their covert organization for its own purposes. The end. That's your story, right?"

"That is correct," Azzur said.

"Wildest, craziest story I've ever heard." Justain chuckled again until he laughed…

And laughed…

And laughed…

And laughed…

Azzur watched Justain's amusement, unsmiling, while leaning against the interrogation room wall in a white, short sleeved guayabera shirt and brown pants. His brown leather satchel waited at his feet.

Justain ended his guffaw fit red-faced. "What are you, the comedian lawyer? But you need to cut the bullshit stalling, advise your clients to give me their real names, and start cooperating. Or I promise, this will not end well for them. Understand?"

Azzur removed his phone from his pocket, tapped a fast message, and lit a cigarette.

Justain grunted in frustration. "I asked if you understood. And you're not supposed to smoke in here."

Azzur's phone rang. He answered it. "Hello…Yes. One moment." He offered Justain the phone. "Your superior would like to speak to you."

Justain smirked. "My superior?"

Azzur blew smoke and nodded.

"Ok, joke man. I'll play along." Justain took the phone and spoke. "Special Agent Justain. Be advised, lying to a federal agent is a felony. Yes…Yes…Yes, ma'am, Administrator Kellin…I do recognize your voice. From all your inspirational speeches…Yes, ma'am…We actually met once when you were Deputy Administrator and you visited the San Juan…Yes, ma'am…Of course, ma'am. Thank you for calling… Have a good day, ma'am." Justain handed the phone back to Azzur. "You have an impressive way of providing your bona fides."

Azzur blew smoke again.

Justain continued with a congenial tone. "I didn't know the Counsel had in office in San Juan. If I would have known, you could've joined our little gossip group. Every Tuesday I have lunch with a Corporation guy and a guy from Mexican intelligence."

"Where are my people?" Azzur said.

"Upstairs in a holding cell."

Azzur flicked ash on the floor. "Bring them here."

CHAPTER 54

An officer brought Molka and Laili back into the interrogation room to Azzur's stoic stare at Justain.

"That's quite an ambitious, if not brilliant, plan," Justain said. "Sorry I messed it up for you."

"Not you, Agent Justain," Azzur said. "Your confidential source. Please pass along my compliments and tell them perhaps I will speak to them personally one day soon."

Justain smiled. "I would if I could. The source is aggressively anonymous."

The officer directed Molka and Laili back to their previous seats across from Justain and moved to re-shackle them.

"That won't be necessary," Justain said.

"They are still in your custody," Azzur said. "Do not give them any special considerations."

Justain nodded, and the officer re-shackled them and handed Justain the key. When he departed, Justain smiled at Azzur and said, "I think this might be a historic occasion. The first time our organizations have worked together."

Azzur, still leaning on the wall, lit another cigarette. "I have personally worked with your organization several times, but at the upper administrative level."

Justain's smile flattened. "Well, maybe next time you and I work together, I will be at the upper administrative level."

"What is your proposal?" Azzur said.

"You identify the yacht, give me its present location, I verify it, seize it, make sure the cargo is aboard, and then just maybe at my victorious press conference, I won't tell the world about your little spy thriller activities here."

"I thought that might be your position." Azzur picked up his satchel and removed a document. "So, I brought along this." He passed it to Justain. "As you can see, that is your name at the top, and I am sure you recognize the name above the signature at the bottom."

Justain scanned it. "A Presidential Executive Order instructing me to keep your operation classified as a matter of national security and under penalty of imprisonment." He smiled at Azzur unconvinced. "Is this real?"

"My prime minster is a very close friend of your president. That took all of a two-minute call to arrange."

"Then you won't mind if I verify it?"

"Call Mrs. Deborah Sheehan at the White House," Azzur said. "She is your president's chief of staff. She is expecting your call."

Justain read over the order again and set it aside. "What's your counter proposal?"

"We will finish our operation as planned and leave."

Justain viewed Molka and Laili. "That order doesn't say anything about your people. I'll need more than a small amount of incentive to cut them loose."

Azzur flicked ash on the floor. "You keep the fentanyl, and I keep the gold."

Justain suppressed glee. "Ok. That's a good start. But…uh…you really don't expect me to just turn my back on 100 million dollars."

"Yes," Azzur said. "Because you will still get your glory and the promotion you desire."

"And you'll get your glory and maybe a promotion you desire and 100 million in easily convertible gold bullion." Justain pushed the order aside. "I don't think so."

Azzur took out his phone. "Then I will ask my prime minister to make another call to your president to tell them Special Agent Thomas Justain of the National Bureau of Narcotics, Caribbean

Division has let his selfish greed and ambitions jeopardize the security of a sovereign state and close ally."

Justain smirked. "You really know how to ram it in deep and make it hurt, don't you?"

"To make it less painful, consider it this way: Getting half the glory is always much better than getting all of the blame."

Justain threw up his hands and smiled. "Ah…what's 100 million dollars between close allies, right? Hell, my agency probably wastes more than that every year from employees streaming internet porn on their work computers."

Azzur blew smoke. "Then we have a deal?"

"Just one question first. What will your special ops team do with the *elusive* Captain Savanna?"

"They have instructions to only detain him and his crew while they extract the hostage."

"Can you arrange for them to hand Savanna over to me?"

"For what purpose?" Azzur said.

"I have plans for him."

"If Captain Savanna were turned over to you, would it seal our agreement?"

"It would," Justain said.

"Then Captain Savanna is yours."

"Then we have a deal, sir."

Justain stood, and the two men shook hands.

Azzur said, "May I talk to my people privately and unrestrained? Afterwards, you and I will discuss details of what will occur tonight."

Justain smiled. "I look forward to it."

Molka twisted her body toward Azzur. "Our weapons."

Azzur addressed Justain. "My people will require all their property to be returned immediately."

"I'll take care of it now." Justain tossed the cuff key on the table and left the room.

Azzur picked up the key and viewed his projects with displeasure.

His projects viewed him with trepidation.

Laili spoke. "I told her not to call and tell you what happened, daddy. I used my one phone call to order a pizza."

Azzur stared down upon her, unamused.

Laili's smile faded. "Fuckers wouldn't deliver it though...I came one day short of completing my part of the task. I'll explain why later. Sorry, daddy."

"Any ideas who set us up?" Molka said.

Azzur blew smoke. "Obviously the same one who informed Agent Justain. However, that can be addressed at a later time. What is the other *major complication* you spoke of on the call to your *attorney*?"

Molka head-flipped a drooping bang. "I couldn't tell you at the time because the officer who gave me my phone was standing there listening."

"What is the major complication?"

"*Outcast* has been moved. Donar Thorsen told us it was seized—along with Paz, his yacht captain, and Caryn Thorsen—by a three-man cartel team. He said they're being held for ransom. He has to sign over his marina to the cartel head by tomorrow morning to secure their release. We did find him being held by two armed men. We eliminated them. Thorsen thinks we're police officers."

Azzur stubbed out his cigarette and lit another. "A more plausible explanation would be Mr. Thorsen lost his nerve and asked the cartel who provided him the fentanyl and gold to come and reclaim it. They have. And the demanded forfeiture of his marina is their inconvenience fee."

"I didn't think of that," Molka said.

"What is the *Outcast*'s present location?"

"They moved her to a remote bay on a nature preserve on this island's northwest coast. But we're on it. We've already reconnoitered it and planned an op to neutralize the cartel team and send Paz and his captain on their way tonight as scheduled."

"Have you delivered Captain Savanna the *Outcast*'s return route navigational information yet?"

"Not yet," Molka said. "I planned on holding it until 5PM today."

Azzur checked his watch. "It is 3:21PM. If you leave now, can you deliver it and be back in time for your operation?"

"Yes. I can be back within two hours."

"Do so. However, do not reveal the events of this day to Captain Savanna. He is to think everything is proceeding smoothly."

"Understood." Molka turned to Laili. "Drop me at my boat's marina, go home and get our gear, including my tac clothes, and come back and pick me up."

"Yeah, ok," Laili said.

Azzur uncuffed his projects. "Your vacations are cancelled, and your bonuses are rescinded. Tomorrow morning, we will all board INS *Geula* in San Juan harbor for their eight-day journey back home and use the time for a deep debriefing. And as to your individual punishments for this security breach: Laili, you now owe me an additional five tasks to fulfill your obligation."

Laili pouted. "Yes, daddy. Sorry, daddy."

"And Molka, upon completion of this task tonight, consider yourself removed from the program."

CHAPTER 55

Consider yourself removed from the program.

Molka tugged at the base of her ponytail as she piloted her boat toward Katelyn.

Consider yourself removed from the program.

Azzur's last words slashed at her heart with endless mutilations.

Consider yourself removed from the program.

Being dismissed meant her little Janetta's murderer would go unpunished—at least by her.

Consider yourself removed from the program.

And that would be hard to live with.

Consider yourself removed from the program.

No. It would be impossible to live with.

Consider yourself removed from the program.

But first she would fulfill her role in the task.

Yes. She would still fulfill her role.

Stubborn honor wouldn't let her walk away.

Then she would go home.

And figure out how to cope with the rest of her life.

Consider yourself removed from the program.

Azzur's decision was cruel to her personally but fair. She knew failure on a task was cause for dismissal from the program. Even though the task would be completed, she had failed by asking for Azzur's assistance.

Although, that couldn't be helped because of Justain and his confidential source. Trying to frame her and Laili as part of a trafficking operation made no sense though. A lot of things weren't making sense. Who had given Justain the false information that had handed him everything he ever wanted and snatched away the only thing she really needed?

Azzur would find out.

He wouldn't rest until he found out.

And then she would love to go see that person and take away something they really needed.

Azzur would never tell her though.

Another unknown life destroyer would go unpunished.

Consider yourself removed from the program.

But maybe there was one small amount of punishment she could leave behind.

When Molka idled into Katelyn's harbor, *Betrayal* and *Vengeance* had been moved out from their protective building to the main dock and were aswarm with crew activity.

In a few hours' time, those men would take their biggest prize only to have him taken away by Flotilla 15. And then to make their loss complete, their beloved captain would be taken away from them by Justain.

Molka docked her boat opposite the hunters and climbed the steps leading to the main villa.

The captain's voice emanated from a speaker beside the door. "Please come in, Lady Molka. I'm in the study."

Molka entered the captain's study to find him at his desk dressed for action. She removed the tiny flash drive containing *Outcast*'s return home navigational information from her pocket and laid it before him. "I believe you've been waiting for this?"

The captain presented his rogue smile. "Only for a lifetime." He picked up a tablet and inserted the drive. After a few swipes, his eyes gleamed. "Mister Cutter!"

Mister Cutter—even more exhausted looking than the last time Molka had seen him—entered from a side door.

The captain handed him the tablet. "It's all here. Let me know as soon as you've chosen our interception point."

"Aye, captain." Mister Cutter departed.

"Lady Molka, you can tell your people everything will be handled just as they wish. And my congratulations on your well-accomplished mission."

"Thank you, captain."

"How fairs Lady Giselle?"

"She's keeping busy."

"Please pass along my greeting, congratulations, and farewell to her."

"I will," Molka said. "Goodbye and…good hunting."

"Thank you and take care, Lady Molka."

Molka didn't move. "Captain."

"Yes, Lady Molka?"

"Captain."

"What's wrong, Lady Molka?"

"Captain, do you happen to have an outstanding issue with the US National Bureau of Narcotics?"

CHAPTER 56

Mister Cutter snorted another double line from his sport cruiser's galley table.

"Damn," Gus said, awakening from his nap on the adjoining couch-bed. "You can do all that and still do your job?"

Mister Cutter stood and rubbed his nose. "This just keeps me leveled out. You have the other thing for me tonight, right?"

Gus stood and stretched. "Yeah."

"And your Belize man will definitely have our money for us soon as we get there. Paid on delivery, right?"

"He already has a buyer in Dubai ready to wire him the cash. But yeah, we get paid on delivery."

"I've got a lot to do to get ready," Mister Cutter said. "So, I won't be seeing you again until after it's over. Keep the curtains closed, and don't dare leave. I'll come and get you."

Gus watched Molka pass by on the dock, heading for her boat. "Hey, I know that bitch. What's she doing here?"

Mister Cutter viewed Molka. "She's one of the ladies' the captain is working with on tonight's prize. She's the one you call the Bitch of Death."

"That's the Bitch of Death?"

"So, says you, lad."

Gus laughed. "She knows someone else I knew." Gus pulled his Glock from his shorts.

"What are you doing?"

"I'm about to give Señor Delgado a present of the Bitch of Death's death and get a pardon and become his new favorite son."

Mister Cutter tagged Gus's jaw with a left hook.

Gus fell.

Mister Cutter picked up Gus's Glock, stepped from the cabin, tossed it overboard, and stepped back inside.

Gus gazed up at him, stunned.

"I'll not have you hurt another woman in my presence."

CHAPTER 57

Molka and Laili parked outside the yellow gate to the Pennington Bay nature preserve at 6:45PM.

On their drive west, they had witnessed an inspiring sunset giving way to a warm, clear, windless, evening.

Perfect shooting conditions.

Both wore their black tactical outfits with slight modifications to their tactical hairstyles. Molka kept her usual high ponytail but swept her bangs right to left across her forehead to keep her aiming eye clear. And Laili double tied her longer ponytail and added a black sports headband to control sweat.

Molka removed a suitcase-sized, yellow bag and two small plastic oars from the trunk, dropped them over the gate, and jumped over herself.

Laili closed the trunk and joined her.

From the yellow case, Molka removed a yellow deflated, folded two-person life raft. She lifted a side flap on it and pulled a red cord. In less than 30 seconds, the raft's self-contained CO^2 inflation system swelled it to a six-by-six-foot octagonal shape.

Molka picked up the oars and grabbed the strap on the raft's front. Laili grabbed a strap on the raft's rear, and they carried it down the long path toward the beach.

DUAL DECEPTION

"I can't believe Azzur kicked you out of the program," Laili said. "I mean, I can, but it sucks for you."

"And it sucks for you; you'll have to survive 24 instead of 19 tasks now."

"You saying I'm not up to it?"

"I'm saying they don't get easier."

Molka and Laili reached the trail's edge overlooking the beach.

They halted at the view, dropped the raft, crouched, and put on their night vision goggles.

"You have to be kidding me," Molka said.

"They're having a fucking beach party?" Laili said.

Molka grimaced. "And they invited well-armed friends."

On the beach below, the 12 cartel men—all slinging AK-47s, AR-15s or carrying sidearms—drank beer and laughed loudly beside a glowing fire pit over which a large, whole pig roasted on a spit.

To the right, about 10 yards down from the festivities, their transportation, a 20-foot fiberglass lifeboat from *Outcast*, sat anchored.

"Damn, that BBQ smells so good though," Laili said. "I'm starving again now."

"Hostages on the ground," Molka said. "About seven meters to the left."

Paz and Captain Fletcher sat in the sand with hands and ankles bound and mouths taped.

"Other guy must be the *Outcast*'s captain," Laili said.

"Probably." Molka adjusted her goggles to full magnification and scanned the *Outcast*. "No lights showing. I wonder if this is all of them?"

"Let's worry about taking these out first," Laili said. "We can crawl as close as we can, toss the flashbangs, and open up."

"Alright," Molka said. "We'll leave the raft here. We can come back for it. But we may not need it now with *Outcast*'s lifeboat down there." She unholstered her Beretta and screwed on the suppressor.

Laili unholstered her Sig and screwed on the suppressor.

Laili offered Molka a flashbang grenade from a bandolier she wore. "Ready when you are."

Molka viewed the flashbang then looked back toward the beach. "I'm ready. But..."

"But what?"

"But firing through grenade smoke in a small well-lit office at close range today was one thing. Doing it at distance while wearing night vision…I'm concerned about our accuracy."

Laili tapped her Sig. "That's why I have 17 in the mag and one in the chamber."

"Fire discipline, remember? We have hostages down there. We can't risk any stray rounds, mainly theirs if we start missing them."

"What do you suggest?"

"Practical shooting," Molka said. "Speed and precision while on the move. Just like the Gary's Shooting World Fall Classic."

Laili smiled and nodded. "I'm down. Which ones do you want?"

"I'll take the six on the left of the pig, you take the six on the right of the pig."

"Nice of them to split evenly like that for us."

"Yes. But during the shoot, if any of them move, we're each responsible for all targets on our own side of the pig."

Laili nodded again. "No problem."

"First one to drop all their targets and make it to the beach alive wins."

"What's the bet?" Laili said.

"How about my old pilot's watch?"

"You mean *my* old pilot's watch. And no way. This is business. That was personal."

Molka racked her weapon. "Maybe the tigress is really just a scared little kitty cat?"

Laili cocked her weapon's hammer. "Say that to me again when you get to the beach. I'll be there waiting."

CHAPTER 58

The rusting green-hulled, 75-foot fishing trawler—accompanied overhead by a relentless seagull squadron—churned through the Caribbean night.

The contractor team operating her had configured the hold to carry two precious cargos: 1,000 pounds of fentanyl and 100, 400-ounce gold bars. Their destination was a rendezvous point 15 nautical miles northeast of Saint Thomas, to which Molka would bring *Outcast* in the next few hours.

Azzur and Justain sat at a small table in a cabin behind the pilot house awaiting their impending glorious victories.

Azzur had freshened from his daytime white guayabera shirt into an evening brown one and Justain had exchanged his suit for a blue NBN logo polo shirt and pressed khaki slacks.

They imbibed with a quality scotch Justain had brought along.

Justain grimaced. "I understand they wanted to make this thing look like a legitimate, working commercial fishing vessel, but did they have to make it smell like one too?"

Azzur blew cigarette smoke. "I don't smell a thing."

"Anyway," Justain said, "you were saying you would use the 100 million to fund otherwise un-fundable operations for your department for the benefit of your country. But how much are you going to siphon off for your, shall we say…personal retirement fund?"

"Even if I were to do something so reprehensibly corrupt, do you think I would confess it to a member of US law enforcement?"

Justain smiled and toasted Azzur. "I'll take that non-confession as a confession. But speaking of corruption, years ago, in Columbia, I had an off-the-record meeting with one of the biggest cartel heads in the world. I'm talking biggest of all time. Why we met is a whole other story. But one thing he told me is, if he found out a member of his organization wasn't siphoning off a little something for themselves, he immediately had them killed. Because, he said, if someone isn't stealing a little from you, it means they're stealing a lot from you. I always respected him for that kind of practical, sensible wisdom."

Azzur took a scotch sip. "We all chose our heroes, I suppose."

Justain flinched, indignant. "The hell, you say. Kiki Camarena is my hero." He poured some of his drink on the deck. "Rest in peace, brother." He checked his social media. "Still at 10,011 followers. By this time tomorrow how many do you think, 100,000, half a million, more? Wonder what it will be like, after one press conference, to go from a lifetime of obscurity and under appreciation to a lifetime of notoriety and admiration?"

Azzur sipped scotch again. "I would never wish to know."

"I'll need to hire a spokesperson to help handle the overwhelming interview requests I'll get. I have to pick and choose which interviews I do. If I do them all, it will look like I'm not doing my job. I'm thinking a beautiful young woman as my spokesperson. Sexiness gets views. I want my brand to pop with the youth." Justain smiled. "You know, I've never worked with, let alone commanded, beautiful young women. You obviously have. What's it like with those two of yours?"

Azzur finished his drink. "Most of the time, beyond maddening."

CHAPTER 59

Molka waited on the beach and lifted her night vision goggles. "Winner says loser carries the raft back to the car."

Laili reached the beach and lifted her night vision goggles. "It wasn't a fair match. One of mine shot back."

"Which is why I took him out for you. Bonus points for me." Molka grinned. "Looks like the old lady still has it."

"Whatever, ugly."

"Lose with class, brat. But before we leave, we need to glove up and fire their weapons into each other. Make this look like a gang dispute or drunken argument gone bad. By the time autopsies and forensics come back on this little island jurisdiction, we'll be long gone."

"Did you bring gloves?" Laili said.

"I always bring gloves. I keep a box in my car. That's a tip for you on your future tasks."

Molka and Laili stepped over and around the 12 dead killers and approached Paz and Captain Fletcher.

They stiffened behind taped mouths.

When Molka and Laili got closer and lowered their weapons, Paz's face cascaded from petrification into confusion.

Molka removed Paz's tape and spoke to him in Hebrew. "Is this man with you *Outcast*'s captain?"

Paz answered in Hebrew. "Yes, he's Captain Fletcher. He's an American. You're Israeli. You've saved us. They sent you?"

"Yes," Molka said.

Paz's eyes teared up. "My country loves me. You two were incredible. My country loves me. They said they were still going to murder us at sea after Donar paid our ransom. And they said their boss was keeping *Outcast* for himself. We were never going home."

Laili spoke to Paz in Hebrew. "But you're going home now. Tonight, Paz."

Line from the yacht bound Paz and Captain Fletcher.

Molka addressed Laili. "I noticed a few of those cartel guys wearing knives. Go borrow one and cut them loose."

Laili trotted to retrieve.

"They're holding Donar too," Paz said.

"Not anymore," Molka said. "He told us where to find you." She removed Captain Fletcher's tape and switched back to English. "Captain Fletcher, is *Outcast* ready to leave immediately?"

"Fueled, provisioned, and ready. But they said they disabled all the radios to keep one of us from sneaking off and calling for help. That's a problem."

"How were they disabled?" Molka said.

"Not sure, but their pilot would, in all likelihood, require them to be operable."

"Can you fix them?"

"I can try," Captain Fletcher said.

Laili returned with a lock blade and started cutting Paz loose.

Molka addressed Paz. "Are there anymore on board?"

"Just one."

"And where's Caryn Thorsen?"

"She's the one on board."

Laili cut Captain Fletcher loose.

"Ok," Molka said. "Get the lifeboat ready to go back to *Outcast*. We'll join you in a second."

Molka and Laili watched Paz and Captain Fletcher jog toward the lifeboat.

"You see Paz's face?" Laili said. "I never seen a person more relieved."

"He still has more traumatic shocks coming tonight, though." Molka retied her ponytail under the goggle's headgear. "With Captain Savanna and then Flotilla 15 coming for him."

"And Azzur getting his mind right about us."

"That might be the worst of all," Molka said. "And apparently, Paz still doesn't know what his yacht is carrying."

"I got that too," Laili said. "He still thinks his kidnapping was only a kidnapping."

"And it's our job to make sure he keeps thinking that. So we have to be careful how we handle Caryn."

"How are we handling her?"

"We're taking her with us," Molka said. "But she might believe she can stay with Paz and keep her dream alive. We don't want her blurting out her and her father's scheme when she realizes what's going to happen."

Laili retied her regular ponytail. "I'll handle her."

Captain Fletcher pulled the lifeboat to *Outcast*'s stern swim platform, allowed his passengers to board, tied off the lifeboat, boarded himself, and headed for the bridge.

Caryn's voice greeted them from inside the main deck salon. "Rafa? I heard all the shooting. Are they dead? Can we leave now?"

"Yes, they're all dead, and we're leaving now," Paz said. "But this isn't that crazy bastard Rafa."

"Baby?" Caryn emerged from the cabin wearing a mortified smile and a white designer halter jumpsuit. "Paz, baby! You're free!" Her face fell on Laili, mortified. "Oh no. Why is she here?" She looked to Molka. "And her too?"

"They're warriors who saved our lives. And before they killed him, Rafa told me the whole reason I had to die was on you and your father."

"No, baby! He's lying! I would never! It was my dad. He—"

Captain Fletcher called from the second level. "They just removed the mics from the radios. I have spares."

Paz called up to him. "Captain, get this thing started, we're going home!"

"You got it!" Captain Fletcher hustled off.

"Paz, you know how these things work," Molka said. "You and Captain Fletcher can't discuss what happened here tonight. Understand?"

Paz nodded with prideful eyes. "I understand my country loves me, and we won't discuss what happened."

Molka gestured toward Caryn. "We'll take her with us, and we need to borrow your lifeboat."

"Keep it," Paz said. "I have two more on board."

Caryn's eyes bulged with panic. "No; baby take me with you. You don't understand. Ok, I have something to tell—"

Laili charged Caryn and put her into a voice-stifling rear chokehold. "Shut the fuck up, you dirty little whore."

Caryn pulled at Laili's arms.

Laili super-tightened the hold.

Paz yelled. "No! Stop that!"

Laili kept her choked and silent. Caryn's face bloomed crimson.

Paz yelled again. "Don't hurt her! Let go of her!"

"Let her go," Molka said. "She won't be able to talk for a few minutes anyway."

Laili released her.

Caryn gripped her throat and coughed for air.

Paz smiled and approached Caryn. "Don't try to talk, baby. I'm going to talk to you. So, just listen quietly, ok baby."

She smiled and nodded.

Paz picked her up and held her gently. "Remember, the first night we met. This is how I carried you to my stateroom and we made love."

She smiled and nodded again.

"Today was supposed to be our wedding night." He carried her to the cabin's entrance. "And this is how I would have carried you over the threshold tonight to make love again."

She smiled and nodded again.

"And this is what I'm doing now."

Paz carried her to the port-side railing, pitched her overboard, and headed for the bridge.

SPLOOSH!

Molka and Laili ran to the railing.

Caryn's head popped up from the bay screaming and cursing and cursing and screaming.

Molka smiled. "I have an announcement. The Davidov-Thorsen wedding postponed from earlier today has been canceled. Permanently."

Laili laughed, raised two middle fingers high, and yelled down to Caryn, "I win, you lose! Game over!"

CHAPTER 60

All the while Molka and Laili fished Caryn from Pennington Bay into the lifeboat and headed for the beach, her screams and curses continued without relent.

But when she viewed the fate of Rafa and his men lying on bloodstained sand, she zoned out into quiet reflection.

Molka and Laili paused to watch *Outcast* light up, power up, retract the swim platform, raise anchor, and rotate toward open water.

As the gorgeous mega yacht slowly moved off, Captain Fletcher sounded two long, airhorn blasts—perhaps salutes to Molka and Laili.

Molka took out her encrypted phone. Per her task instructions, she sent a two-letter message to a preloaded contact number. This would inform Flotilla 15 that *Outcast* had departed Saint Thomas. They would then put Katelyn Island under drone surveillance. When they determined the time they would execute their operation, Molka would receive a return message informing her so she could be in position to seize *Outcast*.

Paz came to the stern railing and waved to Molka and Laili before removing his Team Paz flag from the railing's flagpole and attaching the Israeli flag.

Molka chuckled. "Looks like Paz is growing up and becoming a patriot."

Molka and Laili made Caryn wait in their car's backseat while they staged what would become known locally as the Pennington Bay Massacre.

They returned to the car and found Caryn sobbing. She gulped back her tears and said, "What happened to my dad?"

"He's ok," Molka said. "We're taking you back to your marina. He's waiting for you."

Caryn sobbed again.

Molka started the car and headed east.

Caryn sobbed for another fifteen minutes, quieted, composed, and then said, "Paz said you guys are warriors. Does that mean you're cops?"

"Something like that," Molka said.

"Then you know everything?"

"Pretty much."

"Then you know this wasn't me and my dad's fault, right?"

Laili turned and glared at Caryn. "Didn't I tell you to shut up, whore?"

"No," Molka said. "Let her talk now. What do you mean it wasn't you and your dad's fault?"

Caryn said, "We didn't know once you get into business with these people, they own you. My dad only started running a little weed for them because we had our financial problems. But then they suggested we use Paz to move their fentanyl to the Middle East. And when these people suggest, it's not a request or even an order, it's a life-or-death demand."

Molka said, "And the guys we killed tonight, what's their story?"

"They work for the same people," Caryn said. "The same cartel. My dad panicked. He told them to come pick up their product. He's a naturally nervous man. He didn't want to go through with it. So, they sent those men to recover it and they also demanded Yacht Marina Grande as their inconvenience fee."

Molka and Laili looked at each other and shook their heads impressed. But not by her story, rather how Azzur had interpreted events with complete accuracy once again.

"And that's why they took you guys as hostages?" Molka said. "To make sure your dad signed over the business?"

"No. He was their hostage. Me, Paz, and Captain Fletcher were just in the wrong place at the wrong time. But Rafa told me he never leaves witnesses, and he would keep Paz and Captain Fletcher alive until they got far enough out to sea where their bodies would never be recovered."

Caryn closed her eyes and laid her head back.

After a two-minute silence, Molka said, "That it?"

"Yes," Caryn said. "That's all I can say."

Her confession left out the part about why they found her roaming *Outcast* free—dressed as if she was on a pleasure cruise—and calling out to Rafa about Paz and Captain Fletcher's deaths and about them leaving, though.

Molka considered stopping the car, pulling Caryn out, and insisting that she tell them.

But Molka let it go. They had a task to finish, and that omission didn't pertain to it. Besides, Caryn Thorsen had much bigger problems coming her way.

The moment Caryn stepped from the car, Laili asked Molka to take her to Sapphire Beach Hotel and a few bars in a fruitless search for her "friend" Gus. Molka indulged her for two hours.

Afterward, they considered going to their apartment and packing their clothes to bring along.

On second thought, they didn't want to risk another Justain surprise arrest for more planted narcotics. It had worked once to get half of what he wanted. They didn't put it past him to double down and extort it all from Azzur. The best thing they could do was leave Saint Thomas as soon as possible.

Maybe Mr. Levy would forward their things back home in a month or two. Molka only regretted leaving behind her old pilot's watch, even though it wasn't hers anymore.

DUAL DECEPTION

They arrived at the East End marina where Molka's boat was moored, near midnight. Molka's phone buzzed with an incoming message. She checked it. Flotilla 15's op would commence at 3AM.

Molka and Laili got straight underway for Katelyn.

Fifteen minutes into the 25-minute cruise, Laili—seated in the open bow—finished splitting their 40,000 dollars and placed Molka's half in Molka's gear bag and her half in her own. They didn't want to handle it later after they reunited with Azzur's watchful eyes. She zipped the bags, left her seat, and joined Molka at the central control console. "That dirty little whore Caryn got away with it."

"The Thorsens didn't get away with anything," Molka said. "We already talked about this."

"I mean she got away with what happened to me. I can't prove it, but I know she had something to do with it."

Maybe Molka would tell her about that too. But not that day. She needed a subject changer and had a huge one ready anyway. "I told Captain Savanna we're coming to pick up *Outcast*."

"Azzur's not going to like that. You didn't tell him the reason why, did you?"

"No," Molka said. "But I did tell him about Flotilla 15 coming to rescue Paz."

"Azzur's going to really be pissed about that. Why the fuck did you do that for?"

"Because mistakes can happen on ops. Bad ones. Deadly ones. I've seen it. The captain and his men don't deserve to die from a mistake."

Laili paused to reflect. "Yeah, ok. I can see that."

"And I also told the captain about Azzur's deal to hand him over to Justain. Because the captain doesn't deserve to go down to Justain, not a pompous glory seeker like that. And besides, Justain ruined us."

Laili smirked. "You mean he ruined you. He got you kicked out of the program. Didn't Azzur teach you that vendettas can never interfere with your tasks?"

"Of course," Molka said. "But I'm out. So it doesn't matter now."

Laili cocked her head. "Oh, it matters now. Don't you see how that might have fucked Azzur's deal? When Justain doesn't get the captain, he might declare the whole thing void. Then all he has to do is call his friends in the US Coast Guard to seize the contractor's vessel and keep everything for himself. And don't tell me about the presidential order he's under to cooperate. Once he has a record-breaking fentanyl bust in his pocket and calls a press conference to the tell the world, he'll be a global hero. Their president can't touch him then. If anything, they'll have to praise and promote him."

Molka viewed Laili as if she were a newly arrived extraterrestrial. "Do you always think like that? That's an almost borderline brilliant analysis. You should use that part of your mind more."

"Well, I think you've lost your mind. Because when Azzur finds out what you've done, my next task will probably be killing you."

"I might be killed for what I did, but I dare you to try."

Laili sneered. "There's the Vancouver threat again. I'm still all in to finish that fight."

"Me too," Molka said. "When we get home, let's make it one of the first things we do."

"No. Let's make it THE first thing, ugly."

"Absolutely, brat."

Laili took out and lit a cigarette. After a few puffs she said, "What did the captain say when you told him everything?"

"He said thank you. And then he said he's going to commit one final act of noble piracy and disappear into history and legend forever."

"What the fuck does that mean?"

Good question.

CHAPTER 61

Katelyn harbor was well represented with fine craft when Molka and Laili arrived.

Outcast was moored with its bow pointing outward—an advantageous position and a relief for Molka.

Moored behind *Outcast* was Mister Cutter's sport cruiser.

Opposite them, *Vengeance*—gleaming gorgeous under the harbor lights—waited with all guns still deployed from the raid. And even though Paz had nothing to fear during his capture, the full force showing would have given him the full scare effect and made him appreciate his coming rescue all the more—a thoughtful and thorough touch by the captain.

Betrayal had been put back into the shelter building with the doors closed.

Molka docked and tied off her humble rental at the harbor's far end. They grabbed their gear bags, and Molka led Laili up the terraced stairs and into the villa's wide-open front door.

The once opulent home and been reduced to bare walls and floors in the hours since Molka's afternoon visit.

The captain's voice echoed from the hall. "I'm in the study, ladies."

Except for the captain's desk and a lone chair against the wall—which seated Mister Cutter head down in thought—the room stood barren. The captain waited beside the desk still clad in his pirate costume, including his black bandanna and .45s in their double shoulder holster rig.

The captain smiled. "Good evening, my ladies. Have you news for me?"

"The operation will begin at 3AM, captain," Molka said.

The captain bowed. "Again, many thanks."

Molka dropped her gear bag next to the desk. "Everything go ok with your hunt?"

"We intercepted *Outcast* at 9PM and had her back here by 10. One of our finest hunts. Was it not, Mister Cutter?"

Mister Cutter's head shot up. "Aye, captain. It's all over now but the lies we'll tell about it."

"Well said."

Laili dropped her gear next to Molka's. "How's Paz taking it?"

"Horribly at first," the captain said. "He began to speak of an earlier attempt to take his yacht, but thought better of it and cooperated quietly, if not grudgingly. He spoke with your prime minister and informed me his tribute would be paid by tomorrow afternoon. Or would have, I should say."

"And what about the other revenue stream from Paz we talked about?" Molka said.

"I've decided it's best to shelve that for now," the captain said. "However, he may hear from me concerning it at a future time."

"Where's Paz now?" Laili said.

"He's resting comfortably for his rescue, locked away in the media room. I had the newest version of the *Honor and Glory* video game installed for him. He's playing voraciously happy."

"And Captain Fletcher?" Molka said.

"Poor man's nerves are shot. He asked for a bottle and a bed. I accommodated him."

Molka smiled. "The perfectly attentive host to the end, even though they're now worthless to you."

Four stout, sweat-soaked, crewmen appeared at the study's entrance.

The captain addressed them. "Are we all set, gentlemen?"

One answered, "Aye, captain. We're all set."

The captain opened a desk drawer, removed four thick envelopes, approached the crewmen, and motioned for them to step outside with him. A moment later, he returned empty-handed.

"What will you do now, captain?" Laili said.

"As you can see, I've had a quick liquidation sale. My BVI friend brought over an army of movers and took almost everything for pennies on the dollar. And I've just paid off the last of the crew and cut them loose with my eternal love and affection. They each have enough for 10 years of quiet retirement or two years of noisy unemployment."

Mister Cutter stood. "Speaking of which, captain, if you don't mind, I'll shove off too."

The captain smiled. "We've already settled your remuneration, so there's nothing left to say, except there are good ships and wood ships, ships that sail the sea, but the best ships are friendships, and may they always be."

Mister Cutter's voice cracked. "Aye, captain." He glanced away and departed.

Molka addressed the captain. "Thank you for turning *Outcast* around for me. Getting one of those beasts underway, clearing the harbor, and entering coordinates into the auto pilot is as far as my training got."

"You should have seen her, captain," Laili said. "She had so much trouble with the thruster controls. But they're ordinarily basic to operate, like a video game."

"Yet," Molka said. "You still smacked the dock the first time you tried it."

"It was hot and humid that day. My hand just slipped, ugly."

"Sure, brat."

"Lady Giselle," the captain said. "I don't believe I'll have any further use for these." He removed his shoulder holster rig and placed it on Laili.

Laili glowed with joy. "No way! Thank you, captain!"

"And if you wish, go up to my master bedroom on the third floor and into the left-hand walk-in closet. There's a hidden door at the back. Just push the wall, and it will swing open for you. Inside is a little room with my vintage weapons collection. Take any you like."

Laili glowed with joy again. "Thanks!" She ran off.

The captain sighed, sat on the edge of his desk, and viewed Molka with sentimentality. "Lady Molka, for the invaluable service you have done for me on this night—at great risk to yourself, I fear—allow me to give the rarest of things I can give, that being, the truth." The captain removed his bandana and earring, opened a desk drawer, placed them inside, and shut it.

"My real name is Richard Miller." His voice had reverted to a Midwest American accent. "Most people called me Richie. I was born and raised to working class parents in Savanna, Illinois, a working-class town on the Mississippi. I received a baseball scholarship to prestigious Northwestern University—I was a lefty with a wicked breaking ball. There is no way I could have afforded to attend without the scholarship."

"A lot of very wealthy families in the Midwest send their kids to Northwestern. One of the wealthiest families sent a beautiful daughter there at the same time I attended. Her name was Katelyn. We fell in love. My one and only time. Then I blew out my knee playing in a foolish pickup basketball game for beer money. I lost my scholarship. So, I enrolled in a nearby community college and rehabbed my way back to the pitching mound for over a year."

"Right before my scholarship was to be reinstated, Katelyn met another guy from a fellow rich family. They got engaged and eventually married and moved to Glencoe. That's a very rich suburb of Chicago. I understand she has four teenage kids now. But in our final conversation at Northwestern, she said her decision between me, and the rich guy was a close-run thing. In the end, she said, she chose to be with the man of superior taste, culture, and style."

"I quit school that day and did three years in the navy. Served on a submarine tender. We serviced submarines. Not glamorous, but a vital duty. One of my shipmates, had a post-navy set-up to run weed from Mexico into Florida. He asked me to join him. So, I did."

"We made a lot of money and had a lot of fun. He got himself killed, and I talked to the wrong girl, who talked to the NBN. I did four years in a federal prison. Got an online degree in philosophy and learned to play piano from a wonderful volunteer teacher while I was there."

"When I got out, I went back to weed running. That's when I met Señor Hector Delgado. He was pirating back then, real pirating. He took me under his wing and taught me everything I didn't want to continue doing."

"So I created Captain LJ Savanna: the gentleman pirate. A man with superior taste, culture, and style."

"There is no treasure cave here, or vault, or stash, or secret foreign accounts. From my many prizes, I barely broke even in paying the crew, the staff, buying equipment, maintaining this massive house, entertaining my guests, and keeping all my young, gorgeous ladies happy. Upholding a unique persona is prohibitively expensive."

"Now my island and *Betrayal* and *Vengeance* will be repossessed by the bank. I leave here with nothing but the fondest of memories."

Molka exhaled. "Wow. I'm not sure what to say to all that. If it's any consolation. I'm truly sorry our operation is what ended your run."

"And a fine run, it was!" The captain jumped atop his desk and stood with boots spread shoulder width apart, hands on hips, and face ablaze. He resumed his Captain Savanna accent. "I'll tell you, Lady Molka, here's the life of gentlemen of fortune: They live rough, and they risk a hard death, but they eat and drink like fighting cocks, and when a cruise is done, it's tens of thousands instead of ones of hundreds in their pockets. But most of it goes for good drinks and good fornications, and then it's to sea again with nothing left to show but their shirts. And they wouldn't be happy any other way."

Laili returned carrying a Mossberg 500 Tactical 12-gauge shotgun, a Ruger Mini-14 rifle, and a titanium gold Desert Eagle .50 caliber semi-automatic pistol tucked in her waist. "Thanks again, captain. I'll put these classics to good use." She set them on the floor next to her gear bag.

The captain leapt down from his desk. "I'm glad they're going to someone who will appreciate them. And now, ladies, before I depart, would you favor me with a final drink on the veranda? The final drink I will ever enjoy in my beloved home for these last many years."

Molka smiled humbly. "We would be honored, captain."

Molka and Laili followed the captain down another echoing hall and onto the portion of the veranda that overlooked the harbor.

All eyes fixated on a very large vessel easing away from Katelyn.

Laili spoke first. "Uh…why is *Outcast* leaving without us?"

"That would be Mister Cutter," the captain said. "Evidently, the small fortune he received tonight wasn't enough for him. He also wants a mega yacht to enjoy it with."

Molka slammed her fist on the rail. "And I pardoned that man."

"Well, Lady Molka," the captain said. "You must understand—"

"I know," Molka said. "A pirate's always a pirate." She looked to Laili. "Let's go take it back."

"I'll be leaving on *Betrayal*," the captain said. "However, *Vengeance* is at your disposal for a much faster hunt. Take good caution, though. In the wrong frame of mind, Mister Cutter can be even more fearsome than he looks, and beware of stowaway rats."

"Thank you, captain," Molka turned to Laili. "Giselle, put all those extra weapons in your gear bag, or leave them, and let's move."

"Now if you ladies will excuse me, I really should be leaving myself." The captain presented his rogue smile and kissed each of their hands.

"Goodbye, captain," Laili said.

"Goodbye," Molka said. "Good luck in whatever you're seeking now."

Molka and Laili exited the veranda and headed down the hallway.

Laili addressed Molka. "I'll pilot *Vengeance*, you serve the M60."

"No," Molka said. "I'll pilot *Vengeance*, and you serve the M60. You're the better shot, remember?"

"Shut up, ugly."

"Grow up, brat."

The captain, following behind, called after them. "My ladies, a last thought, if I might."

They paused and turned to him.

"Someday, you will both realize—perhaps after it is too late—that you each carry more benevolence than animus for the other. And that your ongoing conflict has been nothing more than a dual deception."

CHAPTER 62

Outcast ran from Katelyn into a noticeably cooling Caribbean night on calm seas. She had increased her speed but running her down didn't even require half power from *Vengeance*.

Molka positioned *Vengeance* 10 yards back from the mega yacht and slightly to port to stay out of her three-foot wake.

"We can't do this." Molka looked back from *Vengeance*'s controls to Laili who aimed the starboard-mounted M60 machine gun at *Outcast*'s stern.

Laili answered her over the wireless headset. "Why not?"

"We can't fire on her engine compartment. Or any part of her. What if we sink her?"

"What do we do then?"

"How much do you really remember from my yacht piloting classes?"

"All of it."

"Take over," Molka said. "When I tell you, get me close, and I'll board her."

Laili took over the controls.

Molka removed a tactical ladder from the starboard-side rack and positioned herself to attach the ladder's top hooks to *Outcast*'s port-side railing, as the crew had done on the *Tranquility* hunt.

"Ok," Molka said. "Get in as tight as you can."

Laili paralleled the much taller *Outcast*, throttled to match her speed, and ran alongside with a two-foot gap separating the vessels.

Molka's first hooking attempt failed.

So did the second.

And the third.

And the fourth.

And the fifth.

Laili yelled. "Come on, ugly!"

"I'm trying, brat!"

Molka's seventh attempt worked.

The hooks locked over the railing.

Molka grabbed the ladder's sides with both hands, put her right boot on the last ladder rung, put her left boot on the last ladder rung, and started to climb…

Outcast rolled into a port turn and hull-slammed *Vengeance*.

Vengeance rocked and bounced sideways 10 feet.

Molka's boots slipped from the ladder.

The headset fell from her head.

Wave spray soaked her.

She dangled over the Caribbean.

Only her hand grips kept her from falling.

Her wet boots slipped as she tried to get back on the rungs.

Laili identified disaster.

She came in close, allowing Molka to fall into *Vengeance*.

Molka put her left boot on the edge of *Vengeance*.

Outcast rolled into another port turn and hull-slammed *Vengeance* again.

Vengeance endured the same sideways bounce.

Wave spray soaked Molka again.

Her right hand slipped from the ladder.

Her left hand screamed from holding all her weight.

Laili brought *Vengeance* back in to catch Molka's fall.

But Molka got her right hand back on the ladder.

And then her right boot.

And then her left boot.

And then she climbed.

Laili backed *Vengeance* off and got behind *Outcast* again.

Molka reached the ladder's top, tumbled over the railing onto the aft deck, slipped, dropped into a defensive crouch, and recovered from her adrenaline-fueled hyperventilation.

To take control of the yacht, she would have to get to the controls and to the one controlling her, Mister Cutter, on the bridge one level up.

Molka high-kneed the steps to level two. An open door led into a large, salon-type space. At the opposite end, a half open door led to the bridge. She crossed the salon and paused outside the bridge's door.

She really didn't have an issue with Mister Cutter stealing *Outcast*; she accepted that a pirate's always a pirate. But he didn't know the danger he sat on: Justain's fentanyl and Azzur's gold. So he wouldn't like it when she told him he would have to turn *Outcast* over to her with no explanation other than it didn't belong to him.

She didn't want to kill him over it though.

She drew her Beretta anyway.

She counted to herself:

One.

Two.

Three...

She kicked open the door, dove inside, and rolled into a sitting shooter position.

Total darkness consumed the space, except for the dim glow from several control panel GPS screens. Two high-back, leather seats fronted the yacht's wheel and other operating controls.

Mister Cutter sat unmoving in the right-side chair.

But he only observed.

Outcast cruised on autopilot.

The Chartplotter was set for Belize.

Something smelled wrong.

Molka rose and eased toward Mister Cutter's chair back.

His arms hung at his sides.

An empty syringe lay on the deck by his boot.

Molka reached her Beretta forward and used the barrel to spin the chair around toward her.

Mister Cutter's head was tipped back.

His mouth was open, and his eyes were closed.

Molka re-holstered her weapon and checked his vitals.

Shallow pulse and breathing.

She shook him.

No movement.

Beneath his sweat-soaked shirt, his trademark fighting knife was absent from its sheath.

Molka disengaged the autopilot and moved the control levers to the neutral position to bring *Outcast* to a stop so Laili could come alongside.

The deck scuffed behind her.

She turned her head. A gray blur from the darkness whooshed past her face and stuck into the wood-trimmed control panel: Mister Cutter's fighting knife.

She reached for her weapon—too late.

A second object emerged from the darkness—someone swinging a binder holding charts at her head.

Temple impact.

When the stun-stars cleared a second later, she lay on her back with Gus kneeling between her legs and choking her with both hands.

Molka's mind screamed, *Don't let him take your weapon!*

Molka's Krav Maga instructor screamed, *Right hand, throat strike! Left hand, pluck release! Left knee, chest push! Right foot, face kick!*

Molka fired a right punch to Gus's throat.

Gus gasped and pulled back a bit.

Simultaneously, Molka used her left hand to snatch Gus's right hand from her throat, followed by putting her left knee into his chest, pushing him back more, and firing a hard right-boot, kick to his chin.

Gus fell off Molka and onto his side, dazed and still gasping.

Molka rolled back to her feet.

She reached for her weapon again.

She yelled: "Stand up! Hands on head! Do it now!"

Gus complied.

"Keep your right hand on your head and lift up your shirt with your left.

Gus Complied.

"Turn around."

Gus complied.

"Where's your weapon?"

"Cutter tossed my nine overboard," Gus said. "Shit makes you paranoid."

Molka kicked the syringe across the deck. "You give that to him?"

"He begged me for it. A pirate's always a pirate, and a junkie's always a junkie."

"But you gave him a lot more than he wanted. Because you wanted to keep everything here for yourself, didn't you?"

"I didn't steal this big-mother fucker," Gus said. "It was all his idea. You see, he was driving. I charter small craft. I don't know shit about yachts. I was just along for the ride."

"Put everything on the overdosed guy. How brave of you."

"Serious. He's the one who betrayed his captain. He's been doing it for months, selling information to Señor Delgado."

Molka shook her head. "You should have run when I gave you the chance, Gus."

"So, the Bitch of Death's going to call the cops again?"

"Oh, I'm the Bitch of Death? Hmm." Molka kept Gus covered, walked across the bridge, and put her fingers to Mister Cutter's carotid artery. His heart still pumped. "No. I'm not giving you to the police."

"What then?" Gus said.

"We're going down to the main deck."

"For what?"

"For you to answer for the girls of Candyland."

"Fuck that. If you're going to shoot me, just do it right here and drag my bloody ass body downstairs yourself."

Molka stared. "Alright."

Gus's voice broke fearful. "Hold up, hold up, hold up. I'll go downstairs. We can talk. We can deal. I know important people."

"Move."

They moved down to the main deck's aft outdoor lounge area.

Vengeance bobbed along the port side tethered to *Outcast*'s side cleats. The tactical ladder was still hooked over the railing, and Laili climbed up it and aboard.

Laili glared at Molka, and her weapon pointed at Gus. "What the fuck are you doing with him?"

Gus's face pleaded. "Girl, you better help me. She's going to smoke me."

"He tried to overdose Mister Cutter," Molka said. "He might have done it. But I'm neutralizing him for something else. I'll explain what later."

Laili rapidly cross drew the twin nickel-plated .45s and pointed them at Molka's head. "No! Lower that weapon, partner! You can't have him. I'm going to take care of him. He's my friend. Right, Gus? You're my friend."

Gus beamed, lowered his hands, and put his back to the rail. "That's right, girl. We're friends. We're friends because I understand girls from the street like you."

"Don't listen to him," Molka said. "He—"

Laili yelled, "Shut up! And holster that weapon!"

"Ok." Molka complied. Gus Ramos wasn't worth killing for or dying for.

Gus beamed again. "Now take her out. You told me you couldn't stand this bitch. We got a 40-million-dollar yacht here. I know some people in Belize who will buy it, no questions asked, and we can live like kings and queens—for life."

Laili kept her eyes and the .45s on Molka. "We barely know each other, but you judged me anyway. I opened myself up for the first time in a long time and told you deep, personal, shit. Shit I never talk about with anyone. And you still judged me. And maybe I didn't come from a good family like you and get a good education like you, but I'm not the worthless piece of street trash you think I am. And you're not better than me. And on your way down don't forget that."

Gus laughed. "Fuck yeah! Tell her how you roll, girl."

"I wasn't talking to her." Laili spun toward Gus. "I was talking to your punk ass."

She opened fire with both weapons.

The violent impacts pushed Gus back and over the rail.

He died before the splash.

Laili re-holstered the .45s and looked back at Molka. "I lied to you. It all came back to me. All of it. Candyland. I remember every detail."

CHAPTER 63

Vengeance and *Outcast* sat moored on each side of the contractor's stinking trawler anchored at the rendezvous point.

Upon arriving, Molka took Azzur aside and explained to him the Gus Ramos and Mister Cutter situations. The contractor team carried an extensive first aid kit with Narcan and other things to treat opiate overdoses, which said a lot about what they ran across in their work. They stabilized Mister Cutter and said he would recover. He rested in a stateroom. Azzur said he would have a talk with him later and drop him somewhere in Saint Thomas.

Molka suggested a rehab center.

She also informed him that Caryn Thorsen situation had been handled and gave Laili full credit. At least one of them should get a positive review for the task.

Azzur and Justain had moved their celebratory scotch drinking to the *Outcast*'s huge, luxury galley, while deep in her bowels, the contractor's electric tools whined as they fought their way to the hidden compartment and the celebrators double glory.

Molka and Laili joined them at the dining table.

"Paz ok?" Laili said.

Azzur consulted his phone. "No update."

Justain said, "But the operation was definitely a success, right?"

"As I told you, Flotilla 15 signaled that the operation was a success, there were no casualties, and they are on the way back to INS *Geula*. The ship's captain will provide me with more detailed information when their helicopter lands."

Justain smiled. "I can't wait to enjoy the look on Savanna's smug face when he sees my badge."

"What do you have planned for him?" Azzur said.

"Captain Savanna wasn't always a charming rogue. He was a dirt bag running weed from Mexico into Florida with another dirtbag. The other dirtbag got killed, and Savanna got four years federal time. When he got out, he went right back to running weed. At that time, my boss, my superior, Administrator Kellin, was a special agent in Florida, and she spent a year building a case against him. She got indictments and a warrant. Then he disappeared. When he popped up again two years later, he was operating as the Captain Savanna pirate character. The warrant was still good, but he had fans at the Justice Department. That's about the time all those silly pirate movies came out. So, they didn't want to waste any resources going after him. They wanted to be enamored by his daring exploits. But Administrator Kellin wasn't enamored. She was pissed off. He was the one that got away, a career embarrassment for her. And tomorrow, I'm going to make him my present to her." Justain smiled. "Which should nicely cap off my appointment as her deputy."

Azzur's phone buzzed. He scanned the incoming message. "The captain of INS *Geula* reports the hostage rescue team has returned. Mr. Davidov and Captain Fletcher are in ecstatic and appreciative spirits. Mr. Davidov even sung our country's national anthem on the way there."

"And what about Savanna's spirits?" Justain chuckled. "Not so appreciative, I'll bet."

Azzur tapped out another message, waited for the reply, read it, lit a cigarette, inhaled, and blew smoke. "Captain Savanna and his crew were not present on Katelyn Island. It appears they stripped the place empty before abandoning it."

Justain's face fell. "What the hell? Where did he go?"

Molka and Laili exchanged suppressed smiles.

"Both the captain's famed boats are missing," Azzur said. "Since *Vengeance* sits outside, he presumably escaped to somewhere on *Betrayal*."

"An irony not lost on me," Justain said. "Did you screw me?"

"Agent Justain, if I screwed you, you would never know it." He shot a side glance at Molka and Laili. "However, I assure you, I will look into the matter thoroughly."

A coverall-wearing, sweat-dripping contractor entered the galley.

"Have you located it?" Azzur said.

"We have. It's open for your review."

Azzur and Justain arose and smiled ecstatic. And the next time Molka saw men smile so ecstatic would be the second time.

Azzur and Justain followed behind the contractor, and Molka and Laili followed behind them to a lower deck stateroom. The stateroom's disassembled bed and rolled-up carpeting rested in the passageway. Inside the room, two big deck panels had been removed, exposing a large compartment extending down to the yacht's inner hull bottom.

Two other sweating, coverall-wearing contractors knelt beside the opening holding powerful LED flashlights. There wasn't enough space to fit everyone in the room, so Molka and Laili waited in the passageway while still grinning Azzur and Justain entered to gaze upon their prizes.

Justain's voice: "Lord almighty!"

Azzur's voice: "And you are positive there are no other compartments?"

Justain's voice: "Lord almighty!"

A contractors voice: "We ran our videoscopes over every inch, including inside the fuel and water tanks. This is it."

Justain's voice: "Lord almighty!"

Azzur and Justain exited the stateroom frowning tragic. And the next time Molka saw men frown so tragic would be the second time.

Molka and Laili took their places to view what the men had just viewed. They crouched beside the opening in the deck panels with the LED-holding contractors and gazed down at what they illuminated inside it.

The secret compartment did not contain the glorious means to give Justain his long-desired promotion and recognition.

The secret compartment did not contain the glorious means to give Azzur his long-desired operations and successes.

The secret compartment did not contain 1,000 pounds of illegal fentanyl.

The secret compartment did not contain 100 million dollars in gold bullion.

The secret compartment contained just one item.

Tacked firmly to the hull—for none to miss—and displaying defiant black, white, and red—for all to understand—awaited the personal Jolly Roger flag of Captain LJ Savanna.

Lady Molka, I'm going to commit one final act of noble piracy and disappear into history and legend forever.

Molka focused on the flag's smiling skull.

She thought she heard it getting the last laugh.

PROJECT MOLKA: TASK 4

PROJECT LAILI: TASK 1

TASK COMPLETED

CHAPTER 64

Warship INS *Geula* cruised east-northeast from San Juan, Puerto Rico, destination: Port of Haifa.

Azzur—in a black polo shirt and brown pants—and Laili—wearing borrowed blue navy fatigues—sat alone at a table in the ship's wardroom. They watched a laptop streaming a USVI Police press conference live from Saint Thomas Island.

On screen, Hodge—wearing her usual unassuming navy-blue, polo shirt featuring the USVI Police logo—stood at a microphoned podium in a white-walled meeting room. Behind her—in full dress uniforms—stood the police commissioner, assistant commissioner, and both deputy commissioners.

Ten or so female and male reporters sat in seats facing the podium.

A female reporter asked, "Detective Hodge, is it true you found this huge illegal fentanyl load on your front porch this morning with an attached note?"

"This is an ongoing investigation," Hodge said. "And I don't want to comment on that."

"What did the note say?"

"No comment. Next question, please."

A male reporter asked, "Detective Hodge, was the fentanyl related to the deadly apparent drug cartel gunfight last night at Pennington Bay?"

"We have no motive yet," Hodge said. "I'll be heading back to that scene when I'm done here. Who's next, please?"

A male reporter asked, "Several news outlets are reporting that the owners of Yacht Marina Grande, Donar and Caryn Thorsen, arrived in Denmark today and asked for asylum. Do you know why they would have done so?"

"I heard those reports too," Hodge said. "I have no idea." She pointed. "Yes, the patient lady in the back."

A female reporter asked, "Detective Hodge, the RVIP on Tortola announced they are planning a joint statement with your department later tonight on the 'zombie girls' case. Is that accurate?"

"That is accurate."

"Good news?"

Hodge nodded. "Very good news. But that's all I can say now. Next?"

A male reporter asked, "Detective Hodge, there's a petition to make you the next police commissioner. Comment?"

Hodge smiled. "I love the people of the Virgin Islands."

"And is it true your foundation for disadvantaged youths received a very large anonymous donation today?"

"Yes."

"Is it true it's in the millions of dollars?"

Hodge smiled again. "I'll just say, many kids' dreams will come true. One more question, please, and then I have to go."

A male reporter asked, "Any theories on where the fentanyl came from?"

"The National Bureau of Narcotics will be taking lead on this case, and I refer all other questions about it to the new special agent in charge of the Caribbean Division, Special Agent Palmer. But let me just end by saying the people of these islands can take great comfort in knowing they have a guardian angel who cares for them and helps them in ways they'll never know. And I ask them to join me in sending our deepest gratitude and love to this angel, whoever and wherever they are. Thank you."

Hodge stepped away from the podium and the news coverage switched to a female anchor in the studio. "That was Detective

Naomi Hodge of the US Virgin Island's Police holding a wide-ranging press conference after announcing that a record 1,000 pounds of illegal fentanyl was taken off the streets by her department. Getting back to another breaking story on this historic day, long-time Virgin Islands' resident and personality, billionaire financier Jacob Weinberg, was found dead in a Caracas, Venezuela home this afternoon. A police spokesman said the cause of death is an apparent suicide by hanging. Weinberg, age 64, was a fixture at—"

Azzur signed off the stream.

"Thank you for that, daddy," Laili said.

"The decision was not taken lightly. Mr. Weinberg provided substantial financial aid to our country over the years."

"But he drugged and raped me."

"The punishment for that is not death," Azzur said. "You now owe me 10 additional tasks."

"Yes, daddy."

CHAPTER 65

With Puerto Rico disappearing into the late afternoon haze behind her, Molka—also wearing borrowed navy fatigues—leaned on INS *Geula*'s stern railing and finished watching Detective Naomi Hodge's press conference on her phone.

She clicked it off, opened the phone's word processor app, opened the document she had started earlier, and made some final additions to it.

Before they had even left San Juan harbor for the trip home, Azzur had sat Molka down for a debriefing on her final task.

She confessed to informing the captain about Azzur's deal to turn him over to Justain. She had done it to protect the captain and his crew from any accidental harm by Flotilla 15 during their op and to pay back Justain for putting her in the position that had gotten her dismissed from the program.

But she swore she did not tell the captain anything about the Thorsen's scheme with the cartel. As far as she knew, the captain understood that the objective of their task was only to teach the prime minister's wayward nephew a lesson in obedience and loyalty during an election year.

And Azzur believed her. He was a master of lies and liars, which made him an expert at detecting the truth. He then asked Molka to outline her theory on how Captain Savanna could have possibly found out about *Outcast*'s hidden cargo that he had so skillfully pirated away. And she was to present it to him later that evening.

Molka reviewed the document she had prepared to read him laying out her theory:

According to Counsel associate Mr. Levy, Captain Savanna was an accomplished chess player, a game of strategy where sometimes you must think many moves ahead to win. And within the game, the captain's preferred tactic to achieve checkmate is known as the decoy.

But his plan to victory all started with a simple tip.

The captain learned some super rich kid named Paz Davidov, with a mega yacht named *Outcast*, was heading to the USVI. He decided to take them. Just another fat prize to add to the prize wall in his study.

But during his pre-hunt planning, he learned Paz was the prime minister's nephew. He did some much deeper research and formulated a much bolder plan.

Phase One: Make sure Paz and Caryn Thorsen were introduced.

The captain's investigation indicated Paz was highly susceptible to the suggestions of beautiful women. Caryn Thorsen was certainly that. Get those two together and exploitation opportunities would abound. The "bouncer" who introduced them was probably Mister Cutter sent by the captain.

Phase Two: Use Jesse Denmark to suggest to the cartel a wide-open fentanyl market in the Middle East waited to be tapped.

Through his old friend Jesse Denmark—the arbitrator who was trusted and respected by all the cartels—the captain knew about the Thorsen's partnership with the Belize traffickers. And he found out this cartel was aware fentanyl production appeared to be exceeding US demand. So he had Jesse suggest to them they should make a deal to ship their product to anxious buyers in the Middle East.

DUAL DECEPTION

And their partners—the Thorsens, Jesse told them—knew the perfect dupe, Paz Davidov, to move it for them. All they had to do is recommend Caryn marry him. Oh, and offering their new Middle East associates a polite, 100-million-dollar courtesy fee, paid in the form of the easily convertible asset gold bullion, would be a helpful gesture to ease the process.

And so, the Thorsen/Belize cartel/Middle Eastern fentanyl scheme was born.

Note: The captain sending me on the failed errand to bring him Jesse Denmark was probably to save Jesse from cartel retribution when the scheme ultimately unraveled.

Phase Three: Covertly feed the scheme to the Counsel and then covertly suggest to them a way to stop it using himself.

The captain likely used a third-party source (maybe Captain Solomon, who he said he had collaborated with on behalf of American intelligence in the past) to feed the scheme to his American Corporation contacts. They, in turn, passed it along to the Counsel. He correctly anticipated the Counsel would seek to stop it, and then used the same third-party source to suggest to the Counsel how to do so using Captain Savanna as their key asset.

And when the captain learned Agent Justain's informant also found out about the Thorsen/Belize cartel/Middle Eastern fentanyl scheme, he developed a contingency to use Justain too. See Phase Four…

Phase Four: Event shaping.

The captain was Agent Justain's "aggressively anonymous" confidential informant in the USVI. And sometime while Laili and me were out, the captain planted 200 pounds of marijuana in the old bakery under our apartment and removed the window covering so it could be seen. He then gave Justain the tip that we were connected to the yacht he was seeking, and that we also had the incriminating weed. This would allow Justain to get a warrant and arrest us for the weed and put the squeeze on us for the location of the yacht.

This forced me to bring in you, which formed the Justain and Azzur alliance, an alliance the captain would use to embarrass both of our home countries. How could they admit a pirate stole 100 million in gold from under two of their most respected agencies' noses? They couldn't. So they would never reveal to the world the gold existed. And that would make it much easier for the captain to convert it to cash without questions.

The captain was also the one Detective Hodge referred to as the island's "guardian angel." And he used this unknown angel character as an instrument to assuage the guilt of his earlier life of crime by doing good things for a good person, Hodge, who did good things for innocent children.

And as far as Mister Cutter's betrayal, his suspicions were apparent by him keeping Mister Cutter out of the information loop until the last hours on the *Outcast* prize.

He also hinted he was aware of Mister Cutter's association with the dangerous Gus Ramos by two comments he made to me. The first was on my initial visit to Katelyn: Mister Cutter, "doesn't always wisely choose his friends." And the second one was the warning he gave before Laili and me went after *Outcast* for the final time: "beware of stowaway rats."

The only event the captain might not have accounted for was Donar Thorsen losing his nerve and trying to cancel the deal, which caused the cartel's deadly *Outcast* seizure-abduction-ransom situation. But then again, maybe the captain did account for that. He had already put Laili and me in high-pressure life-or-death-type scenarios with my Jesse Denmark errand fiasco and during the Brit smugglers drama. So he knew we could recognize, adapt, and overcome any major unforeseen problems. Which we did.

Phase Five: Collect the reward. No fears. Live your dream.

Just before the captain left, I watched him payoff four stout, sweat-soaked, crewmen who told him, "We're all set." I now assume they had just finished transferring the hidden cargo from *Outcast* to *Betrayal*. The captain then transferred the fentanyl to Detective Hodge's front door and collected his reward: 100 million dollars in gold bullion—less his generous donation to Hodge's youth foundation—which could never be reported stolen because it was dirty money.

As far as the Belize cartel knew, a local cop just got lucky, and their gold was in the same place their seized fentanyl was: the heavy hands of the US Justice Department. And what could they do about it, file a claim? No. Just write it off and forget it. Cost of doing crooked business. Besides, in their operation, that amount was only a rounding error anyway.

Obviously, the captain's stated dream, "the dream of all dreamers, financial security to live free and well for life," came true.

Or maybe his dream was to put an end to the flamboyant Captain LJ Savanna, and he wished to give him a suitably flamboyant—if not spectacular—sendoff into history and legend forever.

Or maybe he just needed the legitimacy to show up at the door of a nice home in Glencoe, Illinois and allow the pretty girl who lives there, named Katelyn, to view the gentleman of superior taste, culture, and style she passed on.

But the captain's plan extracted a heavy price paid too.
People died. Bad people. But people still.
Laili endured more horrendous trauma in her young life.
Mister Cutter lost his sobriety.
And I was removed from the program.

Molka deleted the document.

She would tell Azzur she had come up blank. Because even if her theory was correct—and she thought most of it was—all people would ever do is argue her points to absolve themselves. So why spend a lifetime answering questions about other people's failures?

She had a lifetime of her own failures to anguish over.

Letting down her little Janetta being the worst.

Molka headed below decks for the wardroom. In the narrow passageway, she came face to face with Laili who carried their travel bags over her shoulders.

"Azzur's waiting to talk to you," Laili said.
"I know."
"Did you watch the news?"
"No," Molka said. "I've been thinking."
"Yeah. Guess you have a lot to think about now. But on the news, the captain made a hero out of some basically standard small

island cop by giving her the fentanyl to claim as her own bust. Why didn't he just sell it? They say it might be worth billions."

"He didn't exactly walk away empty-handed. What did Azzur say about that news?"

"Nothing," Laili said. "But earlier he said the prime minister couldn't be happier about the task, and he couldn't be more disappointed."

"He'll get over it. Or not."

Laili's face drooped in disgust. "The captain was such a fool for not selling that fentanyl."

"Sounds funny coming from you," Molka said. "As much as you hate drugs."

"I'm just pissed the captain was lying to us the whole time. Shit, he was lying to everybody the whole time."

"Well, we're all lying to the world to one extent or another. It's only when you get caught lying to yourself that the real trouble begins."

Laili shook her head. "I swear it's getting harder and harder to tell you and Azzur apart."

"How did our bags get here?"

"Azzur had that Levy guy clean out our apartment last night and send them over before we left this morning."

"Nice of the navy to finally give them to us."

Laili dropped the bags on the deck. Each woman unzipped and examined one.

"Ugh," Molka said. "He mixed all our stuff together. And most of your clothes are dirty."

Laili pulled out Molka's old pilot's watch and grinned. "Oooo...look what I found. My trusty, good luck, old pilot's watch." She laid it atop her left wrist for Molka to see.

"Laili...I told you never to wear that in front of me. I wasn't joking. Do not put that on or I'll—"

Laili bowed up. "Or you'll what? Vancouver?"

Molka bowed up. "Yes. Vancouver. Right now, work for you?"

"I'm down. Where?"

"I watched Flotilla 15 fly off a little while ago. So the helo deck or flight deck or whatever the navy calls it is currently available."

"Sounds good," Laili said. "But I don't want to get your blood all over this cute navy guy's shirt. Mind if I change first?"

DUAL DECEPTION

"No. Take both bags with you though. We'll finish separating it later."

"See you up there, ugly."

"See you up there, brat."

Molka waited next to the helo deck and observed the blinking lights of an approaching helicopter. The helo deck landing crew arrived and made ready. Was it the ship's assigned Panther chopper returning? Maybe they had left it in San Juan to make room for Flotilla 15's big Sea Stallion.

She and Laili would have to find another fight venue, though.

But it wasn't a military chopper hovering to land; it was a gold and black, civilian Bell 429.

The pilot landed, powered, down, and waited.

A door in the bulkhead behind Molka opened and Laili approached dressed not for fighting but for flying in a gold flight suit. She carried her gear and travel bags over her shoulders.

"What are you doing?" Molka said.

"Azzur's sending me back to San Juan to get ready for my next task."

"Oh."

Laili blew past Molka and headed straight for the helicopter.

Molka gave her a sarcastic wave. "Have fun, brat."

Laili didn't look back. "Whatever, Molka."

Did she just call me Molka? Ha. That's a first.

Laili opened the pilot-side door. The pilot moved over to the co-pilot seat. Laili tossed her bags in the back seat, took the pilot's seat, closed the door, strapped in, put on headphones, powered up, lifted off, made a smooth, tight turn, and headed southwest.

Good technique. We never talked about flying. Shame.

"Excuse me, miss."

Molka turned to a young navy officer behind her. "Yes?"

"You've been asked to dine in the captain's mess this evening. They're waiting for you now."

"Um...ok. I just need to stop by my cabin and freshen up."

Molka entered the tiny cabin she and Laili would have shared for the next eight days. She moved to her bottom bunk, where Laili had piled all Molka's clothes and shoes while separating them from hers. Molka wanted to find something decent to wear to the captain's mess, but everything was more wrinkled than the navy fatigues she wore.

Molka moved aside another pile and found her old pilot's watch placed on the pillow with care. A handwritten note was tucked underneath it.

Molka read:

I decided I didn't want this. It looks better on you anyway. It's grotesquely ugly. You're really not ugly though. You're ok.

"Thanks. You're ok, too."

Molka tried to swallow back tears.

But she wept as she put her watch on.

Molka arrived at the small captain's mess. However, INS *Geula*'s captain and officers were not present.

Instead, Azzur shared the table with a pair of American fashion models attired in white Israeli Navy officer dress uniforms.

At least they looked like American fashion models, but they were, in fact, Nadia and Warren, hyper-competent US central intelligence service operatives. The same pair who had given Molka much trouble—and to be fair—much help during her Gaszi Sago task.

The blond-haired, blue-eyed, busty, Nadia still stunned. And the brown-haired, strong-jawed, muscular Warren still aroused. They had not changed a bit since she had last seen them in Bermuda.

Nadia smiled at Molka. "*Ketzelah*, you look like hell."

Molka crinkled her nose. "Nice to see you too, *kelba*. Hello, Warren."

"Hi, Molka," Warren said. "I think you look great."

Nadia glared at her partner. "Don't start, Warren."

"Here visiting your old friend, Azzur?" Molka said.

"Actually, we've come to see you," Nadia said.

"About what? I didn't take a penny of Sago's bribe. Ask Warren."

"No; it's nothing like that. I'm going to slap you with the old good news, bad news tactic."

"Wow." Molka yawned, folded her arms, and leaned on the bulkhead. "I can't wait to hear this."

"The good news is, Azzur has just agreed to let you stay in the program."

Molka's eyes shot to Azzur.

He nodded.

Joyous adrenaline recharged Molka's dying heart.

Molka looked back to Nadia. "And the bad news?"

"The bad news is, for your next task, you're working for us. Me, more specifically."

Molka winced. "Oh no."

Nadia smiled. "Oh yes. And I promise you, you're absolutely going to hate it."

KEEP READING!
Molka's Next Task!
PROJECT MOLKA Book 4!

SLAY TIME
A PROJECT MOLKA NOVEL
FREDRICK L. STAFFORD

Available on Amazon!
https://www.amazon.com/dp/B084BQKJNF

Printed in Great Britain
by Amazon